D0893921

KINGPINS

3 3503 00056 6152

KINGPINS

Edited by Cynthia Manson

and Charles Ardai

Carroll & Graf Publishers, Inc.
New York

State Library OF Ohio

SEO Library Center
40780 SR 821 * Caldwell, OH 43724

Collection copyright © 1992 by Davis Publications, Inc.

Introduction copyright © 1992 by Charles Ardai

All rights reserved

First Carroll & Graf edition 1992

Carroll & Graf Publishers, Inc.
260 Fifth Avenue
New York, NY 10001

Library of Congress Cataloging-in-Publication Data is available.

Manufactured in the United States of America

92-05198

Grateful acknowledgment is made to the following for permission to reprint their copyrighted material:

SMALL TALK by Terry Courtney, copyright © 1992 by Davis Publications, Inc., reprinted by permission of the author; THE 730 CLUB by Alan Gordon, copyright © 1991 by Alan Gordon, reprinted by permission of the author; MURDER IN THE FAST LANE by James A. Noble, copyright © 1985 by Davis Publications, Inc., reprinted by permission of the author; all stories previously appeared in ALFRED HITCHCOCK'S MYSTERY MAGAZINE, published by Davis Publications, Inc.

THE ICEMAN COOLETH by T.M. Adams, copyright © 1978 by Davis Publications, Inc., reprinted by permission of the author; MY BROTHER'S KILLER by William Bankier, copyright © 1973 by Davis Publications, Inc., reprinted by permission of Curtis Brown Ltd.; PHILIP MARLOWE'S LAST CASE by Raymond Chandler, copyright © 1959 by Flying Eagle Publications, Inc., © renewed 1986, reprinted by permission of the Executrix of the Estate of Raymond Chandler; THE CAPTAIN M. CAPER by Avram Davidson, copyright © 1970 by Davis Publications, Inc., reprinted by permission of the Virginia Kidd Literary Agency; THE MISFIT by Phyllis Diller, copyright © 1991 by Davis Publications, Inc., reprinted by permission of Arthur Pine Associates; CHARLIE'S VIGORISH by Brian Garfield, copyright © 1978 by Davis Publications, Inc., reprinted by permission of the author; THE WEDDING GIG by Stephen King, copyright © 1980 by Davis Publications, Inc., reprinted by permission of Kirby McCauley Ltd.; KNEECAP CARBONE AND THE THEORY OF RELATIVITY by Keith Peterson, copyright © 1989 by Andrew Klavan, reprinted by permission of the author; HARD LUCK STORY by Richard A. Moore, copyright © 1978 by Davis Publications, Inc., reprinted by permission of the author; THE DARK GAMBLE: END OF THE TRAIL by Hugh Pentecost, copyright © 1977 by Hugh Pentecost, reprinted by permission of the Brandt & Brandt Literary Agency; **THE WEATHERMAN** by Jack Ritchie, copyright © 1976 by the Elks Magazine, reprinted by permission of the Larry Sternig Literary Agency; **EVERYBODY CALLS ME ROCKY** by William I. Smith, copyright © 1976 by Davis Publications, Inc., reprinted by permission of the author; **ANOTHER WANDERING DAUGHTER JOB** by Gerald Tomlinson, copyright © 1976 by Davis Publications, Inc.; **COUGH** by Andrew Vachss, copyright © 1989 by Davis Publications, Inc., reprinted by permission of the author; all stories previously appeared in **ELLERY QUEEN'S MYSTERY MAGAZINE**, published by Davis Publications, Inc.

ACKNOWLEDGMENTS

We want to express our thanks to Herman Graf, who made us an offer we couldn't refuse.

CONTENTS

INTRODUCTION

C'mere.

Yeah, you—with the book in your hands. Don't look so innocent. We know what you're after.

You want the inside story, the dirty secrets of organized crime. You want to read about godfathers and wiseguys, about hitmen and enforcers and life in the underworld. You want to see bullets flying and crimes committed and deals going down.

Well, all right, then. You've come to the right place.

Let's get one thing straight right away. There's a lot of crime in the world, organized and otherwise, and it's a nasty way to make a living. We don't enjoy it.

There are too many headaches—headaches like young hotshots who think they can move up faster by spraying lead around in the ranks. Or like the cops, who will look the other way when you want them to, but not for free. *Big* headaches like all those crusading journalists with Pulitzer Prizes on their minds who think they're above a bribe. They're not. You just have to bribe them with something they appreciate, like their lives.

Headaches.

But there *is* plenty to enjoy about Mob life. There's the money, for one thing, and it's all tax free. Yeah, right, tell Al Capone that. Well, he got nailed—but that was because he was *Al Capone*. Most of us aren't in the public eye quite as much as Al was.

Then there's the bond of Family loyalty. There's the knowledge that you've got power over other people's lives. There's the excitement of living on the edge.

Most of all, there's the simple pleasure of being part of an organization that can get away with murder, literally. What can I say? The rules they make for ordinary people don't apply to us. We're not only outside the system, we're a system all to ourselves.

Don't give me that look. You know you like it. You've got an honest face, but deep down the life we lead excites you.

If that isn't true, tell me why the *Godfather* movies are some of the most successful pictures ever made. Tell me why year in and year out more Mob pictures are always coming out. Not to mention Mob books, and Mob television shows, and Mob computer games. It ain't 'cause we're cute.

It's not because we're flashy dressers, either. It's because we do things the rest of the world only dreams of doing. It's because no one dares to push us around and because even when we're nailed, we go down fighting. We're not your heroes and we're not your friends. We fascinate you. That's a whole nother ball of wax.

And as long as there are stories like the ones you are about to read, we're going to go on fascinating you. Writers like Stephen King, Andrew Vachss, Hugh Pentecost, and Raymond Chandler can take you into our dangerous, secret world so well that it really feels like you're there, inside the Mob.

Look at the table of contents and you'll see what I mean.

In "The Iceman Cooleth" by T.M. Adams, you'll see a Midwestern Don running scared from a hired killer known only as "The Iceman." In "The Wedding Gig" by Stephen King, you'll see a Mob wedding through the eyes of some innocent bystanders. In Gerald Tomlinson's "Another Wandering Daughter Job" and Hugh Pentecost's "The Dark Gamble," you'll see one New York City detective try to track down a missing Mafia heiress and another carry a bloody vendetta to the very heart of the Organization.

In "Philip Marlowe's Last Case" by Raymond Chandler, you'll see the great Marlowe get on the wrong side of the Mob by helping one of their men disappear. He discovers what you and I already know, that there are some people you shouldn't cross—but they discover that Marlowe is a man you don't want to cross either.

More real than this, you don't want it to get.

Some of the writers in this book take a lighter of view of the Mob, of course. (What kind of Mob anthology could leave out comedy? Think of Marlon Brando in *The Freshman* or Jack Nicholson in *Prizzi's Honor.*)

In "The Captain M. Caper," Avram Davidson tells the story of a hapless writer who gets marked for a rubout after being roped into ghost-writing the tell-all autobiography of a Mob turncoat. In "The Weather Man," Jack Ritchie tells the tale of a con-man who pulls an incredible scam on the Mob and gets away with it . . . sort of. And in "The Misfit," Phyllis Diller—yes, Phyllis Diller—tells the story of an unlucky would-be hitman whose career just *won't* take off.

Then there's Keith Peterson's "Kneecap Carbone and the Theory of Relativity," in which a pesky investigative reporter gets a scoop but also gets in over his head . . . and Alan Gordon's "The 730 Club," in which Mob boss Theo the Nut gets himself committed to a psycho ward in order to get out of going to jail . . . and—

And plenty more.

Everything you're looking for is right here: the razor-edged world of organized crime, the bad guys (and girls) who live there, and a little bit of fun at their expense.

And who knows? Maybe you'll even decide you enjoy it so much that you want to become one of us. The door's always open.

Read on.

It's an offer you can't refuse.

—The Editors

THE ICEMAN COOLETH

T. M. ADAMS

The snow had stopped falling at dusk, but the wind was not through with it yet. J. C. Demain, his vest bloated improbably with a lining of one-hundred-dollar bills, was waiting for room service, and brooding about the shortcomings of Democracy.

Think of it. Fourteen months before, a bare majority of good citizens had pulled the wrong lever in the voting booth and so far this winter five men had died as a result. Demain, who had some reason to fear being the sixth, took another sip of his superior sherry and murmured, *"O tempora! O mores!"* (An Ivy League education can be such a comfort—I refer to the taste for sherry.)

Demain's other favorite saying was more plebeian, a dictum of his father's: "If you can't beat 'em, join 'em." It was a more useful saying too: it had brought him here, to these penthouse heights . . .

Johnny Dominetti, heir to the Dominetti rackets fortune, had entered Harvard a check-grabber, a pre-test crammer, an up-and-comer, discussed everywhere, accepted nowhere. But he learned. ("If you can't beat 'em, join 'em.") He adopted the novocaine-overdose manner of inherited money, ran up appalling bills in the right places, allowed his grades to fall to a gentleman's C. He took to collecting jade, porcelain, and expensive redheads.

His name, which he'd changed after his freshman year to J. C.

Demain, came up for membership at two of the best dining clubs. He submerged himself in the underground of the old prep-schoolers he found there, the unnoticed elite of 1960's Harvard. In his senior year he reached the pinnacle, the Polo Team, something so Old Harvard that in the New Harvard it seemed slightly illicit. (His teammates called the sport "this thing of ours"—Demain silently translated the phrase into Italian, and found it good.) Although almost no one followed the game, it was the sport that counted—Demain was a made man.

It was hard to return to the industrial city of his birth and to the family business, which consisted principally of the city's only thriving policy racket. For a few months J.C. was a sort of vice-president under his father; hard times. But a dispute with his silent partners in the Midwest soon divested the elder Dominetti of his life, and he passed on his numbers bank where he had failed to pass on his name.

In his decade's overlordship of the policy business, Demain never saw any reason to revert to his father's vulgar style. There was a remote outpost of Society even here, and he was welcomed into it with friendly yawns. His lack of visible support was, if anything, taken as final evidence of blue blood and blue-chip backing. He had a little suburban estate to house his jade, porcelain, and sundries (one sundry at a time), and a hotel suite in town for entertaining. He drove a Cord, not very often, preferring taxis. He belonged.

His small army of numbers runners took to him less swiftly than Society. They were used to different treatment, to a waiter's percentage of the take, put an extra few hundred tucked into their jacket pockets (with a Latin clasp of the shoulder and a few kind words) any time they needed it—Mama's birthday, weddings, illnesses—like that. Demain paid just a flat salary, generous enough, sure, and a fat annual bonus that came mailed inside little gilt-lettered cards every Christmas, as though he were a real bank president and they the tellers.

The elder Dominetti had also been a more public guy, after the fashion of his kind, contributing heavily to various civic groups and both political parties in a vain attempt to buy respectability. Demain, on the other hand, simply *was* respectable; he donated only to the designated charities of his class (preservation of historical buildings, Radio Free Europe, hemophilia; that sort of thing). Even the police had to be paid off by a middleman; Demain knew the Commissioner, but only to play golf with. And it was this cachet of class that finally won over his new underlings, this scent of attainable legitimacy that drove them into the suburbs, prompted them to trade their flashy Lincolns and Caddys for economy cars and station wagons, encouraged them to have children and put aside money for their college educations.

In short, the whole city had accepted Demain—and then the State had betrayed him.

"Proposition 13," Demain muttered. Snow drifted out of the darkness to burn against the windowpane. There was a knock on the door, and a voice: "Room service!"

Demain stripped off his curiously stuffed vest and tossed it into the bedroom, out of sight. He opened the door and surprised the wizened bellhop behind it with two $50 bills and a folded sports jacket. He spoke rapidly but clearly, "I want you to run down to Santini's and get me a sports jacket like this, only one size larger—but with the same sleeve length. One size larger, understand, but match the color and something like the style. Have one of the salesmen help you pick it out. Do it fast—they're only open until nine—and don't talk to anybody on the way, and you can keep the change, which should be twenty or thirty dollars. Got it?"

The bellhop stammered out his acknowledgment, said he'd be back as soon as possible, and departed. Demain closed the door slowly. So it had come to this. *Buying clothes off the rack.* Nausea gripped him.

Proposition 13 had brought him to this. Proposition 13 had brought the Long Winter. Proposition 13 had brought the Freeze. Worst, and last—as in "last rites"—Proposition 13 had brought the Iceman.

The Iceman, yes. During the same ten years in which Demain had made his modest mark, a less distinguished underworld figure had been carving a reputation for himself. His true name was unknown except to his Midwestern masters; his seemingly anachronistic sobriquet was a reference to the instrument with which he dispatched people who had proved an embarrassment to his employers.

Consider the lowly icepick. Ground to needle thinness, it becomes a sophisticated weapon. Introduced between the ribs at the correct angle, it can stop the heart, leaving a mark the size of a pinhead and a probable verdict of heart failure. Similarly, an inch of blade at the base of the skull can produce an easily overlooked scab and a cerebral hemorrhage not unlike some forms of stroke. Granted, it takes a master craftsman to accomplish this sleight of hand in public, amid a milling crowd. But such a master existed, and if he was expensive, at least his tools were not.

A few years before, at the top of his career, Demain had treasured stories about this legendary hit man, much as shipping magnates like to hear tales of storms at sea. When Demain and his lieutenants got together (there was an office for this; he didn't see them socially), after the books were inspected and the shares apportioned, he would elicit from them the grislier reports that were making the rounds about the Iceman's latest exploits. He had built up in his mind a lurid picture of the fellow: a tall, pale, black-haired man with icy blue eyes and—although theirs had been an equal-opportunity business for some time—a sinister Sicilianesque name. Vito Brevis, he had mentally christened him once; he wished he could forget that now. For now Legislative Proposition 13, the Proposition for the Establishment of a State Lottery, had brought him within days of the Iceman's pointed reprimand.

In the first year of its existence the Lottery had not drastically affected Demain's business. The numbers were cheaper to play, allegedly paid off better, and did not report to the tax man. But the next November a new Lottery Commissioner came up with an innovation, the so-called Presto Tickets, which had the appeal of the old illegal punchboards: one could find out instantly whether or not he was a winner. The tickets were cheap, too. For Demain they marked the beginning of the Long Winter of Discontent.

All November the numbers business plummeted. There was the usual Christmas slump, only worse, and the usual New Year's flurry, only not so good, and then things leveled off at what Demain had to assume was the new average—only about seventy percent of the previous year's weekly earnings.

Even so, Demain need not have suffered. In all the years he'd been running the bank, he had been taking a percentage over and above that allowed him by his bosses farther west. Had he dropped that luxury when business dropped, he could have maintained payments and business relations at their old high standard. But he had not, and now the Iceman had blown in from the Windy City to litter the streets with corpses.

The first killing, that of Deacon LeRoy, one of Demain's top lieutenants, went almost unnoticed. The Deacon's last night on earth was spent watching a telecast of the Lottery's grand-prize presentation. Now, LeRoy was known to feel that the Lottery was not only unfair competition, but blatantly fixed as well. (And indeed, the recipients of grand prizes were good public-relations fodder: mainly sweet white-haired old ladies, black policemen, and young couples just starting out in life.) LeRoy's wife, fearing for his hypertension, had sabotaged the TV that night, but the Deacon stormed down to a local bar and ordered the proprietor to turn on the presentation. As fate would have it, the thousand-dollars-a-week prize that night was won by a sweet white-haired black lady whose son, a policeman, had just got married; LeRoy caused an ugly scene before retiring to the men's room, where he was found later, dead of an apparent heart attack. No one thought much about it at the time, LeRoy's family and associates taking the attitude of "Why look a gift horse in the mouth?"

But when Abby Johnson and Jojo McCloud died of strokes, at a football game and a race track respectively, the word went out on the street as it hadn't in five years: "If you're hot, get out of town—the Iceman cooleth." The Freeze set in. Demain discovered that all the Chicago phone numbers he knew had been changed. His people stopped reporting to him. His operation was being purged, and he, surely, was being kept for last.

When the Iceman wanted to make an example, you received his unkindest cut of all, fatal but unmercifully slow—the thrust of an icepick whose loosened handle came free of the blade at the moment of impact. This allowed the Iceman to walk away with the part of the tool bearing his fingerprints, leaving the pick in the victim and no handle to remove it with.

Demain hadn't the slightest doubt that this was the death reserved for him, and he had a vivid conception of its aftermath.
SOCIALITE VICTIM OF ICEPICK KILLER—how undignified; or
worse: CRIME CZAR SLAIN IN GANG WAR. Oh, yes, much
worse. Please, he thought, let it be SOCIALITE VICTIM . . .

This morning, after one of these morbid fantasies, he had suddenly seen his way out. His former partners were double-crossers;
well, if you can't beat 'em . . . double-cross 'em.

First, Demain had to understand why the Iceman had left him
free while disposing of two more of Demain's top men. Demain
supposed he was being watched as he made his nightly rounds, lest
he escape. He also supposed that the Iceman was waiting for him
to try to remove the numbers bank funds from the safe-deposit box
in which they were believed to rest—in which, as only Demain
knew, they actually did not. Having an aristocrat's distrust of
banks, he had long ago transferred the company funds to a wall
safe here in the apartment. They currently totaled just over
$1,000,000.

This morning he had converted one-fifth of that into the more
portable form of a fabulous emerald brooch (with which he hoped
some day to resume an old hobby), keeping the rest in handily
negotiable one-hundred-dollar bills.

Unless he had waited too long, he could walk away with this
hoard tonight by simply appearing to follow his ordinary schedule.
He would hail a taxi at the same time as usual, but instead of going
to the banquet he was supposed to attend, he would go to the bus
terminal. (Inconceivable that anyone would be watching for *him* at
the *bus terminal.*) He couldn't carry any sort of luggage, of course.
He had to conceal the money on his person . . . a problem.

With a little cramming, he managed to fit all the currency into
the lining of his vest and sculpt it into a human, if somewhat
rotund, shape. But this added bulk ruined the lines of every jacket
he tried on over it, and in the throes of fear he was certain this
would give the game away. The only answer had seemed to be to
send out for a larger jacket . . .

As he rose again to the bellhop's knock, he prayed that this
would do the trick, that the bellhop had not betrayed him, that the
Iceman had not gotten impatient.

Opening the door and looking at the bellhop, a middle-aged,

chicken-necked man with watery blue eyes, he felt relieved. Was this man likely to be in cahoots with the Iceman? Hardly. A glance at Vito Brevis' greasy black locks and flashy clothing, and this middle-American type would be muttering about "hippie punks" and crossing to the other side of the street. Demain's heart warmed to the man. These respectable citizens, colorless but incorruptible, were the backbone of the country.

"Here you are, sir," the bellhop said.

"Thank you," Demain replied, taking the proffered sports jackets and making as if to close the door. The bellhop was standing in the way, all but holding out his palm.

"What did your tip amount to, by the way?" Demain asked flatly. "Twenty dollars, thirty?"

"A whole lot, thank you, sir. Are you sure that's all I can do for it?"

Demain relaxed and said, "Yes. Oh, would you get the elevator and hold it for me, please?"

"Yessir!"

Should have had him hail a cab instead, Demain thought, rushing into the bedroom and pulling on the vest. He tried on the new sports jacket and found it not bad, not bad at all. Before leaving he remembered the emerald brooch and put it in his jacket pocket. Were there any more hard assets around the place? No. Time to leave.

In the hall outside, the bellhop maintained his post at the elevator. The doors were just opening as Demain approached. The bellhop was standing almost in his way, and as Demain squeezed past him the bluejacket gave him a sort of affectionate punch in the ribs, a vulgar gesture of such appalling intimacy that Demain was disoriented with surprise. He stumbled on the threshold of the elevator, grabbed at the bellhop's shoulder for support, and the two of them tottered—almost fell—into the car, jostling the passenger already there. The doors closed behind them.

"Whoa!" said the original passenger, turning around. "Oh, it's you, Mr. Demain."

"Pardon me, Rogers, I guess I tripped," Demain said, recognizing the man in the security guard's uniform. "Going off duty?"

"Yes, sir," Rogers said, smiling because Demain had remembered his name.

Demain knew a mixture of feelings: security first, because armed-and-uniformed Rogers would be at his side until he took his taxi; second, anger at the clumsiness of the bellhop. You tip one of these people and he treats you like a member of his teeming, slum-dwelling family. Although he could hardly hold his ribs and curse in public, such was his desire. Why had the idiot hit him so hard?

"Who comes on duty now, Rogers? Taylor?" Demain asked. Bad form to talk with the staff, but it could not be avoided after stagger-ing into one of them like a drunk. At least it gave him a chance to demonstrate his expertise in the field of staff surnames—*noblesse oblige* and all that.

"No, he's down with the flu, sir. Jackson's filling in for him now." Rogers was beaming at all this attention. Ah, Demain thought, the Little Man has such little pleasures. Thinking of little men, he allowed himself a cool glance at the bellhop, who was fidgeting nervously as the notoriously slow elevator made its way toward the lobby. Demain's hand went reflexively to his probably bruised ribs—and touched something cold and metallic.

He glanced down to see two inches of steel protruding from between his fingers. The slender gleaming shaft was lodged firmly in his jacket, in his vest, and in a wad of hundred-dollar bills beneath, but not in his flesh. He looked up again.

The bellhop smiled sheepishly.

Rogers was saying something about the flu as Demain surrepti-tiously plucked out the icepick blade and dropped it behind him on the carpeted floor. He began to tremble a bit with reaction and then, without knowing what he was going to do, he reached for the little man. With one fluid motion he wrapped an arm around the narrow shoulders in a grim parody of comradeliness, pinning arms to sides. The Iceman looked even more sheepish. The security guard looked at them curiously.

Years of keeping up appearances brought words to Demain's lips. "Do you know who this is?" he asked. He felt the small body next to his go rigid. (As if he could tell Rogers!)

The guard shook his head. Demain babbled on, "My uncle! My long lost uncle . . . Mr. Brevis. An interesting story, Rogers. You see, back in 1920, Grandfather Demain disinherited Mr. Brevis' father for good cause and that whole branch of the family dropped from sight. But my own dad, the Commodore, always wanted to patch things up. Detectives finally came up with a photograph of Uncle Vi—Uncle Victor here, but that was all. Until tonight, when I ring for room service and who should walk in but the man himself? If only Dad were alive to see it." He gave the little man an extra squeeze.

"That's wonderful, Mr. Demain," Rogers said, his honest face awash with sentimentality. "I guess you're going out to celebrate, huh? Sir?"

"Aw, we've been celebrating, Rogers. I guess you could tell that, the way we came stumbling in here." These humiliating fabrications were almost liberating, in a perverse sort of way. Worth thinking about, if he got out of this alive. "We drank everything I had in my room, and then we ordered a bottle of sparkling burgundy from downstairs, and when I tried to open it, what do you think I found?"

"I don't know, sir," Rogers said, grinning widely.

"I found—I couldn't find—the corkscrew, Rogers. No corkscrew!" He actually felt a little drunk. Adrenalin, probably. "So I said to my Uncle Victor here, I said to him, 'Uncle Victor, see if you can open it with the icepick.' And he said, 'Okay,' and do you know what he did?" Rogers shook his head.

"He broke it! He broke the icepick. Show him the handle, Uncle Victor."

The little man just stood there for a moment, vibrating like a plucked piano string, then opened his tight-clenched hand to reveal an icepick handle. A bead of sweat fell onto it, from his nose. The elevator doors opened then, and the little man gave a violent start as light flooded the car.

"Can I walk you to the door, Mr. Demain?" Rogers asked.

"Why, thank you, Rogers, we'd appreciate it." The Iceman squirmed a bit, but Demain's arm had the sinew that only a lifetime of golf, tennis, and swimming can impart. The three of them traversed the mirrored lobby, Demain telling the guard a rather ribald joke—just one of the guys after all.

The air outside was icy, not so much bracing as numbing. (He realized he could have worn—and stuffed—a heavy winter coat.

He need never have called room service.) Rogers was looking for a taxi, but there were none to be seen.

"Where's Charles?" Demain asked, referring to the doorman.

"Running errands, I guess, Mr. Demain," Rogers replied. "Not much work for him out here. Taxi strike, you know."

"Another strike," Demain said. "It's been a hard winter, hasn't it?"

A cold wind blew. The little man squirmed. Demain's arm was getting tired.

Rogers cleared his throat. "What I meant was, you can't get a taxi, Mr. Demain, see what I mean? Do you want one of the guys to bring your car around front?"

Demain made a noncommittal sound. He didn't want to freeze to death standing here, proudly holding the little assassin as though he were some sort of athletic trophy; but on the other hand he didn't know what else to do with him. He couldn't even be sure that the little viper was entirely defanged. He was trying to think of some way to keep Rogers with him when suddenly the Iceman spoke up, like a troll from beneath a bridge.

"Let's take the subway, J.C.," the little man said. Demain tightened his grip, but this only seemed to squeeze out more words. "C'mon, Johnny. We don't want to be late. Let's take the subway."

The last thing Demain wanted to be was "the late" J.C. Demain, and a glance at the shadowed subway kiosk on the corner seemed to threaten as much, should the little man get him there alone.

Demain shook his head as Rogers spoke, "You guys aren't dressed very warm, if you don't mind me saying so. And I wouldn't take the subway this time of night if I was you, Mr. Demain."

Demain's free hand was getting cold. He thrust it into his jacket pocket, flexing it indecisively.

Something pricked his finger.

"There's hardly anybody down there this time of night," Rogers continued. "Anything could happen."

It was the emerald brooch. The pin had come free from the clasp.

"I'll look after him okay," the little man gibbered. "Let's take the subway, kid."

Demain ran his finger along the shaft of the pin. At least an inch and a half long, and sturdy, the body of the brooch providing a sort of handle. The little man looked up at him with longing. Perhaps he only wanted to escape—but wasn't there a touch of calculation there? After all, he was the Iceman and Demain was well aware—proud—of how little he resembled young Johnny Dominetti, street gang scourge of the 1950's. He looked at Rogers and said, "We'll take the subway. I'll be okay."

The Iceman smiled.

Rogers always felt guilty about letting Mr. Demain go off on the subway that night, half potted and all. As he said to his wife later, he just knew, somehow, that Mr. Demain would never be seen again . . .

And the gangland grapevine wondered at the Iceman's latest kill: some unknown bellhop found dead of cerebral hemorrhage in a subway car.

And in a town farther east all the gossip is about this new social lion, this Victor Brevis, who came out of nowhere a few winters back with the right manners, mien, and money. (A familiar face from Harvard, too, although no one can quite place the name.) He married a Schuyler girl (you should see the brooch he gave her) and owned a string of winning race horses until his father-in-law got him that job in the Off-Track Betting Administration.

And now he's been appointed Commissioner of the new State Lottery here, after nearly singlehandedly pushing the idea through the Legislature. If you drop by his office in the capital, you'll see a sign over his desk that reads: IF YOU CAN'T BEAT 'EM, JOIN 'EM.

No one is quite sure what it means.

KNEECAP CARBONE AND THE THEORY OF RELATIVITY

KEITH PETERSON

When I woke up, Guts Manero was picking his teeth with a switchblade. I hate guys who do that. I also hate guys who break into my apartment when I'm sleeping. Guts was not starting the day on my good side.

I groaned and grabbed the cigarettes off my night table. Guts sat on the edge of my dresser, at the foot of my bed. The knife blade scraped and screaked against his enamel.

"Would you stop that? Jesus Christ," I said. I lit the cigarette and blew smoke out at him. "I mean: Jesus Christ."

Guts cast a puzzled look at the offending instrument. But he folded the blade back into the handle and slipped the weapon into his overcoat pocket. "I come here to do you a favor," he said. "Do I get a happy face? Is that a happy face?"

"Don't push it, Guts."

"This is not a happy face, I would say." He had a copy of that morning's *Star* lying next to him on the dresser. He picked it up, weighed it in his hand. "But am I angry? No." He tossed the newspaper onto the bed. "Because you have been a friend to me."

I didn't have to look at the front page. I'd already seen the bulldog, and the headline was the same. It read WITNESS NAILS MAHONEY. The story on page three carried my byline—John Wells.

"Believe me," I told him, "I didn't do it for you. You may not have waxed Capello, but you've buried your share."

Guts shrugged. "All the same, one likes to keep these matters straight. Especially with people whose first name is Lieutenant."

I shrugged back at him. "The witness didn't want to go to the police. She came to me. So you're in the clear for the Capello killing. The door's that way."

"Wait. Wait. Aren't I grateful for this?"

"Uh—yes?"

"Yes is correct. And I have come here to do you a favor, as I said."

I didn't point out that he could have knocked. I smoked quietly and waited.

"I am going to give you a scoop," said Guts Manero. "But you cannot tell it to anyone."

"What *am* I supposed to do with it? Chuckle inwardly?"

Guts raised his eyes to heaven. "At the proper time, when I say so, you will be able to write it. And then you will be ahead of all the others because I did this thing for you—coming here. However, as I am the only person who *could* possibly come here to tell you this, anyone who knows that *you* know will know also that *I* told you. Would this be dangerous to me? I would say yes, if you think having your body placed in a shoebox is dangerous. Therefore, you have to give me your sacred word of honor as a news guy that what I am telling you is off the record."

I scratched my nose. Rubbed my chin. Squinted at the ceiling. Generally did my best to look as if I might not go for it. Guts did not crack under the strain of waiting. Maybe that's why they call him Guts—although I don't think so.

Finally I said: "Oh, what the hell. All right. You're off the record."

"And you are sworn to secrecy until I say the time is right?"

"Yeah, yeah."

"And you will stand by this?"

"Word of honor."

"Angelo Carbone is going to be killed tonight."

"Oh, shit."

Angelo "Kneecap" Carbone was one of the Dellacroce boys, an underboss with a sort of franchise on all the light construction jobs south of Little Jones Street. He was an energetic, flamboyant, and likeable guy who'd once slit a man open from hairline to scrotum just to watch him come apart. Decent, honest, hardworking folks like me kept away from him. But the mayor liked him well enough, and most of the pols in the city and some of its richest developers had been only too pleased to attend his sixtieth birthday party last year.

This Capello fellow, whom Guts did not kill, had been killed instead by a gentleman named Mahoney. Mahoney, it turns out, had been working for Kneecap Carbone and was settling a score that had to do with some renovation work at the municipal building. The upshot, according to Guts, was that Carbone had now been targeted by an avenging angel in the person of Marty "The Bull" Eckstein, who had had an interest in the renovation.

"This evening at four o'clock, like every evening at four o'clock," Guts told me, "Kneecap will go into Maxie's on Mulberry Street. He will sit at his favorite table against the wall and order a cannoli and espresso."

"Yeah?"

"This evening, like every evening, he will be accompanied by his two bodyguards, who will sit at the table by the door. And this evening, like every evening, those bodyguards will be Franco and Caro."

"Right. So?"

Guts slid off the dresser, strolled over to the foot of the bed. Looked down at me. It was quiet for a minute. Beyond the window, four flights down, I could hear the morning traffic on Eighty-sixth Street. I could hear it hissing through the puddles of last night's rain. I could hear horns honking over on Lexington. The lights in the doughnut shop and the Greek diner were probably on already. The neon sign above the stereo store would probably start flashing any minute. People would be hurrying out of their buildings, making for their buses and their subways. The city would be rising out of the night like a great bear out of the high grass. But in here, only the faintest whisper of it reached me. In here, there were the cracks on the wall, the clothes draped over the chair, the thin scarred face of Guts Manero, and his thick voice going on again.

He held a finger in the air. "But will this be just another evening for Kneecap Carbone?" he said. "I think not. Because this evening Franco and Caro will be in the pay of Marty the Bull. Does this sound unfortunate for Kneecap? We can agree: yes, it does."

I crushed out my cigarette. The breath came out of me shakily. I ran a hand up through my hair. Guts kept talking.

"What will happen is this. At exactly four-fifteen, the phone in Maxie's is going to ring. It will be for Kneecap. As always, the waiter will bring the phone to the table behind Kneecap's because the cord doesn't reach. Kneecap will turn around, his back toward Franco and Caro. He will pick up the phone. Marty the Bull will be on the line. He will deliver a message of hatred and revenge appropriate to the situation. Meanwhile, Kneecap's bodyguards will approach and draw their weapons and empty them into the back of Kneecap's skull."

I shook my head. "Man!" I said. But in fact I was thinking: *Man oh man oh man oh man!* I managed to ask, "Just how do you know all this?"

Guts shrugged. "Because of his understandable desire for secrecy and his unwavering and well placed trust in me, Marty the Bull, who has long stood in my way of promotion, had me drive the car while he negotiated this deal with Franco and Caro in the back seat. I, in turn, have placed my trust in you. A token of my appreciation."

"So you can get back at Carbone by having Marty kill him, and get Marty by having the *Star* accuse him of murder."

"Whatever. The point is, you've given your word to be silent. And if you break it, I am a dead man."

"And if I keep it, Kneecap will just be a wistful memory in the pocket of the municipal government."

"That's life in the construction business," said Guts, moving toward the door. "Console yourself with the thought that you alone, of all God's newsmen, will know how, why, when, and where Kneecap died—in plenty of time for the early editions."

The city room of the *Star* was quiet in the late afternoon. Throughout the maze of low-walled cubicles, under the vast banks of fluorescent lights, reporters typed at their computer keyboards almost silently. The wire news came up onto their monitors without the clatter of the old machines, without a sound. The TVs were off and the editors weren't shouting. The place was a living whisper. Even my typewriter—the only typewriter left in the joint —sat untouched.

I sat in front of it, drinking coffee, smoking cigarettes, trying to figure out my next move. It was already 2:00 P.M. Just two hours and fifteen minutes until Kneecap got beaned.

McKay, from featureside, walked by. I flagged him. His round baby face hung over me.

"What would you do," I asked him, "if someone told you, off the record, that there was going to be a murder?"

"I'd call the police."

"What if, by calling the police, you'd cause the death of your source?"

"I wouldn't call the police."

"So what would you do?"

"Okay: what?"

"Thanks, Mac."

He wandered away.

I smoked my cigarette. I drank my coffee. I watched the clock move.

By three-thirty, I couldn't take it any more. I couldn't just sit there and let it happen. I grabbed my coat and headed for the door. I went past the city desk and saw Lansing leaning over Rafferty, looking at his monitor. Her long blonde hair spilled prettily onto the city editor's shoulder, but old Raff's bullet-shaped face remained blank as ever.

"Where to, Wells?" He didn't even look up as he spoke.

"I gotta cover a murder downtown," I said.

"Something come over the scanner?"

"No, it's not for about an hour yet."

He almost reacted. He lifted an eyebrow anyway and shifted his narrowed eyes toward me. Lansing stood straight and stared.

"Something we should know?" she asked.

"Yeah, but I gotta protect a source."

Rafferty leaned back in his chair. His voice was a monotone.

"Wells, my boy," he said, "a reporter's first responsibility is to the society he lives in, the people that he meets, the butcher and the baker, the guy named Joe."

"Can I bring you back a cannoli?"

"Yeah, but don't let them put those little pieces of human flesh in it. I hate that."

I took the subway to Spring and then walked down Mulberry. Painted brick walls pressed in on the skewed and narrow street. Black-iron fire escapes zigzagged over the painted brick walls. Old ladies with forearms like elephants' legs leaned out of ancient windows to watch the scene.

It was June and the neighborhood smelled like garbage. The restaurant scraps left by the sanitation men lay in the gutter, going ripe. Young wives and old wives sat together on stoops and standpipes, fanning the fumes away with their hands. They laughed, and the waiters in white aprons and the maitre d's in cheap suits stood on the sidewalk and smiled and winked at them. Two wiseguys flanked the door of a local social club. They rocked on their heels, their hands in their pockets. Their eyes followed me as I went walking by.

Maxie's was a little place, just a storefront pastry shop between Hester and Grand. It was five of four when I pushed in through its glass door. The place was done in white tile with small round tables of black marble. There were maybe ten of those tables, all of them empty. Only the waiter was there when I came in, standing behind the glass pastry case near the espresso machines. The pendulum of a blond-wood grandmother clock ticked back and forth on the wall above him.

I sat against the far wall, under the map of Italy, facing the door. The waiter came and stood beside me without saying anything.

"A cappucino," I said. I watched the door.

Outside, right in front of the place, a black Mercury Grand Marquis slid to the curb. The blond-wood clock chimed: bong, bong, bong, bong. Caro stepped out of the Mercury's driver's seat onto the sidewalk. He was a broad, muscular man with a razor-sharp widow's peak. Franco got out on the passenger side, into the street. He was a broad, muscular man with a razor-sharp widow's peak, too. Caro opened the Marquis' rear door and out through it stepped Kneecap—a short, waddle-legged man, domed in the middle. A face like a thumbprint, an oval of wrinkly whorls. A black suit worth three weeks' pay.

He led the way in, Franco and Caro flanking his rear. The waiter rushed to pull in the door for him. I was still waiting for my cappucino.

Kneecap seemed to be in fine spirits. He greeted the waiter warmly, slapping him on the shoulder as he passed. Unbuttoning his jacket, he went to the wall opposite me. He sat down at the table there, under the signed photograph of a senator. Franco and Caro, with many a bodyguardlike glance from side to side, sat down together at the table by the door. They stared lifelessly. They stared at me.

I lit a cigarette. I had begun to sweat. My collar had begun to get damp and sticky. I considered the situation. My thinking ran something like this: Oh, shit. Oh, God—oh, no. Oh, shit, holy, oh my God, what do I do now—oh, no. I crooked a finger under my collar and tugged the cloth away from the skin.

The clock on the wall read 4:02. Kneecap was ordering his cannoli. The waiter scurried off behind the counter. Kneecap sat back in his chair. I watched him out of the corner of my eye. He patted his stomach. He sighed happily. He smiled. He said:

"Wells."

"Huh? What?"

"Wells, John Wells."

"Why, hello," I replied, and gave a casual fillip of my hand that sent my cigarette flying into the map of Italy. A starburst of red embers drifted down into the Gulf of Salerno. One stuck and burned a while before it died, leaving a little circle of char on the Isle of Capri. "If it isn't Kneecap Carbone," I said.

Kneecap chuckled, nodding at me. "Heh heh heh." He sounded like a toad with laryngitis. "John Wells. I haven't seen you since my racketeering trial. Or was it my murder trial?"

"Why quibble? The jury didn't."

"Heh heh heh," croaked Kneecap Carbone. "Come," he said. He gave a grand wave of his hand. "Come and sit with me. Share a cannoli."

Gee, I'd like to, but you're going to be gunned down in ten
minutes, I wanted to say. Instead, I said: "Uh—well, I—"

"No, really. I insist."

"Uh—well, I—"

Franco stood up and hulked at his table. "No, really. He insists."

I drew a hand down over my face. It came away wet. I looked at
Franco. I looked at Caro. I looked at Kneecap Carbone. "Oh, well,"
I said hoarsely. "If you insist."

It was only ten paces from my table to his. There was no way to
arrive late. As I crossed the room, I glanced at the clock behind the
counter. It was 4:07.

When I sat down, my back was to the bodyguards. I could still
see the clock over Kneecap's shoulder. The brass pendulum swung
back and forth. Then it swung back and forth again. It kept doing
that. I watched it.

"Heh heh heh," said Kneecap Carbone. His self-satisfied smile
crushed the whorls of his face until the thumbprint became a
prune. The waiter brought him his cannoli and espresso. The plates
rattled on the marble as he set them down.

"And don't forget my cappucino," I called after him.

"So," said Kneecap, lifting his fork. "What are you working on
these days, Wells?"

"A murder," I said. "A mob hit." I remembered Guts Manero and
shut up. I looked at the clock: 4:09.

"Mm," said Carbone around a mouthful of crust. "Violent people. The mob."

"Yeah," I said. "One day you're on top of the heap. The next day,
you're the heap."

"Heh heh heh," said Kneecap Carbone. "Heh heh heh."

I reached for a new cigarette. Its white paper darkened with
sweat as I lifted it to my mouth. I held it steady, aimed a lit match
at the tip. It took a while to make the connection.

Still smiling, with flecks of powdered sugar tumbling from the
corner of his mouth, Kneecap waggled his fork at me. A glob of
white cheese bobbed before my eyes.

"You know," he said, "it's hard to believe today, but it was
thought at one time that I was a member of a criminal organization
myself."

"No. Really?"

"The truth, so help me." He shoveled the cheese into his face.

"You ought to be careful about that, Kneecap," I told him. "Someone might get the wrong idea in a fashion that would cause you to be dead."

He lifted his shoulders, chewing away. Took a quick swig of espresso to wash the stuff down. The minute hand's motion from 4:09 to 4:10 was imperceptible unless your eyes happened to be riveted on the clock.

"What is to be done?" said Kneecap when he could finally say anything. "You know physics, of course."

"I've met Madame Ouspenski. Just to say hello."

"Not psychics, Wells. Physics. Like the theory of relativity."

"Ah. Huh?" I stole a glance over my shoulder. I saw Franco and Caro leaning together across their table. They seemed to be whispering to each other. I turned back. 4:11.

"The theory of relativity," Kneecap was saying. "Einstein."

"Yeah, the carpet guy."

"No. The scientist."

"Oh, yeah—yeah, sure." The sweat ran freely down my temple now, hung for a moment on the stubble of my beard, then dropped onto my soggy collar. My cigarette was a vibrating blur as I brought it to my lips. "Look, Kneecap," I said, "I'd love to discuss this with you, but you're almost dead. I mean, *it's* almost dead. I mean, it's almost deadline. I've gotta go." It was 4:12. My thoughts on the journalistic ethics of the case had focused wonderfully on a reporter's need to get out of the line of fire.

"The theory of relativity," croaked Kneecap Carbone with an expansive wave of his cannoli fork, "is, like, a situation is different depending on where you're looking from. *Capishe?*"

"Listen, Kneecap—Kneester—Cappy—I don't mean to be rude—"

The cannoli fork hovered in mid-wave. "No," said Carbone, lifting an eyebrow significantly, "it's not a good idea to be rude."

I turned to eye the boys again. They sat in their chairs, staring lifelessly, staring at me. It was 4:13. I didn't think they'd let me go now, anyway.

"As I was saying," Kneecap went on, "if you are sitting in a car, for an example, and it cuts a hard Ralph, you think you are thrown on the Louie. But if you are outside the car, then the people inside just look like they keep going forward when the car turns."

"Right. Gotcha. Bye."

"Sit, Wells. Sit."

Slowly, I sat.

"And if you try to figure out your own position, whoa," remarked Kneecap Carbone. "Then you get into Heisenberg's uncertainty principle."

"What a disaster," I moaned.

"You're telling me. This is that the observer, see, always disturbs the situation. So if you're observing the observer, then the observer becomes part of the first thing, the situation. See? Likewise, if you try to become part of the situation, you got a whole different situation on your hands 'cause you're looking at it different. Are you still with me here, Wells?"

"Oh, Kneecap. Oh, Kneecap. Oh, Kneecap," I said. My cigarette had burned to its filter. I smoked the filter. The grandmother clock's minute hand hovered between 4:14 and the fatal minute.

"When you say to me, 'Kneecap, take care lest you are mistaken for an unsavory type of mob person and are whacked, that is to say killed, by goodfellows, that is to say criminals,' then I say to you in the tradition of Albert Einstein, 'Ay, don't get in my face, because we have—' "

The phone rang behind the pastry counter. I jumped in my chair. My cigarette fell to the floor. I clutched the edge of the table with whitening fingers. Unsure whether to dodge or run or sit and hope to be spared, I stayed there frozen, my mind a sheet of white fear.

"It's for you, Mr. Carbone," the waiter said. He had brought the telephone from behind the counter. He set it down on the table behind Carbone.

"Excuse me," said Kneecap. He dabbed at his mouth with a napkin. He shifted, turning his back to me. He picked up the phone. "Yes?" he said. "Why, Marty. Marty the Bull."

I didn't dare move. I didn't dare turn. I sat rigid in my chair, gripping the edge of the table. I stared at Carbone as he murmured into the telephone. I stared wildly at the back of his head. I waited for the black-and-scarlet explosion as he was ripped apart by gunfire. I waited for the lightning flash of pain as I was ripped apart. I wondered if I'd feel the bullets tear into me, if I'd see my own blood on the black marble, feel my own life draining out of me as I went down. I clutched the table and watched Carbone, and the hairs on the back of my neck prickled, waiting for it.

"Well, Marty," said Kneecap into the phone, "I am extremely sorry you feel this way. Yes, I am. But as Nietzsche said: fuhgetabout it, you should live so long." He hung up. The waiter scurried over to remove the phone. Kneecap came around in his chair again until he was facing me. "Marty the Bull," he explained. "A volatile man. Where was I? Oh, yes." He picked up his fork, speared the last of the cannoli, jabbed it into his mouth. He went on speaking as he mashed and ground it. "It's the same in your case, Wells. As a reporter of an event, you can never truly calculate your own effect on that event. There is no sense reflecting endlessly about it. Wherever you happen to be looking from, that's the situation. So I say: be free. I say: live your life. Tell your story, that's what I say. That's the theory of relativity."

He swallowed the last of the cannoli. He chased it with the last of the espresso.

"Well," he said, "since you are on deadline—" He made a gesture of dismissal with his hand. "Uh, I'm done now." He made a rolling, hurry-up gesture with his hand. "Uh, Wells? You can go. Hey, all right?"

I made a noise. If dead men wheezed, that would be the sound of it. I gaped at him. I tried to close my mouth. I tried to loose my hold on the edge of the table. Slowly my fingers slid off the marble. My hands dropped limply into my lap.

"Goodbye, Wells," said Kneecap Carbone.

I nodded stupidly. I stood stupidly. Stupidly, I turned and started walking to the door.

There they were. Franco and Caro. Still sitting at their table, Franco in the chair to my right, Caro in the chair nearest me. I stumbled toward them. They didn't move. Franco stared lifelessly. Caro stared lifelessly. The only difference between them, as far as anyone could see, was that Caro was staring lifelessly because he was, in actual fact, lifeless. I only found this out when I went past him. My hand brushed against his shoulder and he toppled forward to the floor.

I stopped and turned. I looked down at him. He had rolled half over in the fall. His coat opened and I could see, just under his shoulder holster, just under his left breast, the handle of a stiletto protruding from a small circle of damp blood.

I looked up from Caro to Franco. Franco stared at me lifelessly. Then, lifelessly, he smiled.

My eyes traveled away from him, back over the body of his colleague, back to where Kneecap Carbone was reclining comfortably in his chair, his hand patting his cannoli-filled belly. He pushed his plate away.

"You knew," I said.

"Hm?" said Kneecap. "Oh. That. Yes, I knew." He brought his fist to his mouth and belched into it delicately. "But I didn't know you knew. I will have to call back Marty the Bull and tell him this salient fact. It will take care of some other business I had been concerned about."

It was another moment before I found the sense to move. Then I was pushing through the door, pushing out into the spring weather and the narrow street, out into the stench from the gutter and the first subtle darkening of the day all around. Stiff-legged, I stumbled to the corner. I went as fast as I could, leaning forward over my feet. I found the pay phone there, rooted in my pocket for a quarter, and shoved it into the slot.

I pushed the numbers for Guts Manero. I had to warn him. I waited, leaning against the phone stall, gazing at the line of painted brick buildings that ran fading to the north, gazing beyond it at the Empire State Building, which had gone flat and grey against the distant dusk. I heard the phone ringing.

They never even brought me my cappucino, I thought.

I heard the phone ringing and ringing.

EVERYBODY CALLS ME ROCKY

WILLIAM I. SMITH

All sorts of bad things are happening. Al and the people from Vegas are mad. Lola and Ray are running away and if Al and the people from Vegas find them I do not like to think what will happen. George should try to run away too, but it would not do him any good. He knows that and I do feel sorry for George because, you see, it really is all my doing.

The trouble is that people think I'm still stupid, but that's not true. It's just that I can't decide things any more. Big things like who to vote for or little things like what socks to wear.

So George tells me the big things and Mama tells me the little ones and I just do what they say. I always do what people say, not because I'm still stupid but, like I said, I can't decide things any more.

It used to be I could decide things. I decided to become a fighter. I won 30 out of 37 bouts. Only thing, it was the last seven I lost and I kept losing them worse and worse until they wouldn't let me fight any more.

So I went to work for George. I guess you should say I continued to work for George because he was my manager when I was fighting. Only not on paper, as they say, because George is a convicted felon and in our state they won't let convicted felons have anything to do with things as moral as the fight game.

My name is George too, but when I was fighting they called me

Rocky—after Rocky Graziano because I fought like him—and with me working for George, naturally, everybody still calls me Rocky.

Dad, he worked for George too, doing more important things than I do because everybody said Dad was smart. He sure could make money. Really. He made the plates—engraving as they call it —and George handled the distribution, as he calls it. I've still got a special suitcase full of Dad's money and I pass some every once in a while, but only when Mama and I need something important, like food, because if George knew I was passing it he'd get mad and tell me to stop and then I'd have to.

Mama says George is a nice man and I should do as he says so he will keep taking care of us. Mama's near 90 now but she knows George isn't really a nice man. And I know George isn't really a nice man. But Mama doesn't know I know George isn't a nice man and it would be too hard to try and explain it to her, what with her not hearing so good any more. Besides, it's easier doing what George tells me and doing what Mama tells me.

Besides, George is pretty good to me. He won't let other people call me Dummy and he won't let anybody give me drinks, because if I drink I get like I was after my thirty-seventh fight, all mixed up and not knowing what I'm doing or where I am, sometimes for days at a time.

But I do wish George would pay me regular instead of slipping me a bill now and then. Then Mama and me, we'd know where we were and I wouldn't ever have to pass some of Dad's money from his special suitcase.

One thing I do for George is once every two or three months I drive to Vegas with a suitcase full of money. George tells me this has to do with legally accounting for the money, tax-wise and otherwise, but I'm not supposed to understand that. I'm only sup-posed to understand to take the money to Vegas and if anybody like the Feds should want to open the suitcase let them, because unless you know how to open the suitcase the right way everything in it will blow up in one great big whoosh and then, of course, you don't have any money.

But then again the Feds won't have any evidence and money's always what they call expendable, while people like George and the people in Vegas, they don't like to think of themselves as expendable. Of course I know how to open the suitcase the right way, but I'm not talking.

And George and the people in Vegas, they don't trust other people a whole lot, like not at all. But they do trust me because they know I'll do exactly what I'm told and because they think I'm too dumb to know what's what. So you see why I got to let people keep on thinking I'm still stupid, don't you?

Okay, so one day George he gives me the suitcase and tells me it's time to go to Vegas. So I take the money, stop off at my place, which is right across the street from George's Restaurant, to kiss Mama goodbye and pick up some things. Then I head on out to the lot in back of the restaurant where George's got the car parked I'm to drive to Vegas.

On the way out to the car Lola pops out of somewhere with a whole armful of packages and says George wants me to take her home. Now Lola's George's lady friend and he always says to do whatever she tells me. So I take her home even though I'm pretty sure he didn't tell her to tell me to do this, what with me having the money in the car and all.

Then when we get to that fancy apartment building where George rents a penthouse for Lola, Lola she's got all sorts of stuff she wants me to carry up to her penthouse. She tells me to leave that old suitcase in the car because I can't carry that too, along with all her packages. This isn't true because I'm real strong, but I do what Lola tells me, only I keep my eyes open while I'm carrying the packages and, sure enough, just before the elevator door closes on me and Lola and all her packages I see Ray.

Now, time to time, I see Ray with Lola and Lola says Ray's her brother, only he isn't. Or if he is he ought to be arrested for looking at her that way. So there I am with the elevator door closing on me and Lola and all her packages and I see him, just a glimpse, like he's waiting until the door is all the way closed before heading for where I left the car.

Sure enough, when I get back to the car and check the suitcase —which, by the way, I put down on the floor in the back seat so nobody'd be likely to see it unless they were looking for it before I helped Lola with all her packages—sure enough it's not the same suitcase. You'd have to look carefully to see the difference, but I look at everything carefully and I see the difference.

So to be sure, I drive off, park and hurry back real quick, quick enough to see Lola come scooting out the front door of her fancy apartment building and pile into a car driven by Ray. Off they go and there I stand, thinking about it.

Then off I go to take care of a few things. Pretty quick I come back and let myself into Lola's penthouse with a key I got without anybody knowing I got it.

Once I'm inside I head for that fancy bar, with the view of the city behind it, where George likes to sit with Lola those nights he can shake loose from Bonnie Jean, his wife.

At that fancy bar I pour myself out a full glass of the kind of Scotch that George always drinks and I start to swallow it down as fast as I can.

I remember choking on it a couple of times and the next thing I know George is slapping me in the face, yelling at me and asking me where the hell's Lola? I only moan and hold my head in my hands, which is all I really want to do, me not feeling too good at the time.

After a while George leaves off slapping me and starts talking just like I'm not there. "Gone," says George. "Lola's gone. Suitcase, money gone. Gone, gone, gone!" Then George starts cursing.

"Ease off, George. You're going nowhere with that." This is Al talking now. Still I don't look up, but even if I didn't recognize his voice I would have known it was Al because Al's the only one gets away with talking to George that way. "Stop crying and start thinking. Exactly what we got here?"

"We got one hundred thousand plus—missing," says George. "And this dummy here—"

"Stop me if I'm wrong, George," says Al, "but what we got here is your car illegally parked in front of your apartment—"

"Lola's apartment," says George.

"Excuse me," says Al. "Lola's apartment. *Your* Lola, in the apartment *you* pay the rent on, out in front of which sits *your* car. And in *your* car we don't find *your* special suitcase in which is lots and lots of money which is not yours, but is yours to take care of. Do you follow me, George?"

When George does not say anything Al says, "And, George, all this you say is the dummy's fault?"

"She gave the dummy a drink and he took it," says George. "I told her not to give the dummy a drink, never to give the dummy a drink."

"Yes, George," says Al. "So now it is Lola's fault too."

"The suitcase will blow up and burn all the money," says George. "She don't know about that. So she won't get the money. Nobody will. It'll all burn up."

"You can't imagine what a comfort that is to me," says Al. Then I hear someone walking away and I hear a door open and close. Then after a long wait I hear a sigh. Then I hear George get up, for it was him doing the sighing. I stay there very still, with my head in my hands, because I am very much afraid George is going to shoot me.

But he doesn't. He only sighs again and then I hear him walking away. I hear a door close and after a while I sigh.

I sit there for a while feeling very bad, but then I think about how George should not have let me fight those last seven fights and I feel better. Then I decide I will go home and count all my money.

I guess I lied to you, saying I couldn't decide things. I do have a lot of trouble deciding things. It is hard and I don't like to, so usually I don't. Almost never.

One thing I did decide, after I could think again after losing my thirty-seventh fight, I decided George owed me for letting me fight those last seven fights. Then, when George started trusting me to take the money to Vegas, I think maybe someday somebody is going to try and steal it.

At first I would take both suitcases to Vegas, the one with the real money in it and Dad's, which is exactly like the one with the real money in it, exactly like it, and which is filled with Dad's counterfeit money. I would put Dad's suitcase on the seat beside me and George's in the trunk, stuck up back of the spare tire where it is hard to see.

Then, if someone steals the suitcase on the seat, they will steal Dad's and when they open it all Dad's counterfeit money will burn up because, as I said, Dad's suitcase is exactly like George's. Then I will have George's suitcase full of real money and Mama and I will have lots of money and won't have to worry any more and no one will know we have it and everything will be all right.

Only it doesn't work. No one tries to steal the suitcase. Then George meets Lola and I can tell from the fact that I hear George tell Lola things he shouldn't and from the fact that Lola is Lola, that someone is going to steal the suitcase and pretty soon too.

So I change my plan a little. Figuring the stealing will take place around here, every time George gives me his suitcase to take to Vegas I first stop off at home to switch suitcases, leaving George's with the Vegas money at home and taking Dad's with me. Then I drive off and if Lola doesn't try to steal the suitcase, which she doesn't for a while, I come back and reswitch the suitcases and take the real money to Vegas.

And of course Mama doesn't hear me because, if you remember, Mama is awful deaf. And if anybody else sees or hears me coming back, which they never do, I can always say I forgot something and they will not think it strange because people expect me to forget things.

So you see what happens. Lola—Ray really, but Lola told him to —stole the money and gave me yet another suitcase, which to my surprise is filled with counterfeit money. I guess Lola figures when the people in Vegas open the suitcase they will figure George is the one trying to cheat them.

Anyway Mama and I end up with lots of money, real money. Al and the people in Vegas lose lots of money, but I do not feel sorry for them because they can always get lots more. Lola and Ray end up with a burned-up suitcase and with Al and all the people in Vegas after them, but I do not feel sorry for Lola and Ray because they are not really nice people.

I am afraid George will end up gone because he made mistakes and Al and the people in Vegas they don't like people making mistakes with their money. I do feel sorry for George, but not very sorry because, you see, George he should not have let me fight those last seven fights. Even if I am not stupid any more, he should not have done that.

MURDER IN THE FAST LANE

JAMES A. NOBLE

"Mommy, how fast are we going now?" asked little Joel again, leaning across his older sister to get a glimpse of the speedometer.

"Will you quit bothering Mom?" Sissy scolded, pushing him back. "You can't read the numbers anyway."

Alice glanced over at her two children in the front seat and smiled. "Don't be too critical of Joel, honey. Remember, someday when he's your age, he may be a better reader than you."

"That's right," agreed Joel, making a production of folding his arms across his chest and giving his sister a "smarter than you" look.

"Why all this sudden interest in how fast I'm driving, Joel?" asked Alice.

Joel turned away and looked at the tips of his shoes sticking out over the edge of his seat.

"Answer me, honey."

"I can't tell you," replied the boy, defensively.

"Why not?"

Joel hesitated a moment and then said, " 'Cause Charlie told me not to."

Charlie again, thought Alice bitterly. The court had ordered him to stay away from the kids, and here he was sneaking behind her back and telling her children heaven knows what . . . *her* children.

She didn't want them anywhere near Charlie. It was after five years of marriage that she discovered what a cruel, sadistic man he was. Even so, the marriage might have held together had it not been for her discovery that her husband was a gangland enforcer, inflicting pain and punishment on command from mobster bosses.

Alice no longer thought of him as her husband. Even the children called him "Charlie" instead of "Dad" or "Father."

"When did you talk to Charlie, Joel?" The tone of her voice frightened the boy a little.

"Yesterday . . . outside the house."

"What did he say to you?"

"He told me to give you something when you drove us to Mr. Happyland today." Mr. Happyland was Joel's name for the day care center.

"Well, why don't you give it to me now?" asked Alice, giving her son a reassuring smile.

"Not until you're going sixty," said Joel.

"Sixty? . . . You mean sixty miles an hour?"

Joel nodded.

Alice glanced at the speedometer. "We're going sixty-two miles an hour."

Joel reached under his seat belt harness and removed a crumpled piece of paper from his pocket. He held it out and Sissy opened it and passed it to her mother.

Alice began to read in glances while she drove.

Dearest Darling:
  Don't let your speed fall below fifty. I've put a bomb in your car . . .

Alice screamed and dropped the note. The car swerved off onto the gravel of the narrow shoulder, and she struggled to regain control and steer it back onto the highway. It fishtailed briefly, scattering gravel, then finally settled back onto the hard surface. She glanced at the speedometer. Fifty-three. She pressed the gas pedal to the floor and the speed climbed quickly. She held it at sixty-five.

"Sissy!" Her voice cracked. "Pick up the note and read it to me."

"What's the matter, Mom?"

A confused, frightened expression was on the little girl's face.

"Just do it," ordered Alice in a trembling voice. Up ahead, a left-turn signal light of a semi blinked on.

Sissy retrieved the paper and began to read aloud.

" 'Dearest Darling. Don't let your speed fall below fifty. I've put a bomb in your car and attached it to the speedometer cable coming out of the . . .' "

Sissy held up the paper and pointed at a word.

"Transmission," said Alice, sharply.

" '. . . transmission. Sixty miles an hour will arm the bomb, less than fifty miles an hour will det . . . o . . .' "

"Detonate," said Alice, trying not to let her fear creep into her voice. A few hundred yards ahead, the semi pulled into the passing lane, suddenly revealing an equally large moving van in the other lane. Both were moving slowly. Alice let the speed drop to fifty-two. Because of the narrow shoulders and ditches on either side of the two lanes, there wasn't enough room for Alice to get the little hatchback by.

"Come on," she pleaded to the semi, "get around him, please. Hurry."

Sissy continued reading.

" '. . . detonate the bomb. You shouldn't have left me. My life is ruined and you're to blame. I hope you live just long enough to think about what you've done to me.

" 'Hope you remembered to fill the tank. Have a pleasant drive. Charlie.' "

Alice breathed a little gasp as she glanced at the gas gauge. Less than an eighth of a tank was left. At the moment, that was the least of her worries. The two big trucks were side by side, creeping along up a small hill, and she had almost caught up with them. Desperately, she leaned on the horn and began to flash the headlights.

She realized she was faced with a horrible decision. Outside the car, the road surface raced by. The mere thought of forcing Joel and Sissy to jump from the moving car made her tremble.

She considered the possibility that the letter was just a cruel hoax, perpetrated by the twisted mind of a man she once called her husband. If she slowed down . . . She shook her head. She knew

Charlie. If he said he had attached such a bomb to the car, he did it. The bomb and the nightmare were both quite real.

The two huge trucks were now directly in front of the hatchback. Alice made her decision.

The biggest opening seemed to be between the two trucks, but even that space didn't appear large enough. She pushed the accelerator to the floor and the car squeezed into the narrow gap.

The lower corner of the semi's trailer tore the driver's side mirror off the little hatchback while the undercarriage of the moving van snapped off the radio antenna and struck a glancing blow to the corner post of the passenger side window. A spider web pattern suddenly appeared across the right side of the windshield as the glass cracked. The speed of the little car began to drop off rapidly as it scraped its way between the thundering trucks.

The car was barely moving fifty-one miles an hour when suddenly the moving van jerked closer to the shoulder, enlarging the space between the two trucks. Freed from the vise-like grip, the little yellow hatchback picked up speed and passed the two cursing truck drivers.

Throughout the entire ordeal, Sissy and Joel had held on to each other and remained silent.

"Yea, Mommy!" yelled Joel, triumphantly.

Alice leaned on the steering wheel and looked at her brave little boy.

"Yea, Joel," she responded in a exhausted voice.

"Mom, look!" cried Sissy, pointing through the shattered windshield. "There's a police car up ahead."

Alice pushed the pedal to the floor. "Hang on, kids. It's time to get a speeding ticket."

Officer Berry Walker and his partner, Frank Sheppard, looked at each other as the yellow hatchback sped by them doing eighty miles an hour.

"That's the trouble with today's world," said Frank as he flipped on the lights and siren. "We get no respect."

Alice wound down her window as the squad car pulled up behind. She stuck her arm out and motioned for the policemen to pull alongside.

"Fold up Charlie's note and give it to me," said Alice. Sissy obeyed quickly.

As the police car with its two confused officers came alongside, Alice held the piece of paper out. The policeman on the passenger side reached over and took it from her hand.

At first, Berry and Frank couldn't believe what they were reading, but after they called in the license number of the hatchback and realized they were dealing with the ex-wife of a known gangland enforcer, there was little doubt that the threat was real. Just what they could do about it, they didn't know. They called for assistance and then pulled the patrol car ahead of the hatchback to clear the highway ahead.

Alice looked at the gas gauge. The needle was resting just above "E."

"Sissy, take my lipstick out of my purse and write 'gas' in big letters on the windshield."

"But the glass is all cracked."

"That's okay. The policemen will still be able to read it."

"Hey, what's that kid writing on the glass?" asked Frank, looking back.

Berry glanced up in the rear view mirror. "It's backwards writing to you. Look at it in your side mirror."

Frank turned and looked in his mirror. "Oh, no. She must be running out of gas. What the hell we gonna do now?"

Berry pulled into the left lane and slowed down to allow the hatchback to pass. "We're going to push her."

Frank's eyes grew big. "At fifty miles an hour?"

"No, fifty-five. We need a five-mile-an-hour margin of safety."

"What happens when *we* run out of gas?"

Berry looked over at his partner. "Ka-boom," he said, flatly.

Frank picked up the microphone and switched to the P.A. speaker to explain the plan to the driver of the hatchback.

Alice felt the gentle thump as the front bumper of the patrol car contacted the rear of the hatchback. She took the car out of gear and switched the engine off and then quickly switched to the "accessory" position to keep the steering wheel from locking. Alice breathed a sigh of relief when she saw the speedometer continue to register fifty-five miles an hour.

"Why'd you turn off the engine, Mom?" asked Sissy.

"We've got to save what little gas we have left, honey."

"Why? Do you have an idea?"

"Yes, darling. I have an idea." She gave her daughter a reassuring smile. Inside, she wanted to scream.

She realized it wasn't much of a plan and the odds were against her. She knew they would be passing the beach area in a few minutes. She planned to turn off and drive the car into the ocean on the slim hope the bomb and triggering mechanism would fail in the salt water before it detonated. She realized the speed would drop quickly to zero when they hit the water and it was more likely that the bomb would work or, worse still, they might drown. Still, the plan was the best she could come up with at the moment.

When the beaches appeared off to the left, she restarted the engine and raced it as she slowly let off the clutch. A wave of her hand and the patrol car began to back away. She was on her own.

"Brace yourselves, kids," she said as she slowed to fifty-two and turned off at the exit ramp. The ramp veered sharply to the right and the car skidded sideways into the curb. Two wheels jumped the curb and the car ran over a thin metal pole that marked the ramp for snow plows during the winter months. Alice jammed the accelerator to the floor and fought the steering wheel. Suddenly, steam appeared from under the hood. The overtemp warning light flickered and then shone bright red. The pole had punctured the radiator.

As the car left the ramp, it regained the highway leading straight to the beach. The hatchback became airborne briefly as it leaped a small mound separating the road from the beach. The rear hatch suddenly popped open as they came down on the beach. Black smoke began to mix with the steam coming from under the hood. Still, Alice held the gas pedal to the floor.

"Yippee!" yelled Joel.

Out of the corner of her eye, Alice spotted an answer to her silent prayers. She cut the steering wheel sharply to the right. The car slid sideways in the soft sand and began to slow. Still, the wheels were spinning at a furious rate and the speedometer was reading eighty even though they were only moving at about forty miles an hour.

She jerked the wheel suddenly to the left. The right rear tire struck a partially buried log and exploded. Then slowly the little hatchback began to climb the sand dune Alice had spotted earlier.

"Sissy, undo both your seat belts and get ready to jump!" screamed Alice over the roar of the dying engine.

As the driving wheels buried themselves in the soft sand of the dune, the car slowed to a stop. The smell of burning rubber filled the car as the tires spun wildly in the sand. The speedometer was indicating seventy and dropping rapidly.

"Get out!" yelled Alice. "Get your brother out of the car and run. Hurry!"

Sissy reached across her brother and pushed at the passenger door. Sand piled up outside prevented it from opening.

"Go out the rear hatch," yelled Alice as she pushed harder on the gas pedal and lifted Joel over the back of the front seat. The speedometer read sixty. The engine began to miss and sputter.

"Mommy, Mommy, come on!" shouted Joel, half turning as Sissy pulled him away from the smoking vehicle.

Alice pushed at the driver's door with all her strength. Slowly, she forced it open. She could see the patrol car sitting farther up the beach obviously stuck. The two policemen were running toward her. She glanced at the speedometer. Fifty-three. They wouldn't reach her in time.

Quickly, she picked her purse up off the floor and wedged it between the gas and brake pedals, then carefully removed her foot from the accelerator. The speedometer had dropped to fifty-one.

She jumped from the car and tumbled down the side of the dune.

The force of the explosion sent a huge plume of sand skyward. A large fireball appeared from the center of the cloud of sand and raced upward. Alice covered herself as smoldering pieces of the hatchback landed around her.

When the blast had subsided, Alice struggled wearily to her feet and staggered over to Sissy and Joel. She dropped to her knees and took them both in her arms. "You guys all right?"

"Wow!" responded Joel.

"We're fine, Mom," said Sissy.

"Are we still going to Mr. Happyland?" asked Joel.

Alice laughed. "No way, hotshot. Today you guys are all mine." And she hugged them a little harder.

COUGH

ANDREW VACHSS

This business, I know how it goes, the old man thought to himself. He'd been at it a long time. Dead reliable, that's what they always said about him. He kept his thoughts to himself. Nothing showed on his face. The way it was supposed to be. The younger ones come in, take over. In business, you have to make room for new blood. The young ones, they think I don't know that. I know how they think. Cowboys.

He mused to himself, alone in his room. They wouldn't call me in, ask me to retire. I would have done it, they asked me. When you're done, you're done. But they don't know how to ask. No class. It's as if they *like* to do it. Only amateurs like to do it.

I was never one of them. Not a Family man—just a soldier, doing my work. They let *them* retire.

The old man was just back from Miami. The last of the bosses called him down there. The old man thought it was just another job.

"You always done right by us," the boss said.

The old man didn't say anything. He wasn't a talker. That used to be a good thing, he thought to himself, waiting.

"Vito, he don't know you like I do. He's a young stallion. Wants his own crew, you know?"

The old man waited. For the boss to tell him about the retirement plan.

"They think you're past it. Spooking at shadows, hearing things

—you understand what I'm telling you?" The boss puffed on his cigar. He wouldn't look the old man in the face. The old man got it then.

The old man didn't know anything about running. He had always lived in the same place, done the same things. Kept it nice and quiet. By himself.

When Vito called, they said they had a job for him in Cleveland. He knew it was time to show them he could still do it.

His flight was supposed to leave from LaGuardia at nine that night. I've been doing this forever—I know how it's done, he thought. They'll have a man on the plane with me. Take care of business in Cleveland. Sure.

He got to the airport at three in the afternoon. Stashed his carry-on bags in the coin lockers. Checked the schedules. Figured it would take about five trips through the scanners. Bought tickets for Chicago, Detroit, Milwaukee, Pittsburgh. Different airlines. All departing from gates in the same corridor.

He went through the scanner, one of the pieces of the gun buried inside his carry-on. The X-ray machine would show an aerosol can of shaving cream. He left the bag inside, walked back out, patient, taking his time. The old way. The right way. By seven o'clock, he had all the pieces through the scanner. The last time through, he had a garment bag over his shoulder. In the men's room, he put the pieces together and stuffed the soft carry-on bags into the larger case. Then he sat down to wait.

The old man felt the other guy behind him. He didn't look. Smell of some aftershave he didn't recognize—one of those new ones. Like perfume. The old man heard him cough. A dry, hard cough with a liquid center. Like his lungs were getting ready to go. It was better than a photograph.

You have to be sure in this business, it's not a game, you only get one move, the old man repeated to himself. The catechism he learned as a youth. He switched to the no-smoking section on the other side of the departure lounge. The old man didn't catch a glimpse of him, but he heard the cough a few seats down. The young ones, they wouldn't pick up something like that. The old man was a pro.

Eight-fifteen. The old man got up, heading for the men's room.

He knew the shooter wouldn't let him out of his sight. They couldn't be sure he'd get on the plane like some tame old sheep.

Some punk was combing his hair at the sink when the old man went inside. He took the last stall, shut it behind him. Waited.

He heard the cough. In the stall right next to him. He stepped out, bent down quickly, checked under the door. The guy's pants were around his ankles. The place was empty. The old man walked out, letting the guy hear him, slipping gloves on his hands. Checked the door to the men's room. Kicked a little wood wedge underneath to give him a couple of seconds. All the time he'd need.

He stepped back into the last stall and stood on the toilet bowl. The guy was reading a newspaper. The old man put two slugs into the top of his head. Pop, pop. The silencer worked perfectly. He left the gun in the stall.

The old man was back in the departure lounge before they had the first call for boarding.

They'd hear about it. They'd know he wasn't past it. Not some old man who couldn't do the job. He lit a cigarette—the way you do when a job is over.

Then he heard the cough.

THE MISFIT

PHYLLIS DILLER

Always a dollar and a minute late, Frank Pello felt that the business world wasn't for him. Through a contact with Ernie, the bookmaker at the Allegheny Benevolent Club, one Monday morning at Vitello's Restaurant Frank found himself in the presence of Gus Deck.

The most important gangster in that part of Pennsylvania, Gus looked up from his plate of steaming lasagna, liked what he saw in the burly twenty-five-year-old man, and said, "Kid, you want to work for us, I hear."

"Yes, Mr. Deck. It would be an honor."

"I happen to have a little assignment for you. There's a gentleman in Scranton who has a big mouth. Could you do something about that? His name is Joe Styles."

"It would be an honor, Mr. Deck."

"Five hundred. We pay beginners five hundred."

Frank drove to Scranton in his tired Buick and signed in at a dinky hotel on Pittston Street. In his room, he checked out the gun that had been provided him by one of Gus Deck's associates and was satisfied that it would work smoothly and silently.

Frank drove to the Styles home north of the city to check out the area. A crowd had gathered in front of the Tudor-style house. Beyond the tall iron gates, he could make out the flashing red color of an ambulance doppler light. He parked up the block and sauntered back to the crowd. Pleasantly, he asked a man in a bathrobe, obviously a neighbor, what had happened. The man in the bathrobe said, "Joe Styles just drowned in his pool. Heart attack probably."

Two weeks later, Frank again found himself in the presence of Gus Deck. Deck had another problem, this time in Paoli—this chore a little more urgent than the first. Frank rushed off to Paoli. After checking into an even-numbered third-floor room at the Paoli Lodge, he looked out the window and nodded. It was as he'd been told. He could see the back yard where Andrew Cooper spent much of his day enjoying his roses.

Frank assembled his powerful rifle and attached the high-powered telescopic lens. Looking through it right at the heart of the Cooper rose garden, he saw a group of people scurrying about as if in a panic. Puzzled, he sat down and turned on the television set to divert himself as he mulled over his plans.

A special bulletin came on just as Charlie Chan was ready to identify the culprit. In a somber voice, the announcer said, "Word has just come in that Andrew Cooper is dead. While working in his rose garden, he stepped on a live electrical wire that had been temporarily placed in a rose bed by a repairman."

Three weeks went by. Frank Pello found himself in Easton. His Uzi under his coat, he had only to walk into the kitchen of the China Seas Restaurant and decimate Larry Lee. Lee, it seemed, had been encroaching on one of Gus Deck's major enterprises, the ripping off of famous-name garments.

In the alley behind the restaurant, Gus again saw a crowd. In the melange of accents and sounds, he heard someone say clearly, "They'll never bring Larry Lee back to life. Those mushrooms he ate kill you forever."

Frank Pello went home and took a job as a siding salesman.

THE WEDDING GIG

STEPHEN KING

In the year 1927 we were playing jazz in a speakeasy just south of Morgan, Illinois, which is 70 miles from Chicago. It was real hick country, not another big town for 20 miles in any direction. But there were a lot of plowboys with a hankering for something stronger than Moxie after a hot day in the field, and a lot of young bucks out duding it up with their drugstore buddies. There were also some married men (you know them, friend, they might as well be wearing signs) coming far out of their way to be where no one would recognize them while they cut a rug with their not-quite-legit lassies.

That was when jazz was jazz, not noise. We had a five-man combination—drums, clarinet, trombone, piano, and trumpet—and we were pretty good. That was still three years before we made our first records and four years before talkies.

We were playing *Bamboo Bay* when this big fellow walked in, wearing a white suit and smoking a pipe with more squiggles in it than a French horn. The whole band was a little drunk but the crowd was positively blind and everyone was having a high old time. There hadn't been a single fight all night. All of us were sweating rivers and Tommy Englander, the guy who ran the place, kept sending up rye. Englander was a good fellow to work for, and he liked our sound.

The guy in the white suit sat down at the bar and I forgot him. We finished up the set with *Aunt Hagar's Blues,* which was what passed for racy out in the boondocks back then, and got a good round of applause. Manny had a big grin on his face as he put his horn down, and I clapped him on the back as we left the bandstand. There was a lonely-looking girl in a green evening dress that had been giving me the eye all night. She was a redhead, and I've always been partial to those. I got a signal from her eyes and the tilt of her head, so I started threading my way through the crowd to get to her.

Halfway there the man in the white suit stepped in front of me. Up close he looked tough, with bristly back hair and the flat, oddly shiny eyes that some deepsea fish have. There was something familiar about him.

"Want to talk to you outside," he said.

The redhead was looking away. She seemed disappointed.

"It can wait," I said. "Let me by."

"My name is Scollay. Mike Scollay."

I knew the name. Mike Scollay was a small-time racketeer from Chicago who made his money running booze in from Canada. His picture had been in the paper a few times. The last time had been when another little Caesar tried to gun him down.

"You're pretty far from Chicago," I said.

"I brought some friends. Let's go outside."

The redhead looked over and I pointed to Scollay and shrugged. She sniffed and turned her back.

"You queered that," I said.

"Bimbos like that are a penny the bushel in Chi," he said. "Outside."

We went out. The air was cool on my skin after the smoky close atmosphere of the club, sweet with fresh-cut alfalfa grass. The stars were out, soft and flickering. The hoods were out too, but they didn't look a bit soft, and the only things flickering on them were their cigarettes.

"I've got some money for you," Scollay said.

"I haven't done anything for you."

"You're going to. It's two C's. Split it up with the band or hold back a hundred for yourself."

"What is it?"

"A gig," he said. "My sis is getting married. I want you to play for the reception. She likes Dixieland. Two of my boys say you play good Dixieland."

I told you Englander was good to work for. He was paying eighty a week split five ways, four hours a night. This guy was offering well over twice that for one gig.

"It's from five to eight, next Friday," Scollay said. "At the Grover Street Hall in Chi."

"It's too much," I said. "How come?"

"There's two reasons," Scollay said. He puffed on his pipe. It looked out of place in that yegg's face. He should have had a Lucky dangling from his mouth, or a Sweet Caporal. The pipe made him look sad and funny.

"First," he said, "maybe you heard the Greek tried to rub me out."

"I saw your picture in the paper," I said. "You were the guy trying to crawl into the sidewalk."

"Smart guy," he growled, but with no real force. "I'm getting too big for him. The Greek is getting old and he still thinks small. He ought to be back in the old country, drinking olive oil and looking at the Pacific."

"It's the Aegean," I said.

"An ocean's an ocean," he said. "Anyway, the Greek is still out to get me."

"In other words, you're paying two hundred because our last number might be arranged for Enfield rifle accompaniment."

Anger flashed on his face, and something else—sorrow? "I got the best protection money can buy. If anyone funny sticks his nose in, he won't get a chance to sniff twice."

"What's the other thing?"

Softly he said, "My sister's marrying an Italian."

"A good Catholic like you," I sneered softly.

The anger flashed again, white-hot, and I thought I'd pushed it too far. "A good *mick!* I'm a good mick, sonny, and you better not forget it!" To that he added, almost too low to be heard, "Even if I did lose most of my hair, it was red."

I started to say something, but he didn't give me the chance. He swung me around and pressed his face down until our noses almost touched. I never saw such anger and humiliation and rage and determination in a man's face. You never see that on a white face these days, the love-hate pressure of a man's race. But it was there then, and I saw it that night.

"She's fat," he breathed. "A lot of people have been laughing at me when my back is turned. They don't do it when I can see them, though. I'll tell you that, Mr. Cornet Player. Because maybe this little twerp was all she could get. But you're not gonna laugh at her and nobody else is either because you're gonna play too loud. No one is going to laugh at my sis."

I didn't know what to say. I didn't know why he told me or even why he thought a Dixieland band was his answer, but I didn't want to argue with him. You wouldn't have wanted to, either, funny clothes and pipe or not.

"We don't laugh at people when we play our gigs," I said. "Makes it too hard to pucker."

That relieved the tension. He laughed a short barking laugh. "You be there at five, ready to play. Grover Street Hall. I'll pay your expenses both ways."

I felt railroaded into the decision, but it was too late now. Scollay was already striding away, and one of his paid companions was holding open the back door of a Packard coupe.

They drove away. I stayed out a while longer and had a smoke. The evening was soft and fine and Scollay seemed more and more like something I might have dreamed. I was just wishing we could bring the bandstand out to the parking lot and play when Biff tapped me on the shoulder.

"Time," he said.

"Okay."

We went back in. The redhead had picked up some salt-and-pepper sailor who looked twice her age. I don't know what a member of the U.S. Navy was doing in central Illinois, but as far as I was concerned, he could have her if her taste was that bad.

I didn't feel so hot. The rye had gone to my head, and Scollay seemed a lot more real in here, where the fumes of what his kind sold were strong enough to float on.

"We had a request for *Camptown Races*," Charlie said.

"Forget it," I said curtly. "None of that now."

I could see Billy-Boy stiffen just as he was sitting down to the piano, and then his face was smooth again. I could have kicked myself around the block.

"I'm sorry, Billy," I told him. "I haven't been myself tonight."

"Sure," he said, but there was no big smile and I knew he felt bad. He knew what I had started to say.

I told them about the gig during our next break, being square with them about the money and how Scollay was a hood (although I didn't tell them there was another hood out to get him). I also told them that Scollay's sister was fat but nobody was to even crack a smile about it. I told them Scollay was sensitive.

It seemed to me that Billy-Boy Williams flinched again at that, but you couldn't tell it from his face. It would be easier to tell what a walnut was thinking by reading the wrinkles on the shell. Billy-Boy was the best ragtime piano player we ever had and we were all sorry about the little ways it got taken out on him as we traveled from one place to another—the Jim Crow car south of the Mason-Dixon line, the balcony at the movies, the different hotel room in some towns—but what could I do? In those days you lived with those differences.

We turned up at Grover Street on Friday at four o'clock just to make sure we'd have plenty of time to set up. We drove up from Morgan in a special Ford truck that Biff and Manny and I had put together. The back end was all enclosed, and there were two cots bolted to the floor. We even had an electric hotplate that ran off the battery, and the band's name was painted on the outside.

The day was just right—a ham-and-egg summer day if you ever saw one, with little white angel clouds floating over the fields. But it was hot and gritty in Chicago, full of the hustle and bustle you could get out of touch with in a place like Morgan. When we got there my clothes were sticking to my body and I needed to visit the comfort station. I could have used a shot of Tommy Englander's rye, too.

The hall was a big wooden building, sort of affiliated with the church where Scollay's sis was getting married, I guess. You know the kind of joint I mean—Ladies' Robert Browning Society on Tuesdays and Thursdays, Bingo on Wednesdays, and a sociable for the kids on Friday or Saturday night.

We trooped up the walk, each of us carrying his instrument in one hand and some part of Biff's drum-kit in the other. A thin lady with no breastworks to speak of was directing traffic inside. Two sweating men were hanging crepe paper. There was a bandstand at the front of the hall, and over it was a pair of pink-paper wedding bells and some tinsel lettering which said *BEST ALWAYS MAUREEN AND RICO.*

Maureen and Rico. Damned if I couldn't see why Scollay was so upset. Maureen and Rico. Now wasn't that a combination!

The thin lady saw us and swooped down to our end of the hall. She looked like she had a lot to say, so I beat her to the punch. "We're the band," I said.

"The band?" She blinked at our instruments distrustfully. "Oh. I was hoping you were the caterers."

I smiled as if caterers always carried snare drums and trombone cases.

"You can—" she began, but just then a tough-looking boy of about 19 strolled over. A cigarette was dangling from the left corner of his mouth, but so far as I could see, it wasn't doing a thing for his image except making his left eye water.

"Open that stuff up," he said.

Charlie and Biff looked at me and I just shrugged. We opened our cases and he looked at the horns. Seeing nothing that looked lethal, he wandered back to his corner and sat down on a folding chair.

"You can set your things up right away," she went on, as if there had been no interruption. "There's a piano in the other room. I'll have my men wheel it in when we're done putting up our decorations."

Biff was already lugging his drum-kit up onto the little stage.

"I thought you were the caterers," she said to me in a distraught way. "Mr. Scollay ordered a wedding cake and there are hors d'oeuvres and roasts of beef and—"

"They'll be here, ma'am," I said. "They get payment on delivery."

"—capons and roasts of pork and Mr. Scollay will be furious if—" She saw one of her men pausing to light a cigarette just below a dangling streamer and screamed, *"HENRY!"* The man jumped as if he had been shot, and I escaped to the bandstand.

We were all set up by a quarter to five. Charlie, the trombone player, was wah-wahing away into a mute and Biff was loosening up his wrists. The caterers had arrived at 4:20 and Miss Gibson (that was her name; she made a business out of such affairs) almost threw herself on them.

Four long tables had been set up and covered with white linen, and four black women in caps and aprons were setting places. The cake had been wheeled into the middle of the room for everyone to gasp over. It was six layers high, with a little bride and groom on top.

I walked outside to have a smoke and just about halfway through it I heard them coming, tooting away and making a general racket. When I saw the lead vehicle coming around the corner of the block below the church, I snubbed my smoke and went back inside.

"They're coming," I told Miss Gibson.

She went white as a sheet. That lady should have picked a different profession. "The tomato juice!" she screamed. "Bring in the tomato juice!"

I went back up to the bandstand and we got ready. We had played quite a few gigs like this before—what band hasn't?—and when the doors opened, we swung into a ragtime version of *The Wedding March* that I had arranged myself. Most receptions we played for loved it.

Everybody clapped and yelled and then started gassing among themselves, but I could tell by the way some of them were tapping their feet that we were getting through. We were on—it was going to be a good gig.

But I have to admit that I almost blew the whole number when the groom and the blushing bride walked in. Scollay, dressed in a morning-coat and a ruffled shirt and striped trousers, shot me a hard look, and don't think I didn't see it. The rest of the band kept a poker face too, and we didn't miss a note. Lucky for us. The wedding party, which looked as if it were made up almost entirely of Scollay's goons and their molls, were wise already. They had to be, if they'd been at the church. But I'd only heard faint rumblings, you might say.

You've heard about Jack Sprat and his wife. Well, this was a hundred times worse. Scollay's sister had the red hair he was losing, and it was long and curly. But not that pretty auburn shade you may be imagining. It was as bright as a carrot and as kinky as a bedspring. She looked just awful. And had Scollay said she was fat? Brother, that was like saying you can buy a few things in Macy's. The woman was a dinosaur—350 if she was a pound. It had all gone to her bosom and hips and thighs like it does on fat girls, making her flesh grotesque and frightening. Some fat girls have pathetically pretty faces, but Scollay's sis didn't even have that. Her eyes were too close together, her mouth was too big, and her ears stuck out. Even thin, she'd have been as ugly as the serpent in the garden.

That alone wouldn't have made anybody laugh, unless they were stupid or just poison-mean. It was when you added the groom, Rico, to the combination that you wanted to laugh until you cried.

He could have put on a top hat and stood in the top half of her shadow. He was about five three and must have weighed all of 90 pounds soaking wet. He was skinny as a rail, and his complexion was darkly olive. When he grinned around nervously, his teeth looked like a picket fence in a slum neighborhood.

We just kept right on playing.

Scollay roared, "The bride and the groom! May they always be happy!"

Everyone shouted their approval and applauded. We finished our number with a flourish, and that brought another round. Scollay's sister Maureen smiled nervously. Rico simpered.

For a while everyone just walked around, eating cheese and cold cuts on crackers and drinking Scollay's best bootleg Scotch. I had three shots myself between numbers, and it was pretty smooth.

Scollay began to look a little happier, too—I imagine he was sampling his own wares pretty freely.

He dropped by the bandstand once and said, "You guys play pretty good." Coming from a music lover like him, I reckoned that was a real compliment.

Just before everyone sat down to the meal, Maureen came up herself. She was even uglier up close, and her white gown (there must have been enough white satin to cover three beds) didn't help her at all. She asked us if we could play *Roses of Picardy* like Red

Nichols and His Five Pennies, because it was her very favorite song. Fat and ugly or not, she was very sweet about it, not a bit hoity-toity like some of the two-bitters that had been dropping by. We played it, but not very well. Still, she gave us a sweet smile that was almost enough to make her pretty, and she applauded when it was done.

They sat down to the meal around 6:15, and Miss Gibson's hired help rolled in the chow. They fell to it like a bunch of animals, which was not entirely surprising, and kept drinking it up all the time. I couldn't help noticing the way Maureen was eating, though. She made the rest of them look like old ladies in a roadside tea-room. She had no more time for sweet smiles or listening to *Roses of Picardy*. That lady didn't need a knife and a fork. She needed a steam shovel. It was sad to watch her. And Rico (you could just see his chin over the edge of the table where the bride's party was sitting) just kept handing her things, never changing that nervous simper.

We took a twenty-minute break while the cake-cutting ceremony was going on and Miss Gibson herself fed us out in the back part of the hall. It was hot as blazes with the cook stove on, and none of us was too hungry. Manny and Biff had brought some pastry boxes though, and were stuffing in slabs of roast beef and roast pork every time Miss Gibson turned her back.

By the time we returned to the bandstand, the drinking had begun in earnest. Tough-looking guys staggered around with silly grins on their mugs or stood in corners haggling over racing forms. Some couples wanted to Charleston, so we played *Aunt Hagar's Blues* (those goons ate it up) and *I'm Gonna Charleston Back to Charleston* and some other jazzy numbers like that. The molls rocked around the floor, flashing their rolled hose and sounding as shrill as macaws. It was almost completely dark outside, and millers and moths had come in through the open windows and were flitting around the light fixtures. And as the song says, the band played on. The bride and groom stood on the sidelines—neither of them seemed interested in slipping away early—almost completely neglected. Even Scollay seemed to have forgotten them. He was pretty drunk.

It was almost 8:00 when the little fellow crept in. I spotted him immediately because he was sober and dressed better than the rest of them. And he looked scared. He looked like a near-sighted cat in a dog pound. He walked up to Scollay, who was talking with some floozie right by the bandstand, and tapped him on the shoulder. Scollay wheeled around, and I heard every word they said.

"Who the hell are you?" Scollay asked rudely.

"My name is Katzenos," the fellow said, and his eyes rolled whitely. "I come from the Greek."

Motion on the floor came to a dead stop. We kept on playing though, you bet. Jacket buttons were freed, and hands stole out of sight. I saw Manny looking nervous. Hell, I wasn't so calm myself.

"Is that right?" Scollay said ominously.

The guy burst out, "I din't want to come, Mr. Scollay—the Greek, he has my wife. He say he kill her if I doan' give you his message!"

"What message?" Scollay asked. His face was like a thunder-cloud.

"He say—" The guy paused with an agonized expression. His throat worked like the words were physical, and caught in there. "He say to tell you your sister is one fat pig. He say . . . he say . . ." His eyes rolled wildly at Scollay's expression. I shot a look at Maureen. She looked as if she had been slapped. "He say she's tired of going to bed alone. He say—you bought her a hus-band."

Maureen gave a great strangled cry and ran out, weeping. The floor shook. Rico pattered after her, his face bewildered and un-happy.

But Scollay was the frightening one. His face had grown so red it was purple and I half expected his brains to just blow out his ears. I saw that same look of mad agony. Maybe he was just a cheap hood, but I felt sorry for him. You would have, too.

When he spoke his voice was very quiet.

"Is there more?"

The little Greek wrung his hands with anguish. "Please doan' kill me, Mr. Scollay. My wife—the Greek, he got my wife! I doan' want to say these thing. He got my wife, my woman! He—"

"I won't hurt you," Scollay said, quieter still. "Tell me the rest."

"He say the whole town is laughing at you."

There was dead silence for a second. We had stopped playing. Then Scollay turned his eyes to the ceiling. Both his hands were shaking and held out clenched in front of him. He was holding them in fists so tight that it seemed his hamstrings ran all the way up his arms.

"*All right!*" He screamed. "*ALL RIGHT!*"

And he ran for the door. Two of his men tried to stop him, to tell him it was suicide, just what the Greek wanted, but Scollay was like a crazy man. He knocked them down and rushed out into the black summer night.

In the dead quiet that followed, all I could hear was the little man's tortured breathing and somewhere out back, the soft sobbing of the fat bride.

Just about then the young kid who had braced us when we came in uttered a curse and made for the door.

Before he could get there, automobile tires screeched on the pavement down the block and a car engine roared.

"It's him!" The kid screamed from the doorway. "Get down, boss! Get down!"

The next second we heard gunshots—maybe as many as ten, mixed calibres, close together. The car howled away. I could see all I wanted to reflected in that kid's horrified face.

Now that the danger was over, all the goons rushed out. The door to the back of the hall banged open and Maureen ran through again, everything jiggling. Her face was even more puffy, now with tears as well as weight. Rico came in her wake like a bewildered valet. They went out the door.

Miss Gibson appeared in the empty hall, her eyes wide. The man who had brought the message to Scollay had powdered.

"What happened?" Miss Gibson asked.

"I think Mr. Scollay just got rubbed out," Biff said. He looked green.

Miss Gibson stared at him for a moment and then just fainted dead away. I felt a little like fainting myself.

Just then, from outside, came the most anguished scream I have ever heard, then or since. You didn't have to go and peek to know who was tearing her heart out in that street, keening over her dead brother even while the cops and news photographers were on their way.

"Let's get out of here," I muttered. "Quick."

We had it packed in before five minutes had passed. Some of the goons came back, but they were too drunk and too scared to notice the likes of us.

We went out the back, each of us carrying part of Biff's drum-kit. Quite a parade we must have made, walking up the street, for anyone who saw us. I led the way, with my horn case tucked under my arm and a cymbal in each hand. When we got to the truck we threw everything in, willy-nilly, and hauled our butts out of there. We averaged 45 miles an hour going back to Morgan, back roads or not, and Scollay's goons must not have bothered to tip the cops to us, because we never heard from them.

We never got the 200 bucks, either.

She came into Tommy Englander's speak about ten days later, a fat girl in a black mourning dress. It didn't look any better than the white satin.

Englander must have known who she was (her picture had been in the Chicago papers, next to Scollay's) because he showed her to a table himself and shushed a couple of drunks at the bar who were sniggering.

I felt really bad for her, like I feel for Billy-Boy sometimes. It's tough to be on the outside. And she had been very sweet, the little I had talked to her.

When the break came, I went over.

"I'm sorry about your brother," I said, feeling awkward and hot in the face. "I know he really cared for you—"

"I might as well have fired those guns myself," she said. She was looking at her hands, which were really her best feature, small and well formed. She had a musician's fingers. "Everything that little man said was true."

"That's not so," I said uncomfortably, not knowing if it was so or not. I was sorry I'd come over, she talked so strangely. As if she were all alone, and crazy.

"I'm not going to divorce him, though," she went on. "I'd kill myself first."

"Don't talk that way," I said.

"Haven't you ever wanted to kill yourself?" she asked, looking up at me passionately. "Doesn't it make you feel like that when people use you and then laugh about it? Do you know what it feels like to eat and eat and hate yourself and then eat more? Do you know what it feels like to kill your own brother because you're *fat?*"

People were turning to look, and the drunks were sniggering again.

"I'm sorry," she whispered.

I wanted to talk to her, to tell her I was sorry too. I wanted to tell her something that would make her feel better, but I couldn't think of a single thing.

So I just said, "I have to go. The next set—"

"Of course," she said softly. "Of course you do. Or they'll start to laugh at *you*. But why I came was—will you play *Roses of Picardy?* I thought you played it very nicely at the reception. Will you?"

"Sure," I said. "Glad to."

And we did. But she left halfway through the number. And since it was sort of schmaltzy for a place like Englander's, we swung into a ragtime version of *The Varsity Drag,* which always tore them up. I drank too much the rest of the evening and by closing time I had forgotten all about it, almost.

Leaving for the night, it came to me that I should have told her that life goes on. That's what you say when someone's loved one dies. But, thinking about it, I was glad I hadn't. Maybe that's what she was afraid of.

Of course now everyone knows about Maureen Romano and her husband Rico, who survives her as the taxpayers' guest in the Illinois State Penitentiary. How she took over Scollay's two-bit organization and worked it into a Prohibition empire that rivaled Capone's. How she wiped out the Greek and two other North Side gang leaders, swallowing their operations. Rico, the bewildered valet, became her first lieutenant and was supposedly responsible for a dozen gangland hits himself.

I followed her exploits from the West Coast, where we were making some pretty successful records. Without Billy-Boy, though. He formed a band of his own after we left Englander's, an all-black Dixieland band, and they did real well down south. It was just as well. Lots of places wouldn't even audition us with a Negro in the group.

But I was telling you about Maureen. She made great news copy, not just because she was shrewd, but because she was a big operator in more ways than one. When she died of a heart attack in 1933, the papers said she weighed 500 pounds, but I doubt that. No one gets that big, do they?

Anyway, her funeral made the front pages—more than anyone could say for Scollay, who never got anyplace past page 4 in his whole miserable career. It took ten pallbearers to carry her coffin. There was a picture of that coffin in one of the tabloids. It was a horrible thing.

Rico wasn't bright enough to hold things together by himself, and he fell for assault with intent to kill the very next year.

I've never been able to get her out of my mind, or the agonized, hangdog way Scollay had looked that first night when he talked about her.

It's all very strange. I can't feel too sorry for her, looking back. Fat people can always stop eating. Poor guys like Billy-Boy Williams can only stop breathing. I still don't see any way I could have helped either of them, but I do feel sort of bad every now and then. Probably because I'm not so young as I once was. That's all it is, isn't it? Isn't it?

THE WEATHER MAN

JACK RITCHIE

I made a notation. "You say the marriage ceremony is scheduled to take place at ten o'clock tomorrow morning?"

Juliette Carmichael nodded. "I know that's rather short notice, but I just heard about you yesterday. I'm getting married at St. Leo's and I'd like it to be a nice sunshiny day. The reception will be in the afternoon."

"I'm sorry," I said, "but I really can't guarantee receptions. That is a field unto itself. My province is only the marriage ceremony."

She accepted the limitation. "Well, *mainly* I'm concerned about the wedding. I wouldn't want it to rain."

I consulted several of my charts and then ran a finger down a logarithm column.

"It's truly amazing how you're able to predict the weather," Miss Carmichael said.

I agreed. "It is a gift which I try to use for the benefit of mankind." I multiplied 22,826 by 4,426, pondered over my slide rule, and then did a little long division. "I'm afraid that there's a slight inharmoniousness in the Fourth Quadrant of Spencer's Mobile Infraction."

"Oh, dear. You mean it's going to rain?"

I smiled reassuringly. "No. I positively guarantee that there will be no rain during the marriage ceremony itself. However—" I tapped the sheet of paper containing my calculations "—there *is* a chance of some cloudiness."

She showed considerable relief. "Well, what's a few clouds, any-way? Just as long as it doesn't rain. That's a bad way to start off a marriage, you know."

"Who's the lucky man?" I asked routinely.

"Terrance Renfro," she said, and wrote out a check for one hundred dollars.

When she left, I went back to my crossword puzzle.

It is my profession, my trade, my bag, to predict the weather—particularly for weddings—and I do this with an accuracy of over ninety-six percent.

How am I able to achieve this near-miracle? Really, it's quite simple.

I always predict fair weather. Always. Or to be more precise, I predict that it will not actually *rain*.

To begin with, according to weather statistics for this part of the Midwest, there are—on an average—only six days in the month of June which one might describe as "rainy."

Therefore, by predicting fair weather, my chances of being correct are immediately twenty-four out of thirty—or eighty percent.

But I go further.

I predict *only* that it will not rain "during the ceremony," which almost always takes place between the hours of eight and twelve in the morning.

And since it does not rain twenty-four hours a day, even on "rainy" days, a bit more mathematics will show that the chances that there will be rain during any particular four-hour segment of the month come to less than four percent.

And if it does rain?

I cheerfully give my clients double their money back—which, of course, occurs less than once in twenty-five times.

I had just finished my crossword puzzle when I heard the outer door to my waiting room open and close.

I let seven or eight minutes pass—one must not appear too eager to shear the sheep—and then opened my office door.

I found a young bespectacled man who studied me earnestly.

"Are you the weather man?" he asked. "The one who predicts the weather or double their money back?"

I acknowledged that. "With ninety-six percent accuracy."

He seemed impressed. "Ninety-six percent? In my book that means there's more to it than just predicting. You must have the *gift* to make the kind of weather you want."

I laughed deprecatingly. "People *have* said that about me."

He nodded. "Nobody is right ninety-six percent of the time without some kind of an inside track. Right? When you want sunshine, you *get* sunshine. And when you want rain, you *get* rain." He pushed his glasses back up the bridge of his nose. "And I want rain tomorrow."

Frankly, no one had ever asked me for rain before. I was curious. "Why?"

"I'm sorry, but that's personal. I just want a nice steady soaking rain tomorrow."

It wasn't that I was unwilling to take his one hundred dollars, but the odds were overwhelming that I would just have to give him double his money back tomorrow.

"I'm sorry," I said, "but I've already promised someone else sunshine. First come, first served, you know."

He fixed me with a steady eye. "I am not a person who haggles. I'll give you four thousand dollars if I get rain tomorrow."

Four thousand dollars? That did change the picture a bit.

I could take his money and leave town tonight. Four thousand made the move worth it. Besides, I'd practically milked this territory dry, anyway.

I rubbed my jaw thoughtfully. "Well, if rain is really *that* important to you, I just may be able to swing it."

He took out his checkbook and began writing. "You won't have any difficulty cashing this at the First National. I've already spoken to the people there."

When he handed me the check, I saw that his name was Terrance Renfro.

Terrance Renfro? And he wanted rain tomorrow?

I was mildly shocked. "You *want* rain on your wedding day?"

He flushed slightly. "It's sort of a tradition on my side of the family. It rained when my parents got married, and my grandparents, and my great-grandparents. I wouldn't want to break the chain. It's bad luck."

After he left, I went immediately to the bank and cashed his check. I returned to the office with the intention of gathering a few personal belongings before leaving town and found a tall, heavy-set man with hair greying at the temples waiting for me.

"Are you the weather man?" he asked.

I admitted as much and he studied me. "Do you know who I am?"

"I'm afraid not, sir," I said.

"The name is Carmichael. Mike Carmichael."

It came to me now where I'd seen his face before. In the newspapers. It was reported that—in a subterranean fashion—he controlled the north side of this city. Or was it the south? Actually, I didn't suppose it really mattered, except to the people living there. I felt distinctly uneasy in his presence.

"What was Renfro doing here?" he demanded.

I could see no particular point or profit in denying Renfro's visit. "He wanted a weather prediction."

"And what did you give him?"

"I said it would rain tomorrow."

Further wheels meshed in my brain. Mike Carmichael? Juliette Carmichael? Was she his daughter? And Terrance Renfro his future son-in-law?

I yielded to the impulse to perspire. I had predicted fair weather for Carmichael's daughter and rainy weather for his son-in-law. The contradiction was clearly embarrassing and could possibly lead to pain.

I laughed quickly. "I predicted a sunny *morning* for your daughter and rain in the *afternoon* for your son-in-law-to-be."

He regarded me skeptically. "You're telling me that you can pinpoint weather like that?"

I pointed to my slide rule, my charts, and the other various window dressing. "It's all quite complicated, but an exact science."

"How much did you charge Juliette for the sunshine?"

"One hundred dollars. My usual fee."

"And Renfro?"

I hesitated a fraction of a second. "One hundred dollars, of course."

He leaned over me slightly. "I got other information. Now tell me why Renfro would pay you four thousand dollars for rainy weather?"

My throat was quite dry. "He told me he was getting married and it's a tradition in his family that it rains *sometime* on the wedding day. I promised him rain *only* for the afternoon."

Carmichael winced with disbelief. "He gave you four thousand dollars just for predicting rain?"

I dabbed at my forehead with a handkerchief. "I seem to have an unexplainable *influence* on the weather and some of my clients are so grateful for my services that they *insist* on paying me a bit more than the usual fee."

Carmichael rubbed his neck. "What Juliette sees in that dimwit, I'll never know. I got the feeling he's up to something. I'd ask him myself, firm-like, but he'd run to Juliette and she'd yell at me." He moved to the hall door. "But I'm keeping my eye on him. And you."

When he was gone, I hurriedly stuffed a briefcase with the things I intended to take with me and then glanced about the reception room to make certain I had left nothing of importance behind.

I frowned at the racing form lying on the magazine table. Who had left it there?

I paged through the booklet and found that it covered tomorrow's races at Sportland Park. A green ink-mark had been made beside one horse in each race.

Renfro had signed his check with green ink, hadn't he?

I studied the form again. Evidently Renfro played the favorite in each race—except for the fourth, where he picked a horse named Watercress.

Watercress had been out six times and never in the money. The form gave odds of fifty to one.

Why would Renfro pick favorites in all of the races except the fourth? Did he know something? I thought it over. Horses. Watercress. Long shot. Rain. A wet track.

Could Watercress run in the mud? *Really* run in the mud? A man could make a killing if he had inside information like that.

And Renfro was willing to part with four thousand dollars to make it rain.

The killing would have to be made off-track, of course. Any large amount of money bet on Watercress at Sportland Park would immediately bring down the odds before post time.

And off-track betting on the north side—or was it the south?—was controlled by Mike Carmichael.

But obviously Renfro wasn't telling his prospective father-in-law about the coup. That meant that Renfro was going to marry Carmichael's daughter in the morning and double-cross Carmichael in the afternoon.

I sighed at the iniquity of man and also at my inability to provide rain on command.

When I reached my apartment, I packed a suitcase and opened the door to the hall.

Carmichael stood outside. His eyes went to the suitcase. "Going somewhere?"

I cleared my throat. "I just received word that my favorite Uncle Mortimer in Portland passed away and I was about to attend his funeral."

Carmichael shook his head. "Let Uncle Mortimer get put away without you. Stay in your apartment until I say different."

I went back to my apartment and closed the door.

Obviously Carmichael had decided to keep an eye on me until he found out what Renfro was up to.

After an hour, I opened the door again. Carmichael was gone, but one of his representatives had taken his place. The short burly man stared me back into my apartment.

I tried again at intervals, including two and four o'clock in the morning. The faces changed, but the principle of guarding me remained the same.

Saturday morning dawned bright and clear. Juliette would have a perfect day for her wedding.

I phoned the corner restaurant and had breakfast sent up, but I found I couldn't eat it.

At eleven, as I was mixing my third bourbon and soda, I glanced out of the window. The sky had begun to darken.

At a quarter to twelve, it began to rain. A steady, soaking rain. One that could make a race track really sloppy.

I glanced at my watch and took a long drink. What time was the fourth race at Sportland Park? Probably about three.

I sat down at the phone and put in a call to Joey Evans in Peoria.

"Joey," I said, "I'd like to put five hundred on Watercress in the fourth at Sportland Park."

There was a pause while he evidently wrote that down. "Haven't heard from you in a while."

"Been traveling."

"Watercress? Looks like a dog to me. Five hundred? You never put down more than a couple of tens before."

"I know, Joey. But last night I dreamed about watercress sandwiches and then this morning when I picked up the form, there it was. Watercress in the fourth. You got to play something like that, Joey."

He could understand that. "All right. Five hundred on Watercress."

Next I dialed Ed Leonard in Madison, Weiss in Milwaukee, and Kramer in Rockford. Five hundred here, four hundred there. I spread it around, making certain, of course, that none of it was laid down in Carmichael territory, whichever it was. When I was through, I had four thousand bucks on the line.

I made myself another drink. Now what about Carmichael?

When Watercress came in and his bookies got hit big by Renfro, he would ask questions until he got answers.

But Renfro probably had plans to get out of town fast, safe, rich, and possibly with Carmichael's daughter.

That left me here, the patsy.

Carmichael was bound to decide that somehow Renfro and I were in on the deal together. It wasn't too hard to imagine what Carmichael would do to me.

I took courage in a few more drinks and then opened the door to the hall.

The short burly man was back.

"I've got to see Carmichael right away," I said.

He shook his head. "Carmichael's at his daughter's wedding reception. Whatever you got to say will wait."

"This is a matter of life, death, and especially money," I said. "Lots of money, and Carmichael will be doing the paying if I don't get to him in time."

It took my guard a full minute of jaw rubbing and head scratching to make up his mind. "Okay," he said finally. "Let's go."

He took me to the Westerland Hotel where Juliette Carmichael's wedding reception was being held in a packed hall on the third floor.

He caught Carmichael's eye across the room and pointed to me. Carmichael frowned, then nodded and made his way through the mob.

When he and I were alone in a small room off the main hall, he scowled. "Well?"

"I now know why your son-in-law wanted rain so damn bad," I said. I showed Carmichael the racing form and explained the entire setup.

Carmichael's face darkened. He opened the door and spoke to the burly man just outside. "Get that little bastard Renfro and bring him here."

When Renfro was escorted into the room, he didn't look at all happy, especially when he saw me.

Carmichael did the talking, and when he was through Renfro's mouth hung open.

"But, Dad," he said, "it's really nothing like that at all. Yesterday morning when Juliette told me she was going to this weather man, it gave me a *brilliant* idea. The weather man *guaranteed* double your money back if you didn't get the weather he predicted. I checked with the weather bureau and they said there wasn't a ghost of a chance of rain this weekend. So I went to the weather man and ordered *rain* for today. Don't you see, Dad? I knew positively it wasn't going to rain and so he'd have to give me double my money back. Eight thousand dollars."

I blinked. Was Renfro really that simple? That naive?

Carmichael waved the racing form in front of Renfro's nose. "Do you deny this is your green ink?"

Renfro frowned at the form. "I thought I forgot that in the weather man's office. I always play the favorites, except I had this dream about watercress sandwiches. But even then I only bet two dollars like I always do."

Carmichael grabbed the phone on the corner table. After a few calls, he put down the receiver. He seemed slightly incredulous. "There hasn't been any heavy betting on Watercress with anybody in my organization. Also, the fourth race at Sportland was just run and Watercress came in sixth."

Sixth? I felt distinctly ill.

Four thousand dollars down the drain on a damn horse that couldn't run in the mud—or anywhere else, for that matter.

Carmichael glared at his son-in-law. "Didn't it come to your keen mind that the weather man would probably skip out of town with your four thousand?"

Renfro frowned. "Do you think I should have checked him out with the Better Business Bureau first?"

"One other thing," Carmichael said.

"Yes, Dad?"

Carmichael pointed to the window. "It's raining."

Renfro nodded sadly. "It looks like you can't even trust the weather bureau these days."

Carmichael indicated the door. "Go join the lucky bride."

When Carmichael and I were alone again, he studied me. "Everybody's missed the real point but me. You said it would be sunny in the morning and it was. You said it would rain in the afternoon and it did."

He offered me a cigar. "Even the weather bureau with all its fancy instruments couldn't call that. So maybe you got something going for you. Maybe you really got the power to call the weather any way you want it, rain or shine."

He lit the cigar for me. "Suppose I got myself a real good horse that runs terrific on a wet track and I keep quiet about it? And suppose *you* provide the rain on the day I need it? Something like that could be worth twenty grand to me."

Twenty thousand? To make it rain? And suppose it really *did* rain on the day Carmichael wanted? I could parlay that twenty grand into—

I took a long drag on the cigar and smiled at Carmichael. Yes, there was still one born every minute.

THE CAPTAIN M. CAPER

AVRAM DAVIDSON

Abel Serles hurried along Sixth Avenue. Partly he was looking for an answer to the problem of Sally and partly he was looking for a place where he could buy a necktie for not more than a dollar. Without realizing it in his haste, he let the necktie move into first place and then stopped thinking about Sally altogether.

Usually Abel Serles did not wear a necktie, nor did he usually wear a suitcoat.

There had once been a time when he had regularly worn both—both pressed to a fare-thee-well; but then the irresistible force met a movable object: Serles, who had been writing evenings and Sundays for over a year, had in one week sold not just his first story but his first three stories!—and spectacularly failed to meet the quota required of all sales personnel at Banting Brothers. It had been a case of you-can't-fire-me, I-quit—and the firm had let him have it *his* way because old Mr. J. B. Banting didn't approve of unemployment insurance, to which he, Abel Serles, would have been entitled if he'd been discharged.

Old J. B. Banting didn't approve of most of the social changes which had occurred in the U.S.A. since John Quincy Adams had died on the floor of the House with an Abolitionist petition in his pocket and what has been described as "a smile like the Peace of God" on his face.

At the present moment, however, Abel was thinking of a different kind of unemployment insurance. Either Seventh or Eighth

Avenue might have been a better bet for what he was seeking—
though absolutely not Fifth Avenue or any of the streets farther east
—not for a dollar necktie! However, Sixth Avenue was on his way,
uptown toward West 44th Street and the lobby of the Algonquin
Hotel; and he scanned every store window as he zipped along, not
without some rueful recollection of the drunk who searched the
north side of the street for the quarter he'd dropped on the south
side, because the light on the north side—

The old chestnut ceased abruptly to be applicable as he saw,
between a store selling factory-rejected classical phonograph
records at $1.50 each and a shop which printed "newspapers" with
the customer's own name in the headline of his choice (*Manny Hits
Town, Pretty Girls Leave*), a place selling just what he was looking
for: NECKTIES! NECKTIES! GOING OUT OF BUSINESS! 99¢
AND UP.

The "and up" he could forego, but the sales tax would cut into
his money. Somehow, Serles felt, the Algonquin was not the place
where he wanted to go grubbing in his pockets for loose change.
He did the grubbing right then and there, finding—thank the Lord!
—enough odd pennies to cover the tax and give him four one-
dollar bills back for his fiver.

"I'll take this one," he said, not quite snatching the very first
cravat he saw, this first one being an imitation plaid in colors
gaudy enough to cause another rising of the clans; but the first one
he saw which would pass muster. The Algonquin wasn't all that
particular—and Godfrey Bland wasn't particular at all. Not about
neckties, at least.

"Yessir, very nice, how about some—"

"Don't bother to wrap it up." Serles seized the tie and strode out.
It was hot in the street, which was being ripped up again, and the
air was thick with asphalt smells and automobile fumes. He adjusted the tie as he continued his rapid pace north. It was 4:15;
Godfrey Bland always arrived at 4:00 and would have had at least
two drinks by now; he would leave at 5:00 for his home in Great
Shores, Long Island. It was imperative that Serles should meet him
after he had somewhat unwound from a hard day at the literary
agency—shouting his demands for escalator clauses and movie,
TV, stage, radio, ballet, and Punch-and-Judy rights for the United
Kingdom, Australasia, and Luxembourg over the transcontinental

and transatlantic telephones as if trying out for the finals in a hog-calling contest—and before he started winding up again for the trip back to Great Shores, where dwelt Mrs. Godfrey Bland (who raised show collies) and where whatever he was likely to find cooking on the stove was likelier to be for the collies than for Godfrey Bland.

Yes, between 4:15 and 4:45 was the best time to be in the Algonquin lobby—if you were Abel Serles, that is, and wanting to see Godfrey Bland.

For weeks after his first and tripartite success as an author, Serles had stuck so close to his typewriter all day that when he emerged in the evenings for food and frolic, all the dry-cleaning places were closed; but such was his zeal, his pleasure, and his absorption in his new profession that it was almost a month before he had occasion to discover that they were all closed. His tie and suitcoat, which he'd donned automatically each night, were by then pretty bad. He had flung them in the closet he kept chiefly for flinging things into, kicked off his no longer glossy Thom McCanns, and—shirt-sleeved and stocking-footed—invested in the far, far less formal kind of clothes sold in little stores that never closed, the kind of clothes (he realized with exultation and a sense of infinite release) that he had always wanted to always wear.

And *"Abe!"* she had said. *"You look so* different *tonight!"*

That had been five years ago. Both suitcoat and necktie had been cleaned since then, but not frequently and not recently. Five years . . . "A lustrum!" as Frederic H. Beard would have said—and did, when opportunity offered. Old Fred Beard, muffled to the eyebrows in unshorn hair and whiskers, cosuitor (so to speak) of Sally —Old Freddie Beard, perpetual student, financing his perpetual studies by writing learned articles about the hilts, tangs, blades, bindings, and what-else-have-you of Japanese swords, on which he was perhaps the nation's leading authority—Old Freddie, how he would snort and how he would scorn if he knew on what purpose his former schoolmate was now hastening.

Stopping just long enough to adjust the necktie, Abel turned into West 44th Street. He hurried on, cursing the erratic memory which had allowed him to remember the necessity for a suitcoat—wrinkled though it was, it would serve—but to forget the equally necessary tie. The lapse was costing him the price of at least one drink, but that couldn't be helped: without coat and tie he could not be served in the Algonquin, and without being served in the Algonquin he could not hope successfully to talk business with Godfrey Bland.

Thirty years past, the Algonquin had been the height of fashion as a literary and theatrical center. Abel Serles had not seen its lobby then. In fact, he had barely been born. Alexander Woollcott was just a name to him, FPA only a set of initials. Unlearned as he was in hotel lobby décor of that period, it nevertheless seemed to him that the place could hardly have changed much, and he liked its small and crowded old-fashioned lobby. He also liked the fact that you could get drinks served to you right there—but he didn't like either a tithe as much as did Godfrey Bland, who was sitting in his usual place at his usual hour: heavy-set, redfaced cherub with curly gray hair, looking into his drink as if it might be a crystal ball and he, crystal-gazer, seeing therein strange things which for all their seeming strangeness yet failed to surprise.

Also, as usual, on the table in front of him was a half-eaten sandwich. A cynic might suppose it was fortification against finding nothing to eat in Great Shores except perhaps a pot of bubbling horse-meat intended for the supper of Great Shores Midlothian Dukie and the latter's current consorts; but Godfrey had another explanation. "It's not the booze that does you in," he said. *"It's the not-eating.* The boys and girls whose livers turn green and kick out on them, it's not because they drank, you know. It's because they forgot to eat! Malnutrition! But not me. No, sir. True enough, when Godfrey Bland eats he always drinks—but when Godfrey Bland drinks he always eats!"

Frederic H. Beard, hearing Abel repeat this once, had raised his eyebrows. "In other words, 'A sandwich a day keeps the A.A. away.' Maybe so, maybe so."

Bland looked up as Abel came to his table, and thrust out his lower jaw in greeting. "Hello, Abe. What are you doing here with this bunch of phonies?"

Abel knew better than to presume on Bland's description of the Algonquin habitués, being well aware that Bland reserved such criticism for himself. "The West Side for morning, the East Side for afternoon, and the Village for evening," Abel said.

Bland cocked his head and moved his mouth reflectively. "Well, as philosophy, it has its faults. But as an aphorism, it'll do. Emil! What are you having, Abe?"

Emil, white-jacketed, hovered over them. Abel had a *shtick* he'd been waiting for the proper occasion to use. It might as well be this one. "A double Demerara," he said.

Emil beamed, Bland stared. "What in the name of Vishnu is even a single Demerara?" he demanded.

"Very fine rum, sir, from British Guiana," Emil said, "*Very* fine rum. No ice, of course, sir."

"Of course not," Abel said virtuously, no sacrifice being too great for his art.

Bland looked impressed, as he was meant to be. "Well, I suppose you might as well drink it while you can still get it," he said. "Look what happened to Cuban cigars . . . British Guiana, hey? A government headed by a *dentist,* for crying out loud! You know what's the trouble with dentists, Abe? They've all got inferiority complexes because they're not doctors."

Emil returned with the double Demerara and a drink to replace the one which Bland had by this time finished, which was nominally a martini—although Abel knew that no vermouth was ever allowed to come near it—and Bland drank up, with a gesture to Abel to do likewise.

The rum wasn't bad, although Abel would rather have had it with lots of coke, lots of ice, and half of a lime.

He had paid for this round, allowed Bland to pay for the next. Whether or not he would be able to afford the third, Abel was uneasily unsure. Perhaps it wouldn't come to that. And Bland babbled on.

"I don't know what's the matter with most of you writers," he said, waving a plump hand to a publisher's editor who had just come in. "Think you're a bunch of artists, for crying out loud. Want to know something? You're not. Artists either have patrons or else they go and starve in a garret and are happy about it. Writers don't want to starve, not that I blame 'em, and they don't have patrons, not that they should. Writers are—most of 'em—*small businessmen*—that's what they are. None of you want to admit it, though. Some of you, you can write fine, but you can't meet a deadline to save your lives. Now, what kind o' way is that to run a small business?

"Tom Carp, you take Tom Carp, a *lovely* writer. But—look—I come to him, I call him up, I say 'Tom, I've got an assignment for you. Two sex novels. Good terms, good advance. Six months to write 'em. You can use a pseudonym. What do you say?' 'Swell,' he says, 'swell.' And then I find out he's got three other assignments, he's two months past the deadline on one, a *year*—for crying out loud!—past the deadline on the other, and *two years* past the deadline on the third."

He picked up his glass, moodily set it down again. "So of course I had to say, 'Sorry, Tom.' Made me feel rotten, because he's a *lovely* writer. Too good for sex novels, but, then, there you are. Now, I've got four or five guys I could get like *that*. Clients of mine, too, which Tom isn't, any more than you are. And they'd meet the deadlines with time to spare. So what's the trouble? The trouble is, they're rotten writers, that's the trouble. Good enough to write one of these crummy little items that pay $500 for all rights. But not good enough for what Clay and Curtain have in mind. They're branching out, had good luck with Crime and Science Fiction; now they want to try Sex. Of course they want something better than ordinary hackwork."

Godfrey Bland brooded a long moment. Then he smiled, somewhat twistedly. Another of his troubles was, he said, that business was too good. All his clients, the topnotch ones, were up to their navels in contracts for books. Meanwhile, he had contracts of his own to supply books for eager publishers.

He had called up or tried to call up other writers, clients of other agents, or acting as their own agents—he wasn't greedy for the measly ten percent—and with what results? Bob Bigelow couldn't take time off from his play, Saunders Pierce (*né* Siegfried Poltz, and who could blame him) was doing a series of biographies of famous women for a hardcover publisher, Nissim Stone was in Spain doing research, and so it went.

"Hmmm, yes, I see your problem," Abel Serles said. He sighed.

"*Sophis*ticated sex novels, that's what these have to be."

"Hmm, yes, I see—"

"Not just *love*—love is for animals, only human beings can appreciate lust. But *sophis*ticated lust, you understand."

"Well—"

Abruptly, Godfrey Bland ceased staring into his glass of gin, swung his head around and looked Abel Serles in the face. "What are *you* doing these days, Abe?" he asked.

"I'm working on some short stories, Godfrey."

The literary agent jerked his head back, stared at the younger man reproachfully. "Short *stories*? What a disgusting phrase. Short stories haven't been economical since—since—well, not for years. All right, I grant you," his tone was indulgent, "that short stories are more economical than poems. True. But nobody tries to make a living out of poems. Novels!" He prodded Serles with a fat red knuckle. *"Novels!* That's where the money is!"

Things were beginning to move. Bland almost always had assignments to give out, and when he didn't, he knew who did.

"Sex novels, you mean?" Serles asked, his tone somewhat amused, somewhat scornful—and his mind on his unpaid rent and empty refrigerator.

Bland raised a cautionary finger. "So*phis*ticated sex novels. Otherwise, why would I bother? What are you worrying about? Your reputation? Use a pseudonym. I think we've got a couple of housenames you could choose from, or make up your own. What the hell, fellow, *you're* sophisticated! Anyone who knows a brand of booze *I* never heard of, *has* to be. One thousand on signing the contract and another thousand on delivery of an acceptable manuscript—can you beat those terms? No, of course you can't. What do you say?"

"Well—"

"Come around to the office tomorrow morning. If you need an advance we can arrange for you to have something right away. What time is it?" Abruptly his mood changed. "I've got a train to make. I'll rush like hell, and then it'll stop in Brooklyn for an hour to contemplate its navel or something. Oh, well. See you tomorrow, Abe. *Emil!*" Godfrey Bland paid the tab and plodded out.

It had all gone as Serles had hoped. Not that he hoped, exactly, for two sex novels; but he would have taken anything that came down the pike: juveniles, health fads, Cuban exposés pro or con, the role in the Civil War of the Confederate Bureau of Weights and Measures, or fast-moving novels of crime in which the hardboiled detective hero shoots the erring blonde one inch to the right of her appendectomy scar; such was the urgency of Abel's financial situation.

He sat in a mildly pleasant daze induced not only by success but by two double Demeraras on an almost empty stomach. Authors, editors, agents, publishers, PR men, Girls Friday in a wide variety of shapeliness, actors and actresses and old ladies from Dubuque came and went, gabbling and silent, and off in one corner a man with a beard calmly changed a little baby. Serles was observing, with academic interest only, that it was a little boy baby, when someone gestured to him from halfway across the lobby. Wobbling only in the slightest, he went over.

"I'm Jack Foster," said the gesturer. "We met, briefly, at Bob Bigelow's autographing party when his book came out." It was the publisher's editor to whom Bland had waved earlier.

"Oh, yes, you're with—" The name of the firm failed him.

"Samuel Rice. We're still kind of new. We're young, but we're growing daily. How about a drink?"

Abel shook his head. "I've paid the cocktail hour all the obeisance it's going to get," he said. "But if this is on the expense account I'll have a sandwich."

"All right," Foster said equably. "Let's go in the restaurant. I'm in the mood for a cool green salad myself." He was a thin man in his late thirties, with dusty brown hair.

They talked about Bob Bigelow's book for a while, then Foster asked—almost inevitably—what Abel was working on "these days." And was told. The editor gave a tiny sigh. "Short stories aren't in our line, I'm afraid. We just might bring out a volume of newly discovered tales by Edgar Allan Poe, then again we just might not. Nonfiction is our chief product. When I say product, that's just what I mean—not to underrate the books, you understand; but we sort of specialize in items by people who've got something to say but who aren't professional writers and don't know how to say it. We provide them with professional assistance—"

"Ghosting, you mean?"

"Ghosting, I mean," Foster said, still equably. "The actual writer gets an acknowledgement in the credits somewhere, but none of this *As Told To* stuff, which makes the author of the first instance sound like an illiterate, which he sometimes is. And then we publicize. We publicize very, very much. You may or may not remember, but we are Samuel Rice *Associates*. We've got all kinds of associates in all kinds of media, and when we puff a book, believe me the book *stays* puffed. It sells and sells and sells. Are you interested?"

"Yes."

"You're not doing anything for Godfrey right at the moment?" He ate salad as Abel explained that Bland had made him an attractive proposal to which, however, he had not definitely committed himself. "All right," said Foster, spooning up a dab of dressing. "If you definitely uncommit yourself, and Godfrey isn't sore about it—and he's enough of an old pro himself not to be—you can call me tomorrow for an appointment. I can't tell you now what it is, but I can tell you that it's a lot better than sex novels. There's more money in it, for one thing. And for another thing, you write some piece of paperback tripe, it's dead three months after it hits the stand, and who remembers who wrote it? Whereas a credit like this one, even if you don't get your name on the cover—well, it's a hard cover, not a soft one. And you know what a difference *that* can make."

Abel did. "I'll be in touch," he said.

He heard voices as he came up the stairs of the old three-story red-brick Greenwich Village building he lived in. Sally Stone was in his apartment, and so was Frederic Beard—the latter, on the telephone.

Sally and Fred were often together—had been, in fact, together when Abel first met her. Were they together rather more these days than Abel, now he came to think of it, really liked? He thought they sort of were, then realized it wasn't that so much as that he himself was not so often alone with Sally as he would have liked to be. Their friendship had been casual and comfortable and, at times, very warm indeed: "honest" was the way he had liked to think of it. Was? Had been. Not that it was now *uncomfortable*, far from it; but Abel had a while back grown aware that his own *unwillingness* to become more deeply involved with her was resulting in her own *willingness* to become less deeply involved with him; and to this problem he had as yet found no answer.

". . . nobody in this country," Old Fred was informing his invisible communicant, who might be anywhere from Point Barrow to Chula Vista, but what difference to Abel?—Fred always paid for his own calls; "and only one man in Japan. He lives in Izo Prefecture, I think, I've got his name and address somewhere at home, and so far as I know he's the only one who still does hilt bindings in the Eighteenth Century Satsuma style. Shall I look him up for you? All right, I'll do that, Dr. Bolzack. And I'll see what dates the polisher has open for your swords, too. Goodbye." He turned around and said, with satisfaction, "We eat."

"Good" said Abel. "But we won't have to wait till Dr. Grulzack or whatever his name is sends you a check—I think I've got a good assignment waiting for me tomorrow."

And Sally said, "We eat. But not because of your assignment tomorrow. I brought a bag of goodies with me *right now*." She was a statuesque brunette, which was just as good as a statuesque blonde any day, with a possible edge in that she was less likely to suffer from sunburn.

"I will now kiss you," Abel said, and did so. It wasn't Sally who had said, that time, "Abe! You look so *different* tonight!"—that one had gone to live in a cave in Guadalajara with three Peace Marchers. Now, from the pride of paper bags on the table, Sally produced two kinds of smoked fish and two of soft cheese, a jar of cold sorrel soup, butter, ice cubes, whiskey, mixer, and Bialystockers—those succulent onion rolls which start out to be doughnuts and then change their minds.

"What is the decision of the caucus?" she asked.

"We eat!" declared Fred and Abel with one voice, Abel adding that he would emit shrill little squeals of delight if he could get his voice up high enough, and Fred wanting to know what the occasion was. The occasion, she informed him, was Quahog State Bank and Trust Company of Boston Check Day. The men gave three cheers for the Quahog State Bank and Trust Company of Boston, then three more for Edward Erastus Leverett XXVth.

Sally, serving out the goodies, acknowledged the cheers on behalf of the absent honored. "I will say—and this is my sincere advice to all poor working girls—if you ever must marry and divorce, by all means let it be to and from a Boston Brahmin with more apartment houses than he knows what to do with. Edward

Erastus Leverett XXVth is a *gentleman,* and I'm sure I no longer begrudge him his mother complex in the slightest. The poor man has to have *some* hobby. Dear, dreadful old Mother Leverett, with her diamond dog collar and her spastic colon; oh, well. Dinner is served."

"Any news?" Fred asked presently, his vasty beard flecked with crumbs which he carefully brushed onto his plate.

"Don't ask me," Abel demurred, reaching for another moist, pink, delicious flake of kippered salmon. "I haven't read any periodicals at all lately, except for a copy of the Sam Jones Junior High School Alumni Review, which my sister was kind enough to send me. Ask Sally."

Sally protested that she never read newspapers any more. "Not even the *Village Voice* or *The Realist.* I can stand only so many exposés of Tammany Hall and Organized Religion. However, let me see, I did catch a news program on TV this afternoon. Oh, yes." She nodded, began to tick off her fingers. "Liz has gone excommunicado again. There was another coup in North Dong Dunc. The U.S. government is either not going to raise taxes or not going to lower them. Somebody else is saying wicked things about the Mafia. And there was a baseball game, but I forget who played, or what the score was."

Abel made himself another drink. "Well, Fred," he said, "so now you know."

But Fred only snorted.

The premises of Samuel Rice Associates occupied two floors over a chi-chi barber shop specializing in blond rinses for aging young men and the showroom of a renegade Zoroastrian who sold imitation *objets d'art* from the Nether Orient. The elevator smelled of shampoo and curried fish, but the publishers' office was air-conditioned and nice. Two men who didn't look at all like writers sat on facing benches in the anteroom and surveyed Abel bleakly as he approached the receptionist's desk, then lost interest when she confirmed his appointment.

Jack Foster, on seeing Abel Serles enter his office, frowned slightly, as if feeling a slight pain somewhere, the location of which momentarily eluded him. Then his face cleared.

"Were you able to satisfy Godfrey?" he asked. Abel assured him that Godfrey had taken it philosophically. "Well, let's go in, then," said Foster. But he did not rise. "I don't remember if I told you or not, but this is all on the q.t., whether you take the job or not. If that isn't agreeable to you—"

Abel said it was perfectly agreeable. Foster nodded, got up, and led the way into another room, which opened off his office. Seated therein was a man behind the desk, who, was, Abel assumed, Samuel Rice; a man in front of the desk, who had on a flowered sports shirt and goldrimmed spectacles; and two men sitting in the corners of the room on the other side of the desk.

"Sam," said Foster, "this is Abe Serles, about whom, et cetera."

Mr. Rice said something affable. The man in front of the desk looked on with interest. "Abe," Foster went on, "this is the gentleman with whom you will be working, if everything figures out satisfactorily. Meet Captain Marryat."

It seemed to Abel that he could scarcely have revealed much surprise, but the man in the flowered sports shirt burst out into a hearty Ha Ha! as they shook hands. "He don't believe it!" he guffawed. "Well, that's okay, why *should* he? One thing I can't stann, I can't stann a dope. Please ta meetcha."

"My pleasure, Captain Marryat." Serles could, with just a little effort, picture him on the poopdeck of a gravel barge.

The "captain" laughed again. Rice and Foster smiled faintly. The two men in the corners facing the door did not change their expressions, which were expressionless.

"Yer all right, kid," the "Captain" said, taking Abel's arm just below the elbow and giving it a squeeze. "You do know who I am, do ya? Am I c'reck? One a them writers, all a time in a nyev'ry tar, huh! Well, at's all right, never mine, you'll loin. See, leave me explain the situation to ya. These two gentlemen, Mr. Ice and Mr. Foster, they toll me yer not suppose to know my rill name jus' yet. So *I* figure, what the hell, I'll have some fun witcha. Om gunna be like a writer myself, ain' I? So Om entitle' to a pseudonymph, ain' I? *Okay.* See, when I was a kid I read this book, *Masterman Ready,* by Captain Marryat. Wadda book! *Robinson Crusoe,* you can have it. Dull as a dishwasher. *Swiss Family Robinson?* Kid stuff. But *Masterman Ready?* Great! So I figure, I'll call myself Captain Marryat. Okay?"

Abel said that it was okay with him. "Captain Marryat" hit him a friendly blow on the shoulder, repeated that he was "all right," then turned to the publisher. "Well, does he take the contrack?" he asked.

Rice cleared his throat. "Maybe Mr. Serles should know a few more details before he makes his mind up. Captain, uh, Marryat— how should I put it—has led a very interesting life—"

"*Maron!*" said Captain Marryat.

"—and now he has retired and plans to go abroad for a little while. Now, it seems to us that the story of his life and, uh, professional career would make a very interesting book. He will provide the facts, you—if it'll be you—will write it, and me and my associates will publish and publicize it. That's the general picture."

Captain M., who had been nodding and smiling, suddenly spun around. "I don't wantcha ta think I can't *write,* now, kid. I can write. Gimme a pencil. Anybody got a pencil?"

"Your word is sufficient for me, Captain," Abel assured him.

And so the conference proceeded.

The terms, Ricewise, were not grandiloquent in the extreme, consisting of the same $2000 offered for one of Mr. Godfrey Bland's much-despised sex novels. Bland (or his publishers, Clay and Curtain), it is true, did offer a rising scale of royalties dependent on subsequent editions and their sale, and Rice did not. However, no one ever expected the Bland books to *have* subsequent editions, whereas with Rice—

"You get a straight royalty, it doesn't go up and it doesn't go down. How come?" Rice asked and Rice answered. "Because our books don't sell on account of the writing. They sell because we push them. And a fixed royalty on a book that's pushed the way we push books is a lot better than a paper rise in royalty on a book which is not pushed. That's the picture."

Serles thought that he had seen better pictures, but there was some truth in what the publisher said. And by this time he was rather intrigued. Captain Marryat's "interesting life," whatever it was or had been like, sounded as though it might be much more interesting than confecting even a sophisticated sex novel. Or even two. And then the "Captain" himself had offers to make.

"You'll be woikin wit *me,* kid," he said. "Up in *my* place. It's a pretty classy place, aircondition', private bar, the works. Yull be eatin wit me, yull be eatin what I eat, an', kid—lemme tellya—I eat *good.* An when somebuddy eat wit me, they never even *see* the bill. *Okay?"*

"*Okay."*

Captain Marryat beamed again as Abel dodged his punch. "Drawr up them papers fer the kid to sign," he directed. "I gotta go now. My masewer comes at noon." Suddenly there was no trace of geniality in his face or manner. He leveled his forefinger at Abel Serles. "Ya gotta keep ya mouth shut. Ya know that, dontcha?"

Jack Foster said, smoothly and swiftly, "Mr. Serles is aware that he is contractually obligated to maintain strict secrecy in this whole matter."

For a moment the face of Captain Marryat remained blank. Then he beamed again. *"Okay!"* he said. He snapped his fingers. The two men in the corners rose as one. "Which way the elevator? Left? See yez all again."

Abel did not linger in Foster's office. The latter told him that the contract and a check in advance of the advance would be ready in the morning. Outside, Abel automatically took a left turn. There was an elevator there, all right, but it was not the one he had come up on, and it said *Freight.* For a moment he stood there, thoughtfully. Then he pressed the button. The freight elevator rose slowly, was empty, descended slowly. The cellar was equally empty, and so was the alley—which let to the street behind the one which the building's lobby opened onto.

It was only when he was on the bus that he realized he hadn't seen in the Rice reception office, on leaving, the two men he had seen there on entering. It struck him, in retrospect, how very much in manner and looks they had resembled the two men sitting watchfully in the corners facing the door of the inner office. Had the man who called himself Captain Marryat made a slip of the tongue when saying that the elevator was the one on the left? Perhaps he had meant the one on the right. But, if so, wouldn't Foster or Rice have corrected him?

Captain Marryat, plainly, was either circumspect or circuitous or both—and, equally plainly, he did not move unaccompanied. It was not likely that the hush-hush surrounding the ghost-writing arrangement was the result of an ordinary shyness or delicacy of feeling on the part of the protagonist of the memoirs-to-be.

Abel got off the bus at Washington Arch and walked across the Park. For once its scenes failed to hold his interest—not the playing children, the pretzel and ice-cream vendors, the chess and checker players, the bohemians and beatniks, the old Italian women in their black dresses, the tourists from East Weewaw, Wisconsin, the pipe-smoking artists with canvases under their arms, the girls with their long hair, the fey young men walking their weeny dogs—none of it. And at the kiosk abaft the Sheridan Square subway station he did something he hadn't done in a long time: he bought a newspaper.

It was hours and hours too early for the coffeehouses to be open, so he went into a bar, ordered a beer, took it to an empty booth, and sipped at it while he turned the pages of the *Daily News*. He found what he was looking for, in the center photographic spread. A man was walking down the front steps of a public building and shielding his face with his hat; but enough of the face was exposed for Abel Serles to recognize it as that of Captain Marryat, so-called. The two-line caption convinced him that this not really nautical person had indeed lived "a very interesting life."

And it also informed him who, in Sally ex-Leverett's words, had been saying wicked things about the Mafia.

Frederic the Beard was in the apartment again, leafing through a sheaf of photographs of sword-tangs, and comparing them with inscriptions in an old Japanese book printed on soft Chinese paper.

"Did you get the assignment?" he asked.

"I guess so."

Fred scratched his beard, of which there was enough to have supplied a quorum of old-style Mormon Elders. "What's it for?" he asked.

"I am contractually obligated to maintain strict secrecy in this whole matter."

"Oh, come off it! What's it about?"

"I am contractually obligated to—"

"Oh, foosh!" said Frederic Beard. He went back to his inscriptions. "Oh, well," he said, after a moment, "as long as you eat."

Abel did indeed eat, his first meal at Captain Marryat's place being a late breakfast consisting of three kinds of eggs, four of fruit juice, fried flounder, prosciutto ham, Canadian bacon, fresh whipped butter, six kinds of bread, four of pastry, seven of preserves, peanut butter, hot muffins, and Irish, English, Dutch, and American gin—these last to go with the fruit juice.

"Eat up, everybody," directed Captain Marryat, addressing Abel, the bodyguards, and a thin British secratree with white eyelashes and a rabbit nose. "Eat up, everybody—costs me a fawchin."

Everybody ate up.

The place was a penthouse overlooking the East River, with better trees growing on its terrace than Abel had seen at several country estates. He had a room just refurnished for him as a private office, with its own private bathroom; and Captain M. informed him that a bedroom was available for him as well, should he desire to spend his nights there—and informed him, also, that should Abel desire not to spend them alone, he, the host, had Telephone Numbers.

The breakfast having been eaten and its remains cleared away with dispatch by several silent servitors who had presumably been lurking in the woodwork, Captain Marryat said, with a belch and an apology, "Awright, where were we now, doll—I mean, escuse me, Miss Meadowes-Humphrey?"

And Miss Meadowes-Humphrey, after having riffled her steno pad, said, in the voice of one who reads recipes aloud on the Home Program of the BBC, "The icepick murders of the seven Sijjy Brothers in Greenpoint, Mr. Sullivan. Having been lured there under the pretense of discussing the possibilities of heavy investments in the ice-cream and dry-cleaning industries, the brothers—ah, here we are: 'Louis, the fat one, squeal like a pig, so—' "

This recitative, which might, as far as tone was concerned, have been concerned with novel methods of confecting things from leftover rice pudding, hard-cooked eggs, and anchovy paste, was interrupted by her employer's snapping his fingers in a chagrined fashion. Miss Meadowes-Humphrey stopped as if she had been switched off.

"Did I say Greenpernt?" he addressed one of his samurai.

" 'Ats what chew say, Big Smith."

With a sigh and a rueful shake of the head the Captain corrected the location to Red Hook. "I got, like, confused. Greenpernt was where them udder brudders got boined. Sorry, Miss. Change it, please."

Captain Marryat, alias Mr. Sullivan, alias Big Smith, turned to Abel. "The lady, here, she type up a bunch of this stuff that Mr. Ice awready seen. So while we go on, she takin' dictation, why don' you go inna yer office and look it ova? See what it needs, like. In udder woids, kid, get stahted. *Okay?*"

"Very well, Captain," Abel said.

Marryat-Sullivan-Smith snapped his gross fingers again, and the lady at once said, " '—*so we give him a couple more to shut him—*' " The door closed behind Abel and on the sad story of the seven Sijjy brothers.

Neatly arranged on the desk was a wealth of writing materials ranging from an electric-tape typewriter to a battery of gold-pointed fountain pens. There was also an embossed-leather folder of manuscript typed on paper of so good a quality that Abel had never even seen anything like it before. He seated himself in a chair of complex contours which almost adjusted itself to his back and buttocks, and drew the folder of manuscript toward him.

The author's style, at least at first, appeared to have something in common with that of Holden Caulfield. "Where my parents come from and where was they born is nobody's G.D. business and anyway they both die in the influenza epidemict in the First Worlds War and after that I'm on my own"—that was the arresting first sentence. It seemed a shame to have to change it, Abel thought.

What the manuscript possessed in forceful style, however, it lacked in organization. Plunging from the death of the author's parents and his entry into independence, it veered off from his escape from a denominational protectory into an account entitled *Nitty Gerundive Who Place a Tax on All the Cherry Syrup for New York City during Prohibition* to a description of several Syndicate conferences "holden" to consider the opportunities offered by coin-operated television; thence to an interminable apology for the author's rather intimate acquaintance with the world of crime, which was, in effect, a refusal to apologize at all; followed by thumbnail biographies of 137 big and little hoods, alive and dead.

Thereafter was a chapter on fixing municipal governments and police forces and insuring their staying fixed, a graphic description

of several episodes in a Chicago gang war in the early thirties, a
patriotic digression on the United States as the land of opportunity,
and the "true facts" about Al Capone, Justice Crater, Tammany
Hall, Las Vegas, someone called Little Iggy, Rum Runners' Row,
Arnold Rothstein and thirty-odd more persons, places, and things.

Abel leaned back thoughtfully in the form-fitting chair, and it all
but clutched at him passionately. As he seized the desk for support, his hand slipped and clawed open a drawer. Regaining his
balance, he pulled the drawer farther open, revealing a cedarwood
box full of fat brown cigars with Cuban accents. First he lit one,
enjoying every rich molecule of its smoke. Then he slowly made a
sandwich of two sheets of quasiparchment and a piece of imperial
carbon paper, fitted it into the giant typewriter. He switched on the
current.

For a moment his fingers brooded above the keys. Then they
descended.

In 1932 Al Capone poured two glasses of wine and said to me

There would be lots of places for flashbacks, and lots of flashbacks for those places.

He wondered what there would be for lunch.

Abel had not taken advantage of the offer to spend the night at
the penthouse, and consequently he was quite surprised the next
morning when the doorman of the posh apartment building po-
litely stopped him and said, "Sir, Mr. Sullivan isn't here any more."

Abel stared at the man in the uniform of a Latvian admiral. "Not
—Did he leave any message? My name is Serles. You mean he
won't be back at all? Moved out? No message? Well, I'll be darned."

Blankly he moved down the street, with vague notions of calling
the Rice office. Would he still collect his money? Not likely. It had
been *very* good food, too. A tug rounding the point of Welfare
Island hooted mournfully.

As if in echo, a passing car sounded its horn briefly. Then again.
He glanced at it. In front were two of Captain Marryat's sideboys.
They neither looked at him nor moved at all, that he could see, but
the car slowed down and the back door opened. Abel got in.

They drove uptown, crosstown, downtown, uptown again. At
one time he almost caught the driver's eyes in the mirror, but the

eyes weren't looking at him. At length the other man in front murmured an address. The car slowed down again, Abel got out, the car picked up speed and turned down a side street. He was only a few blocks from the address.

The building was a big old West Side Hotel dating from the architectural era of Stanford White. No name having been mentioned and Abel not having thought to inquire for one, he paused for a moment at the desk, nonplused. The mousy, hollow-chested little clerk, strands of colorless hair swept across his bony skull, looked up at him in silent inquiry. Light glinted on his glasses. An elderly woman with blue hair scanned the pigeonholes for mail, found none, turned and said to Abel, "Go have children," and went away.

Sullivan? Smith?

Probably not. On impulse Abel asked for Captain Marryat. The result would have utterly surprised him, had he never made an intimate purchase from a timid pharmacist. The clerk seemed to melt in upon himself, dropped his eyes, faded rather than moved away from the desk, and furtively consulted a register. He then ebbed back to the desk, still not looking up, and whispered, "Ten-o-three. Use the house phone next to the cigar stand."

No method actor assigned to interpret someone with a guilty secret would have played the role quite like that, but Abel was convinced—convinced, too, that the secret had an earlier origin than the migration of Captain Marryat to the Hotel Bellepaise.

The cigar stand, presided over by a fat man in a grizzled mustache and a stained vest who made no concessions to the underarm deodorant trade, was just what it appeared to be, and even had a tiny blue-tipped gas jet in a brass sconce for customers to light their smokes at.

"Still ring-ing," said the operator.

Then, very quickly, *"Yeah?"*

"Abel Serles."

"C'mon up."

Abel went up.

"All new people onna tent' flaw," said the shriveled elevator man.

"Oh, yes?"

"Sure. All re-renovated. Air-conditioned. Ready lass week. But they move in lass night. *Tent'* flaw. Watcha step."

Abel wondered how many other hideyholes were even now in preparation in case another flight of the Tartar Horde should prove indicated. The two men who had driven him from the East Side were already on guard in the corridor; they looked up with their usual sliding, opaque glances. One yawned, another picked at his fingernails. Abel walked on down to Room 1003 and knocked.

The new suite was a mixture of fake French Provincial and midwestern Swedish Modern, as if two rival interior decorators had come to an uneasy truce. The Captain and his staff were once again at meat; he informed Abel that he was just in time, and invited his participation. "Good steaks," the Captain said. "They fly 'em up from Youraguay. Go on. Take. Take."

In a few moments Abel was as greasy about the chops as his host and Miss Meadowes-Humphrey, and then became sticky as well, investigating what was beyond doubt the largest selection of melons he had ever seen in his life. The primest, which fairly swooned away on his tongue in sheer delight, bore on their bosoms roughly printed little tags which might have been Arabic, Persian, or Pushtu. After prawns, mussels, *écrivisses,* wild strawberries, and other goodies, followed by tiny cups of *cawwa* and brandy, Captain Marryat fired his usual salute to the excellence of the meal, then turned to business.

"I read yer stuff, kid, an' it's okay. Ya think it'll sell a lotta books? Bestseller?" Abel said he hoped so, but that it was impossible to predict. Conditions in the book trade, he said, were very fluid. Captain Marryat frowned. "Mr. Ice, he give me his woid, him an' his partners would promote it."

"I'm sure they will."

"Well, *okay,* then. Yer office is over on this side now. Let's see whatcha can do. Miss, where we at?"

Meadowes-Humphrey cleared her throat with a little whinny, peered into her notes. "Assignation of Machine-gun Jack McGurn with a daughter of Senator X, Mr. Sullivan. *'Jack was shacked up with—'* "

The new office was as soundproof as the other. The furniture and equipment were not identical—the typewriter, for example, was pearl-gray instead of lime-green—but it was just as good. The cigars were green instead of brown. Abel looked once at the Hudson, then read over his previous day's work, then turned to the source material. This time he didn't have to put paper into the mill, it was already there. He lit his cigar and gazed at the pseudo-Utrillo on the wall facing him. Then he set to.

When I was setting up slot machines in Louisiana I learned that not every donation to a "parish" has to do with religion, and

Sally had not once been married to a Bostonian for nothing.

"Where do they get off charging prices like that for the drinks in a place like this?"

Abel grunted. "That's the tax for not having to watch old movies. You always pay more in a bar without TV."

She fussed a while more, then sipped her Scotch sour, watching him. "Has your assignment gotten you down?"

"No, why do you say that? It's probably the best assignment I've ever had."

"Then how come you're so grim?"

He gnawed at a potato chip. "Well, if you must know. I was almost run down by a car on Sixth Avenue today, and besides that it scared the hell out of me, it's made me think about the vanity of human wishes, and what is our life but a dunghill, smoke, and all that sort of thing. And if I'm grim, that's why."

She gave a great bosom-swelling sigh—and instantly he became less grim. "Look! There's Fred. *Fred!*"

The moment was gone before it had well arrived, and Fred Beard came towering through the bar, angrily brushing away at the clouds of smoke.

"It's outrageous," he growled, crowding his legs under the table.

"Yes. Pity they don't all chew, or take snuff." Abel was feeling crotchety.

Fred stared at him. "What are you talking about? Oh. Smoke. No. Thesis typists! Idiots! I rupture myself earning the money to pay the cretin—and then she types eleven copies without numbering the pages. Eft. Toad. Gelded sow. And now I've got to number eleven times a hundred twenty-five pages by myself!"

Sally took his hand and patted it. "Never mind, Fred. We'll hold a numbering party, the three of us, and get it done for you in an hour or so. Maybe later tonight. Won't we, Abe? . . . Poor Abe, he's feeling grim. A car almost ran over him today."

Abel glowered, having had other plans or at least hopes for later that night with Sally, and ignored Fred's clucks of sympathy. Suddenly his drink gave a lurch in his hand. Fred and Sally, having noticed nothing, chattered on together. And the voice in the booth behind him repeated, "Where is Big Smith?"

"Who in the hell is Big Smith?"—a second voice.

"Some crook they're looking for. That's what the headline says. 'Where Is Big Smith?' "

The second voice obviously couldn't care less. "Where is Bug Stuart, that's what *I* want to know. Why doesn't he get his big fat backside over here? I haven't got all night."

Muttering something about going to the head, Abel got up, observed what newspaper was on the table in the booth behind, and promptly went out to buy a copy.

Where Is Big Smith?

The subject or object of one of the biggest undercover manhunts in recent years, ex-Syndicate stalwart Harold "Big" Smith—alias Jerry Sullivan, alias Popo Bogarty, and many other aliases—was still hiding out in parts unknown today. Earlier this week he sang like a canary to this newspaper's reporters and presumably made many Syndicate ears ring, because he immediately dropped out of sight again. Syndicate hatchetmen would like to know where he is. So would State Senator Elbert Dibbler (Rep., Chenango County), chairman of the Committee on Urban Crime. So would Police Commissioner Brenahan, crusading Congressman Cutler

Abel had just resettled himself at the table, glowered at Sally cuddled up into Fred's beard, and taken his drink in hand again, when it gave another lurch.

"*Where is Big Smith?*" a voice boomed.

"*That is the question which*—click."

"Turn that damn radio down," one bartender directed another, a second after it ceased to be necessary.

Sally separated herself from the country's leading authority on

Japanese swords. "Abe," she said, "what you need is a good night's sleep after that awful shock today. Fred and I are going over to his place and we'll do the page numbering all by ourselves, don't you bother. You just drink some hot milk and go to bed."

He watched them wordlessly as they went out. Then he paid for his drink and left. On the way home his moody eye was arrested by the blue flicker of a TV screen in an open bar. "—and that's the scene in North Dong Dunc. On the *home* scene the big question of the moment continues to be—Where is Big Smith?"

Abel cursed. And went home to bed.

He dreamed of the squabs they had had for supper at the Bellepaise, a giant pot of them, stuffed with wild rice, and garnished with bacon, peppers, mushrooms, and flaky black bits of truffle. The squabs twittered (do squabs *twitter*? part of his mind wondered) petulantly throughout the dream meal, and then began to scratch at the pot. The scratching became a scraping, grew louder. For some reason everything was dark, and then Abel realized he was wide-awake and in bed and that the scratching and scraping was coming from his rear window.

The pillow hit the floor with a faint noise as he leaped, so to speak, into a sitting position. Someone shouted, *"What's that? Who's there?"* and he recognized the voice as his own. There was a silence, then the slap-slap of feet on the fire escape. He jumped out of bed, tripped, regained his balance, and rushed over, flinging up the window with a bang. *"Police!"* he cried. *"Police! Police!"*

The police, who arrived somewhat later than immediately, consisted of a pair of neat, well-spoken young men. "There you are," said one, pointing. "Jimmy marks. How do you like that? Didn't even tap the joint first, to make sure there was nobody at home. That's what we mean," he said, turning to Serles, "by 'the nerve of a burglar.' "

Something suddenly and belatedly occurred to Abel. "I'll tell you something else they didn't tap first. And that's the window. It wasn't even locked."

Both policemen laughed heartily. "Well, that's the way those addicts are," said one. "They even forget their rudimentary intelligence."

"You're sure it was an addict, officer?"

The officer nodded. "Bound to be. These cheap burglaries—I mean, beg your pardon, but this apartment is no fur loft or jewelry store—they're always the work of an addict. That's what narcotics does to you, undermines the very fabric and basis of society. If I had my way, anybody caught even for a first offense, pushing—the firing squad. Hey?"

"That's where you are *wrong,* Alfred," the second policeman said, softly and earnestly. "That has *never* solved a problem yet and it never *will.* The *only* answer is to make these preparations *legal,* like they do in Siam or wherever it is. Then these unfortunate people would not be obliged to come climbing through this gentleman's window in the hopes of stealing his typewriter at half-past two in the morning."

By the time they concluded their sociological discussion and had left, Abel found he was no longer tired. So he walked across town to the vicinity of Tompkins Square and woke up Fred Beard.

The sword sage peered through his tangled locks and muttered and snorted. "Is Sally here?" Abel asked.

"No, she went home. I thought she advised you to do the same."

"I did, but there was no milk to heat. I thought I'd borrow some of yours."

"Foosh," said the Beard. "Oh, I suppose you might as well come in. Don't sit *there!* Those are my notes on steel analysis of the early Tokugawa Era—"

"Did you number the pages?"

"Yes."

"I'll bet you did . . . What do you think, Fred? Do squabs twitter?"

After a restless several hours on Fred's sofa he returned home to shave, there having been no equipment for such purpose in the Beard's establishment within the memory of man. He found his place in ruins. The chairs had been smashed, the mattress slashed, likewise the pillows and couch, the typewriter was a tangle of broken keys and springs, shattered dishes were everywhere . . .

"Well, maybe I was wrong, Alfred," one of the policemen said on their second visit. "*This* is not a narcotics-type incident at all. *This* looks like a classical revenge-type bit. Remember that place over on Perry Street? There was this psychology student, female," he explained, turning to Abel, "who had been living with a would-be poet who was under psychoanalysis. That situation finally broke up, then he dropped out of his analysis, and then he decided that it was all her fault, so he went over to her new place of residence and—"

Abel interrupted him. "I'm quite sure," he said bitterly, "that none of my ex-girl friends is responsible for this."

"Ah," said Alfred, gently rebuking him, "but what Patrolman Roberts was just going to explain to you before you got abrupt, see, this nutty kid picked the wrong apartment to wreck. Maybe that's the same case here. Now, the super tells us that the party downstairs is on Fire Island, the party upstairs is in Provincetown, and the party across the hall, *he* was just coming home from having been out all night just as we were coming up the stairs. So there was nobody around to hear anything. *What* a mess!"

Bemused and bewildered, as well as not a little outraged, Abel Serles took the IRT uptown and arrived at the Bellepaise in time for early breakfast, where he was mildly surprised to see Miss Meadowes-Humphrey already on duty, pouring the tea and buttering the scones or shew-bread or whatever they were. A wicked and unworthy thought entered his mind. Could it be? Could they be? —namely, Miss Meadowes-Humphrey and Captain Marryat? No, no, impossible; surely those albino eyelashes, those meagre measurements, could hold no illicit (or even, damn it, *licit*) attractions for one so obviously designed by Nature to seek for depth of chest and breadth of hip.

"How ya comin?" was the Captain's question. Miss Meadowes-Humphrey continued nibbling rapidly. No, no, nothing more than too many years ill-nourished on spotted dog, bubble-and-squeak, jam tarts, thin milk in thick tea, oleaginous chips and cabbage, cabbage, cabbage, were responsible for her early appearance at the Captain's table. Abel decided to keep his troubles to himself, and joined in on the crisp brown trout which had only the previous day been swimming in some cold mountain stream.

"Ya look tie-ed, kid."

"Didn't get much sleep last night."

Captain Marryat gave a lewd chuckle, and they presently parted for the day's work. The noon meal was subsequently served up by a high-class wholesale Rumanian restaurant. Abel partook copiously of the mushk-steak and the jellied calves-foot, but thought there was really more eggplant than he cared to encounter even in such various forms. He wondered if the Captain's gourmet learnings were undermining his own simple writerly tastes, always before so readily satisfied with what was cheapest and to hand. As a background accompaniment to such soul-searching the television demanded: *Where is Big Smith?* And the radio echoed: *Where is Big Smith?*

"Leave 'em fine out," grunted the missing man, stuffing himself with Balkan desserts. Abel left him and his stenographer recapitulating the bloody end of one Fat Dempster, who, as luck would have it, was run to earth at night in a meat-packing plant in East New York, New Jersey. Abel spent the rest of the day trying to organize the memoirs as they related to the nonfashionable suburb of Cicero, Illinois, during the late twenties. And when he opened the door of his apartment that evening, an explosion flung him back against the hall wall and broke several windows.

"Faulty wiring there," said the detective later, chidingly. "Obviously that was meant to go off when you opened the *kitchen* door. Otherwise, why would they have put it in the kitchen?"

Abel felt sickish and aching, but there appeared to be no fractures. "I'll speak to the electricians' union," he muttered.

The detective surveyed him with eyes as bright and alien as a bird's. "This is the third attempt at your apartment in twenty-four hours, isn't it? Come on, you must have *some* idea who or why?"

Abel shook his head. He made a little speech. He had lived in Greenwich Village for six years, in this same house for four, in the apartment for three. In all that time, he said, he had never even so much as been troubled by a friendly drunk; and he had *no* idea whatsoever.

The detective listened, giving little ornithological nods. As soon as Abel had finished he said, "Come on, you must have *some* idea who or why?"

Feeling bruised and ill, wanting to lie down, Abel, as soon as he could get away from the birdy man, went out. He got a taxi and went up to Sally's place in Chelsea. He was feeling increasingly sick and shaky, and the thought that she might not be in was the greatest fear he could imagine.

But she was in.

He had on numerous other occasions sought her there for a friendly drink or a friendly talk; but he never before had sought her or thought of her as refuge, home, or healing.

As he did now.

She screamed on seeing him, and Frederic H. Beard, who had been joining her for a light supper, leaped up in such alarm that a piece of egg yolk fell onto his ample beard. "Abe, what happened?" they cried, almost together.

"I want to lie down."

Together they helped him into bed, took off his shoes, and then, as he began to shiver, covered him with blankets. Sally got him to drink a shot of brandy, and then she repeated, "But what *happened*"

"They tried to kill me."

"*Who?*"

"The Mafia."

Fred and Sally stared at him. Then she said, "But, Abe, listen dear, that's only a tiny little outfit over near Bleecker Street. They just get a rakeoff on cigarette machines. I *know* one of them, Patsy Something-or-other, such a nice little man. They don't try to *kill* people."

The shakes had begun to diminish. "I don't mean that Mafia. I mean the real Mafia. The Syndicate. They tried to kill *me.*" And he told them of what had been going on in his apartment, and she gave a little scream.

"What about that car that almost ran you down?" Her fingers made a paling over which her large frightened eyes peeped.

"Oh, God! I forgot about that." He wanted to say, Give me some more brandy, but all he got out was "Gick." So he pointed a quivery finger until they poured him another. His friends were patient people: they let him get about half of the second shot down before asking the obvious question, namely, Why did the Syndicate want Abel Serles killed?

Abel pondered. Between bed, blankets, and brandy he was now beginning to feel warmer. And better. "Well, I'm not supposed to say," he said.

"Oh, come *on!* What is this, the Code of the Underworld? Sally, talk sense to him—"

"Abe, dear—"

He squirmed in his bed. Was he really bound to keep silence

unto the grave? No. Absurd. "Listen. You know all this recent business about Where Is Big Smith?" Sally nodded, Beard blew out of
the corner of his mouth a scornful snort which fluttered the end of
his piratical mustachio.

"It's everywhere—newspapers, TV, radio. Disgusting. Two hundred ancient and priceless specimens of the Japanese swordsmith's
craft are scattered around this country in the houses of people who
picked them up as mere souvenirs at the end of the war, and
nobody lifts a finger to have their whereabouts so much as identified—and look at all this hullaballoo about a cheap crook who—"
He stopped and seized the sides of his vast beard with both hands.
"Don't tell me!" he exclaimed. "Don't tell me. *You?*"

Abel nodded. "Me. I know where he is. That's why they're trying
to kill me."

Sally sat down on the side of the bed, suddenly and heavily.
"Oh, my. Oh, dear. Things like this never happened in Boston.
What are we going to *do?*"

Fred was shaking his head. "That doesn't make sense, Abe. Assuming the Syndicate knows that you know where he is, wouldn't
they try to get you to *tell?* First by bribery, most likely, then by—
well, *force.* But they wouldn't try to *kill* you. Furthermore, *how* do
you know—"

Abel said, "Because I've got the assignment to ghost-write his
memoirs, and they don't want the publicity . . . I wish to hell I'd
never taken the job. It seemed like fun until all this started."

But Fred was still shaking his head. "It *still* doesn't figure, Abe.
Now, I'm no authority on the Mafia, but from what I've heard and
read, they don't operate that way. They seem to keep their killings
confined either to their own members or to people they try to
victimize who won't hold still for it. After all, you're only one
among many, many people who are trying to expose the Syndicate.
The cops, Congress, the State Legislature, the newspapers, so on.
They're not trying to kill *them.* Why would they want to kill *you?*"

Abel shook his head. For some reason the thought of the many
magnificent victuals served up to him at Captain Marryat's table
came to his mind. The condemned man had eaten not only a
hearty breakfast, but tasty brunch, gourmet dinner, and exotic supper as well . . . He repeated now, to his friends, what he had said

to the detective: all the years he had lived in Greenwich Village without trouble, and now—

"First, someone tries to run me down. Then someone tries to break into my apartment, then someone *does* break into my apartment—and wrecks it—maybe looking for an address, maybe just to warn me. Then somebody plants a bomb in my kitchen. Who else could it be, if not the Syndicate?"

Fred cocked his head, still dubious. Sally was wide-eyed. "But," said Abel, "hey, listen . . . Wouldn't even gangsters be smart enough to know that killing the man who's writing the exposé would result in *more* publicity, not in less?" It didn't make sense, Abel felt that himself. But what did, in this whole evil-crazy business?

Fred and Sally continued to debate the matter. Abel closed his eyes. He was aware that he was falling asleep, but felt no desire to do otherwise . . . He awoke with the smell of coffee in the room —plain, good, ordinary supermarket coffee, the kind Sally used; nothing exotic, very much like Sally herself. "Hey, can I have some of that?" he called. It was broad daylight.

"Well, you certainly caught up on your sleep," she said, coming in with two cups. "Which I'm very glad of. Oh, you looked just *terrible* last night. Well. Now we have to decide what you're going to do. Of course you're welcome to hide out here as long as you like. *Or.* Edward Erastus has this eccentric cousin—of course, *I* always got along just fine with her—but anyway, she owns this island off the coast of Maine, and I'm sure if I call her she'll be happy to put you up. She's really very nice."

Abel shook his head. "I'm going to make a phone call, okay?" She nodded, and he dialed the offices of Samuel Rice Associates.

Jack Foster refused to believe he was serious at first, but, convinced at last, was obviously disturbed. "I'll talk to Rice right away. Don't hang up." He was back almost at once. "Rice says to waste no time, but go to the police at once—"

"And tell them everything?"

"Everything."

"Well, fine, then. I guess you'll be hearing from me soon. I hope." He turned to Sally. "The bossman says to tell the police."

She seemed uncertain. "Well . . . whatever you think Abe; anyway, you can always stay here, or go to Pogunquit Island. But let me know, whatever happens. And if I'm not here I'll probably be at Fred's."

It was another item in his unhappiness that he knew she probably would be.

A dazed-looking woman with a black eye sat on the bench in the precinct house; three young men with shiny black hair and leather jackets to match were slouched in chairs, snickering aimlessly when they caught one another's eye; and an old man scanned a racing sheet. The desk sergeant was engaged in easy discourse with one uniformed and two un-uniformed men, but looked up at Abel's approach and said, "Well, what's your trouble, fellow?"

Now for it. The giant disclosure. "I know where Big Smith is," he said.

All four burst out laughing.

"I mean it," Abel cried, outraged.

"Oh, boy, what a bazzazz," said one of the plainclothesmen. "So you know where Big Smith is. Goody, goody for you. Well, now, you go and tell that palooka that Lieutenant Dick Murphy said, 'Hello' and wants to know who-in-the-hell spread all this talk that the Commissioner wants to see him. Strictly an unofficial inquire-y."

Abel gave a little hiccup of astonishment, at which the four laughed again. "The Commissioner *doesn't* want to see him?"

"Naah. What *for?* That big boob hasn't done nothing illegal since he shot his own big toe in Evanston, Illinoise, thirty years ago. Trying to shake down a candy store or something. And he served his time for that. *I* don't know what all this *Where Is Big Smith?* malarkey is all about. Do you?" He addressed one of his friends, who shook his head.

Lieutenant Murphy proceeded to inform Abel that Big Smith owed his connection with the Syndicate entirely to the fact that he had once been married to the late sister of one Vinny, a middle-upper rank Syndic, who kept him around for laughs.

Abel swallowed. "Then how come he blew the whistle on them? I mean, aren't *they* after him? I mean—"

Murphy shrugged. "Big Smith was strictly a run-out-and-get-me some-coffee or give-Tommy-a-hotfoot character, until he made a lot of money in the market. He loves to eat and he loves to play these cheap, common practical jokes, and he loves to shoot off his mouth and talk himself up. And that's all there is to Big Smith, and only some dumb apple-knocker like this upstate Senator What-ever-his-name-is would think different. Those dumb apple-knock-ers are always looking for a way to insult the City and not have to reapportionate the Legislature, anyway. So, if that's all you come to see us about, thanks, and maybe you'll excuse us now, and we'll get on with something important."

As Abel stood in the doorway, poised for the street, he heard one of them repeat, "Where Is Big Smith?" and they all burst out laugh-ing again.

Serles walked slowly along, trying to figure things out. He con-sidered one thing with another, and it seemed to him that a certain configuration was beginning to become dimly visible. Half a block later, he saw a public telephone, and, on a sudden decision, went into the booth.

"Mr. Bland is on the telephone to London," said the girl at the switchboard.

"Let me speak to one of his assistants, then. George or Mary or Sanford."

He wasn't quite certain which one was talking to him a few moments later, but he identified himself and asked, "Do you know who the 'associates' of Samuel Rice Associates are? I'll explain an-other time." The distant epicene voice of George or Sanford or perhaps Mary named several. Abel thanked him, or her, and hung up.

He then dialed again, rapping impatiently on the tiny shelf, until he heard Jack Foster's voice. Yes, said Abel, he had been to the police. And if Foster, Rice, and Captain Marryat would like to hear about it they could damn well meet him in the office in an hour.

"Listen," Foster said, "you can't—"

Abel hung up.

The Captain greeted him with a wave of his hamlike hand and a large "How ya doin?" Rice expressed instant sympathy, and was about to say more, when Abel overrode him.

"Lieutenant Dick Murphy said to tell you Hello," he addressed

Captain Marryat. "He says you're a big palooka and you haven't broken a law since 1939."

"Hoddaya like that fa noive! Listen—"

Abel turned to Rice. "This whole buildup about 'Where Is Big Smith?' is a clever piece of publicity cooked up by your associates in radio, television, and newspapers—that's the gimmick, isn't it?"

Rice nodded. "Coming along very nicely too. Should help get a big price for the movie rights, and maybe a TV and magazine series, too."

Abel said, "And it would have been even more helpful publicity if I'd told the police all about the attempts on my life, wouldn't it?"

Rice stared, frowned. "You mean, you *didn't?* You mean—now just a minute, here. I don't like the tone of your voice at all. You mean you think *we* were behind the violence?"

Foster said, "I can assure you straight out—we had nothing to do with it."

"No, Jack, that you didn't, and maybe your boss didn't. But what about Captain Marryat here? God knows I've given a lot of thought to the whole thing. It *had* to be wrong, my thinking it was the Syndicate doing all that to me, because the Syndicate would be smart enough to know it would only create *more* publicity. Well, who then? Obviously—" His gaze settled on his sometime collaborator.

Captain Marryat bounced to his feet and thrust his hand at Abel, who danced away from it. "Yer awright, kid!" the Captain boomed. "Ya gotta good head on ya! What-the-hell. We're *lookin'* fa publicity, ain't we? We wanna sell lotsa books, don't we? Me an my udder pals, we wooden hoitcha, not fra million dollars! Laugh it up, kid. Laugh it up. I mean—jeest, you musta look funny, dodgin' that cah!" He ha-ha'd happily. "I mean, if we *wanneda* kill ya, we could of. As fa that liddle cherry bomb—"

Abel turned to the bookmen. "I've had the corpuscles scared out of me three times and my apartment wrecked twice. My zeal for my art doesn't include having either happen to me even once. In short —I'm through. You're welcome to what I've already written on your tame hood's life and times."

Foster, in a tired voice, said he was sorry; his employer shrugged. "We won't need what you already wrote. Writers aren't hard to find. Just return your advance and—"

Serles stared at him for a moment. Then he said, "I tell you what, Mr. Ice. We'll compare the damage to my apartment with the amount of the advance, and if there's any difference in your favor, I'll give it to some worthy cause. Gentlemen and Captain Marryat, goodbye."

As the door closed behind him, Abel heard Captain Marryat having the last word, and a mournful one it was. "Kid's got no sense a yuma," said Big Smith.

It was a hot day, and Abel, proceeding north on Fifth Avenue, felt every degree of it. There were several things that badly wanted taking care of.

His apartment was one of them, but he could put the basic repairs in professional hands and leave the rest for later. There would have to be a "later"—for one reason because someone else would be consulted in the restoration, and for another because he felt he both required and deserved an immediate vacation.

If Sally's eccentric-ex-cousin-by-marriage was so sure to have been willing to put him up on Pogunquit Island by himself, it was exceedingly likely that she would put him up accompanied by Sally (Fred, after all, could make do with his swords); and he intended to put this pleasurable prospect before the former Mrs. Edward Erastus Leverett XXV in reasonable hopes that she would not remain so-styled for very much longer. Life, after all, was too short for him to go on keeping one of its most important facets at arm's length forever.

But repairs to and replacements for the apartment, as well as transportation in comfort to the State of Maine, would exhaust what remained of his finances. Certainly he could write while he was there—after a decent interval, that is—but he would have to have something assigned him to write, and an advance against this assignment to finance the rest of his holiday.

His honeymoon . . .

He looked at his watch. It was 3:43. Without hurrying he could catch Godfrey Blank at just the right moment, over his late afternoon cup in the lobby of the Algonquin Hotel. If he were in luck he might still be able to get those two sophisticated sex novels for himself after all—or possibly—why not?—a better assignment. Hadn't he been settling for second-best and worse long enough?

It was at this moment that another and sudden thought occurred to him. Clasping his hand to the front of his collar, he discovered that he was not wearing a necktie. He also realized that he was not on Sixth Avenue, but on Fifth.

Without a moment's hesitation, and with only the briefest mental acknowledgment to Captain Marryat, Abel Serles strode into the lavish interior of the nearest swank haberdashery, and made a sizeable donation to a worthy cause.

"Nothing gaudy," he directed. "Just your best plain silk foulard."

MY BROTHER'S KILLER

WILLIAM BANKIER

There wasn't much for me to do around the dry-cleaning shop. There never is. Once in a while, when I've just come back from a hit out of town, I drop by and pick up the bank book and take it over to the bank where I deposit the $5,000, which is what they usually pay me, to the credit of the shop's current account. It's what Vince Angelino calls "washing the money." But apart from that, the two girls I've hired to run the place do it all. Mainly I look in to establish that the shop is mine, because that's the whole idea —a legitimate "cover." But the little hole in the wall depresses me, the way most things have for the past year, so I soon get out of there.

On this day I walked up the street to the Cherub Bar and started the treatment. A little early this afternoon; it was only three o'clock. The treatment has been going on as long as the depression. It consists of drinking a lot of whiskey and looking at the young girls swaying and nodding to the loud rock music until I begin to feel the way I used to. It takes me about an hour.

I don't get involved with these kids. All I do is stare and eventually smile a bit and then turn back to my drink. It's a young bar, but they're getting used to this fat old guy with the red face who comes in and perches on the end stool.

"Same again, Mr. Regan?"

"Same again, Dallas."

He looks like no other bartender I've ever seen. His shoulder-length hair is held back by an Indian headband. They tell me he's a small-town boy and he took the name of Dallas so we'd never forget what happened to John F. Kennedy. Maybe that's why I like him. I'm a small-town boy, too, and Regan isn't my real name either.

I've never really liked my life. There was a time, though, when I didn't mind it. There was excitement. The trip to a strange city was always a lift; like a pro-ball player I was always off to Chicago or L.A. And I do what I do because if it isn't me, somebody else would do it. You can't change the world.

But now I have to fight my way up every day. Is this what it means to be 45 years old? If it wasn't for the booze and the girls to look at I swear I'd go home and put the muzzle of that automatic in my mouth.

By eight o'clock I had eaten half of the good steak the management sells cheap to make sure we stay there and keep drinking. Which I fully intended to do. When out of the crowd came a tall good-looking man, peering at me under the flat of his hand like a frontier scout.

"It is, it is!" he said. "It's my big brother, Ross!"

I grabbed his hand. He felt good. "Alex, what are you doing in town?"

Looking at my brother after all these years, I felt a surge of warmth in my chest. Part of me wanted to grab him and hold onto him, but I couldn't bring myself to do it. Vince Angelino and his crowd are always kissing their brothers, but Alex and I weren't brought up that way. Still, the feeling was in me, and I think I saw it in his eyes, too.

"It's the Congress of Suburban Mayors. You knew I was elected Mayor of Clearwater last year, didn't you?"

"No. Congratulations. When you moved to the big city you really made it, eh?"

"Clearwater's just a suburban community. But yes, it's important. A lot of money lives there. A lot of power."

I ordered drinks and Dallas brought them.

"There you are, Mr. Regan."

"Regan?" Alex said. "No wonder I couldn't find you in the phone book. What's the matter with Cumberland?"

"It's a business thing. I'll explain later. How the hell are you? You look great, really great."

It was after nine when we decided to get in a game of snooker pool. Just like the old days. There was a place with tables down the street and I took my brother there.

How quickly the years fell away. Standing in the shadows around the table, or leaning into the bright light close to the brilliantly colored balls on the rich green surface, we found conversation unnecessary and replaced it with the calm, simple statements of the game.

"Blue in the side."

"Twice across."

"In off the pink."

And there were the old comedy lines, made more precious by years of repetition.

"This table leaks."

"Sold the farm."

It was as though we were back in Baytown, at Lafferty's Poolroom, having a quick game after school. I could almost imagine we'd finish the game, hurry home for supper, then head down to the church for choir practice.

I found myself humming our favorite hymn, the Welsh tune, *Aberystwyth.*

"Jesu, lover of my soul, Let me to Thy bosom fly . . ."

Alex straightened and we stood facing each other, unselfconscious, me singing the melody while he did the tenor part. We kept our voices down, not to disturb the few others in the pool room, but it didn't matter to us anyway. This was serious: we were reliving our past.

> *"Safe into the haven guide,*
> *Oh, receive my soul at last."*

I was disappointed to learn, as we walked from the poolroom to Alex's hotel, that my brother had given up going to church. The subject flowed naturally from our memories of the choir.

"It used to be important for a politician to be seen regularly in church," he said. "But not so much any more. I just show up at Christmas and Easter."

"I go every week. Even when I'm out of town."

We were passing under a street light and I saw Alex's faint smile. It's remarkable how a guy can change. We both used to care about God. Now I still do, but he doesn't. I feel very definitely that a Supreme Being orders our lives and that we are accountable to Him at the end.

You might think that strange, considering the kind of work I do. But what I do is right. I never accept a contract until Vince Angelino tells me why the man has it coming. In a way I am doing His work by punishing the wicked here on earth.

Alex and I bought some food and took it up to his hotel room and ate it, watching a late movie on television. An old Laurel and Hardy film which I'm sure we saw together at the Belle Theatre on its first run. A movie cost us ten or twelve cents in those days, I don't remember which, and we always went on Saturday afternoons.

Now, sitting in front of the TV screen with a sandwich in my hand and my little brother in the dark beside me, it was like being home. I could imagine my mother, who didn't like television, sitting alone in the kitchen, chain-smoking, and yelling out, "When is that thing finished?"

I left late with a promise to call Alex after his meetings the next afternoon so we could do it all again tomorrow night.

In the morning I was awake and shaving before it got through to me. My depression was gone. Maybe I should consider moving to Clearwater so I could spend more time with my brother. That's my problem—being too much alone. I'm a family boy at heart. Of course, I knew it would never happen. They would never allow me to leave town. They need me.

On my way to get breakfast I stopped at the newsstand on Eagle Street to pick up a paper. It was a beautiful sunny day and Davey's voice rang out on the warm air.

"Morniiiiing Gazette!"

I got in the stand with him just out of habit. Whenever I have time, I stay in there with old Davey. It's like visiting his home. He expects me to come in.

There was just room inside for me to open the tabloid to the sports section. I helped myself to a doughnut; Davey always has a bag of jelly doughnuts in there.

"See Hank Aaron hit another one."

"Yeah. He'll catch Babe Ruth."

"Think so? I don't think so."

People came by and put dimes on Davey's tray and he pushed out papers to them.

"Say. Know who I saw getting off the train this morning? Kosk."

My ears pricked up as Davey knew they would. There are only a few specialists in my business and we know each other by reputation. Kosk comes in from Cleveland once in a while to do a contract here. I never work in my own town just as Kosk never works in Cleveland.

"I wonder what he's here for?" Davey asked. Davey is the only man in the world who knows what I do. Besides Angelino. Davey doesn't really know, he suspects. I live with it because I know the police could burn him and he'd never squawk.

I shrugged and turned the page. But I was really curious. So I went and had coffee and then telephoned Vince Angelino. It's never easy getting through to Vince. He had to call me back on another phone because he's scared of wiretaps and I suppose he's right. I told him what I had heard and insisted I wanted to know more. Because Vince was a little coy.

Finally he said, "Okay. It's a politician who won't cooperate. One of those mayors here for the conference. He's making it very hard for the organization in Clearwater. We've tried to talk to him but he refuses to listen. So . . ."

I felt very cold all of a sudden. "What's this guy's name?"

"Cumberland. Alex Cumberland."

I went and sat in back of the dry-cleaning shop and thought about what I should do. If I warned Alex, he wouldn't believe me. To convince him I'd have to prove I am what I am. I can't do that. He thinks I'm a legitimate businessman and I want to keep it that way.

Even if he did believe me, what could he do? The police can't protect him. Not against Kosk. And if he went back to Clearwater, Kosk would follow him.

The only thing would be for Alex to stop holding out. Contact the organization and say he'll go along. But I knew Alex would never do that.

I used to resent my little brother sometimes, but at the same time, I was proud of him. Right was right to Alex. He wouldn't cheat on an exam. He wouldn't take things out of stores. We all did, but he wouldn't. He was like a model of what the rest of us should be and though we couldn't measure up, we needed him as a comparison.

I believe God puts people like that among us. If you know my brother Alex, you can't say the human race is naturally bad.

When I had thought it all over, it seemed clear what I had to do. I went back to Davey's newsstand and asked him a question. Yes, he had kept an eye on Kosk. He had gone to a roominghouse on Arbour Avenue. Not far from Alex's hotel, I thought.

I went and stood on the corner of Arbour where I could see the roominghouse door. It was a long wait. I used the time to improve the suntan on my face. I look better in the mirror behind the Cherub Bar when my face is tanned.

It was mid-afternoon when Kosk came out of the roominghouse. He had been pointed out to me once before, years ago. As I had suspected, he started walking in the direction of Alex's hotel. I kept a block between us, only hurrying when he turned into the hotel entrance.

Inside the lobby I saw him on the house phone. He didn't speak, so I figured he was checking Alex's room and found it empty. When Kosk went to the elevators I hit the stairs. Alex's room was on the third floor, close enough for me to be there first.

In the corridor I waited around a corner. I heard the elevator door open and close. Footsteps on the carpet. Then a familiar sound. I glanced down the hall. Kosk was using a plastic strip to force the lock and get into Alex's room.

When he was inside, I took a chance. I had to. I went to the room next door and rapped lightly. Again. No response. I was lucky. Taking out a credit card, I did the same job Kosk had done on Alex's lock.

Inside I went to the window. A full-length glass door slid open to let me out onto the narrow balcony. I had looked out Alex's window last night and had seen the rows of balconies connecting room to room. I had left his open then. As I climbed the rail dividing the balconies, I hoped he hadn't closed it.

Again I was lucky. Not only was the glass door unlocked, it was open a couple of feet, the floor-length drapes billowing slightly into the room. I was not sure where Kosk would be, but I had a hunch. I peered past the drape and saw I was right. He was on his belly on the floor behind the bed, facing the door and with his back to me.

I came in quietly. He saw the movement of a shadow on the floor, turned, and saw my gun aimed at his head. The silencer on the barrel told him a lot.

"You ain't a cop."

I shook my head.

"Then you must be—But listen, this is an official job. If you're local, you must know Angelino. He put out the contract."

At close range Kosk turned out to be an ordinary little guy. His suit was cheap and I could smell his perspiration. His glasses had been broken and one shaft was held together by adhesive tape.

"Have you got something against me?" he asked.

I shook my head again.

"Then you must be protecting Cumberland. Okay. You've done it. Just let me walk out of here."

I said, "Angelino would never let you walk away. He's paid you for the hit. You'd have to follow him back to Clearwater." Without expecting to I said, "I can't protect my brother everywhere."

"Your brother? Does Angelino know that? Talk to him. Talk to your brother. I don't know what the problem is, but can't you work it out?"

There was a key in the door. It opened quickly and the lights snapped on. It was Alex, a brief case in his hand. He wasn't stupid, my brother. He stayed cool. Closing the door, he moved slowly to where he could see Kosk lying on the floor.

"Ross, what is this?"

"This guy was waiting to kill you. I found out."

"How did you find out? And how come you have a gun?"

Kosk was looking desperate. And crafty, with a witness in the room. He stood up. "This is all a mistake. I'm getting out of here."

I leveled the gun. "Stand still."

Alex yelled, "Ross, stop!"

"He's a hired gun," I yelled back. "There's a contract out on you."

My brother turned to Kosk and smiled. "Oh, I see. The syndicate. The police reorganization I'm bringing in. Yes. And it may spread if I keep pushing it." He turned back to me. "But I still don't see your involvement."

Kosk said, "Your brother is a hired gun, too. There's no other way he could know about me."

"Is that true, Ross?"

I didn't say anything.

There was an expression on Alex's face I had never seen before. Cold and hard. "All right. I don't need mob protection to survive. The first thing I do is call the police." He went to the phone.

Kosk glanced at me. I said, "Don't do that, Alex."

"Why not?"

"There's too much happening here. I'm involved. No police."

Alex looked straight at me and I saw the simplicity of the situation in his eyes. Men with unlicensed guns are against the law. Police must be called. There is right and there is wrong.

"I have to call them, Ross." His voice was quiet. "You know that."

"Kosk," I said. "Take the phone from him."

Kosk snatched the phone from Alex's hand. For good measure he tore the wire out of the wall.

"Then I'll go and call from the desk." Alex turned. "This whole thing has to stop right here."

As he walked to the door I felt a helpless rage boiling up inside me. It seemed to come from deep down and from years ago. You couldn't tell him anything. You couldn't reason with him. Bloody, sanctimonious, holier-than-thou—

The gun popped twice, then again. Alex put his hands against the door, leaning there, supporting himself, then his knees bent and he slid to the floor.

Kosk was looking at me, wild-eyed. He expected the worst. When he saw nothing else was going to happen, he quickly stepped across Alex's body, opened the door, and was gone.

Now I am sitting at the Cherub Bar, trying to deal with the voice in my head. I have had three drinks, doubles, and still the rage inside me goes on.

"Are you all right, Mr. Regan?"

"I'm fine, Dallas."

"You sure?"

"It's okay. I'm all right."

The question is, what to do? I know now who killed my brother. It was Kosk. He came here from Cleveland with a gun and he murdered him. Alex did not deserve to die. He was a good man. He always did right and there was no wickedness in him.

I know what I will do. I will go to Cleveland knowing that my enemy can be found there. And in time I will find him.

Then, as the instrument of God's justice, I shall confront Kosk. And the guilty shall be punished.

ANOTHER WANDERING
DAUGHTER JOB

GERALD TOMLINSON

Melva Dominic was a daughter of Manhattan, of the Depression, and of the man known as Charlie Corkscrew, a squat serious hunk with shoulders like the U.S. Sub-Treasury Building. Charlie picked up his nickname when once, early in his speakeasy days, having left his basic weaponry at home, he settled a barroom brawl in Murray Hall with a corkscrew. Fatally.

Charlie's more refined persuasive techniques involved the use of a Thompson submachine gun. He became so adept at chopping down moving targets from a careening LaSalle that the Boss of All Bosses smiled on him. Charlie smiled back. Foolishly.

One night early in Herbert Hoover's reign, following a noisy, four-corpse fracas in front of Angie's Rainbow Gardens on Lexington Avenue, the speeding LaSalle threw a rod while crossing the Queensboro Bridge on its way to the mob's hideout in Jackson Heights. In the back seat of the car police found Charlie clutching a velvet-lined cello case that did not contain a cello. The interior of the case was very warm; so was the Tommygun.

The jury glowered, its twelve members unbought, and Charlie gnashed his teeth at the verdict. His pregnant wife Bootsie wailed, vowed a deep and abiding love for her caged turtledove, and shortly thereafter moved in with a curly-headed capo across the Hudson.

Despite Charlie's pleas, no one in the mob sped north to talk turkey to the governor. Charlie fretted and fumed. The state fed him and fried him. Ashes to ashes.

Little Melva, heiress to these woes, was born on Black Thursday, 1929, just four days before Charlie walked the last mile at Sing Sing, a date that Melva's mother afterward called Sizzling Monday. Wryly.

It was small wonder that Melva Dominic, a deceptively demure-looking brunette with wide innocent eyes, strayed from the path of the righteous. Too soon adrift, with a mother who, on her curly-headed capo's death from .38-caliber puncture wounds in Deal, New Jersey, lived at the Hotel Dixie and went by the stage name of Cosmic Raye, Melva soon knew everything worth knowing, and some things not worth knowing, about Times Square and West 52nd Street.

At the age of 14 Melva whistled the Dixie goodbye. Her mother, ever ready for a party, threw a champagne bash for Melva on her departure, the affair ending in a grand finale with Mama, Cosmic Raye, née Bootsie, dancing the hootchie-cootchie on a marble-topped coffee table at the guttural request of Frankie Brown Eyes Slade.

Melva, on her own, soon took up residence with Private Jethro Henry. USMC, AWOL, a gawky recent emigre from Parris Island, who supported the two of them in a certain raffish style in a Greenwich Village walkup, using a pair of loaded dice backed up by a pair of brass knuckles.

It appears that Melva truly loved Jethro, for when the United States Marines tracked their young private to his Bleecker Street lair, she joined Jethro in a mad flight to Tijuana, Mexico. For a few weeks Melva entertained her fellow gringos by appearing onstage in scanty attire at the mob-owned Maximilian Club.

Jethro had fallen ill the first day in Mexico after eating a meal of chicken *mole,* and, unaware of Melva's stage triumphs, succumbed in less than a month to a violent case of Montezuma's Revenge.

Back in the states, Melva drifted from town to town: Newport, Kentucky; Gretna, Louisiana; Cicero, Illinois; Phenix City, Alabama. She never wanted for male companionship in these out-of-the-way places. Fresh-faced, doll-like, she attracted admirers the way a Lady Beaverkill lure attracts trout.

And then in 1962 she dropped entirely out of sight.

Which is why, some years later, a Wall Street lawyer for Mrs. John Morland Olmsted made the trek to my agency's fourth-floor office on 47th Street, west of Broadway. I'm a private investigator, the man who runs the World-Wide Detective Agency, or so say the black letters on my frosted-glass door. The agency consists of yours truly, Matt Coleridge, 48, and a twenty-nine-year-old secretary who thinks she loves me.

The widow Olmsted's mouthpiece was one of those starchy, bloodless, snowy-haired gentlemen whose taste in booze runs to sherry and whose preference in broads runs from nonexistent to bizarre. He had a nervous little laugh that punctuated his sentences like fizzled firecrackers.

"Mrs. Olmsted is a very wealthy woman," he said by way of introduction.

"Prunes."

The lawyer started, momentarily taken aback. Then he caught my meaning. "You're quite right, Mr. Coleridge. Prunes, grapes, and avocados. Mrs. Olmsted's late husband, John Morland Olmsted, owned a controlling interest in the Intercontinental Fruit Company. Upon his death, Bootsie—Mrs. Olmsted, that is—became sole heir. She is now in her early seventies, in failing health, and she wishes to leave the bulk of her estate to a missing daughter. A woman named Melva. Melva Dominic."

I hauled a fifth of bourbon from the bottom drawer of my scarred metal desk. "Drink?"

"Thank you, no."

I poured a water glass half full of Kentucky's pride, leaned back against my swivel chair, and put away a jigger or two. "Another wandering daughter job, eh?"

"I beg your pardon."

"This Melva," I said. "She didn't like living on Sutton Place? She worked up a social conscience going to Miss Porter's School? She thought John and Bootsie were kingpins in the international capitalist conspiracy?"

"No," the lawyer said thoughtfully. "Nothing like that. Melva ran away more than thirty years ago. Back when Bootsie was called Cosmic Raye, lived at the Hotel Dixie, and sent her daughter to P.S.

191. In those days Bootsie performed every night except Monday as an ecdysiast at the Cosmos Club on West 52nd Street."

"A stripper."

"If you prefer."

"She's come up in the world."

"She will leave a sizable fortune to her daughter Melva, if Melva can be found. The bequest is somewhere in the neighborhood of eighty million dollars."

"That's a very classy neighborhood. Not many grifters living there. Where was Melva last seen?"

The lawyer built a pyramid with his parchment-white hands. "She was last seen on a street near her apartment in North Las Vegas. Fifteen years ago."

He went on to tell me the life stories of Charlie Corkscrew Dominic and Bootsie Foote Dominic Olmsted. He gave me a couple of dog-eared photos of Melva at 14. He agreed to a nip of bourbon when I showed him, first, the label and, next, a clean sparkling shotglass. Then he tottered out, leaving Melva's snubbed-out trail to me.

I tried all the usual sources—departments of motor vehicles, municipal tax collectors, boards of elections, Julius Blumberg's outfit, Infosearch, Fidelifacts, even the Ouija board I keep in the top drawer of my rusted file cabinet.

Nothing.

In March 1962 Melva Dominic, a thirty-two-year-old blackjack dealer and sometime showgirl at The Fortinbras Hotel in Las Vegas, had vanished completely. Like a gonfalon bubble, as the poet would say.

After checking out the allowable expenses with Bootsie Olmsted's lawyer, I hopped a night flight to Vegas.

Three days later, bleary-eyed from bird-dogging, blackjack, and booze, I dragged my tired remains to McCarran Airport and slept soundly through a daytime flight to New York. I had acquired a $3000 debt, which I was pretty sure Mrs. Olmsted would refuse to pay. I had learned nothing new about Melva Dominic beyond the fact that she once lived in Apartment 2-C of the Sloan Arms in North Las Vegas.

On my second day in the Vegas sunshine I got myself a second shadow, also known as a tail.

He was a tall lean guy with a pockmarked face, gunfighter-blue eyes, and a handlebar mustache. He wore a glittering cowboy shirt open at the neck to reveal a chestful of yellow hair. He was about as smooth as Bowery bar whiskey when it came to tailing me, but he was persistent. He followed me right onto the DC-10 to Kennedy.

I've never liked being tailed. It reminds me too much of my own daily routine.

When I don't like something, I let people know.

At Kennedy I made my move. I cornered my newfound friend in an otherwise empty men's room, wedged him back between a sink and an air blower, and dug the barrel of my concealed Beretta into his navel.

"What gives?" said Harry Handlebars with a charming show of teeth, as if he hardly cared.

"You tell me."

"What's to tell?"

"You've been two steps behind me since I left Caesar's Palace yesterday. Why?"

He winked. "Why not? You're a likable guy."

I rammed the Beretta deeper into his abdomen. "Talk."

"Sure, Coleridge. Anything you say. I could recite a poem. How about 'The Rime of the Ancient Mariner'?"

"No poems, Harry. Just a straight story. What're you doing on my tail?"

He shrugged. "Mr. Eff says I follow you, I follow you."

Mr. Eff was a man I'd heard about. He was a favorite of Meyer Lansky and Moe Dalitz. Mr. Eff's well-manicured hooks had scratched their way into every operation on the Strip since Bugsy Siegel, Las Vegas visionary, flagged down four slugs at his girl-friend's pad in Beverly Hills in 1947.

"Why does Mr. Eff want you to follow me?"

"He's looking for his little Melva."

"Melva?"

"Haven't you heard, Coleridge? You're supposed to be looking for a well-stacked dame, about five-foot-two, named Melva Dominic. Mr. Eff, he's got the same idea."

I turned that over in my mind. "Why?"

"Mr. Eff gives order, Coleridge. He barks orders. You ever heard

him? He sounds a lot like a wolfhound. Looks like one, too. He
don't confide in me or nobody else."

"So?"

"So all I know is you're a New York gumshoe named Coleridge.
You're looking for Melva Dominic. Mr. Eff is looking for Melva
Dominic. I'm glued to your shirt-tail in case you find her."

"Simple as that."

Harry Handlebars stared past my shoulder. "You learn fast. Hey,
there's a big bimbo behind you wants to dry his hands."

It was an old trick, but I fell for it. I turned. And there he was,
sure enough, a big bimbo behind me who wanted to dry his hands.
The bimbo started to apologize.

"Can it," I muttered. It was as much his men's room as mine, I
figured. I sidestepped the big fellow's Florsheims and left.

My secretary had opened the office at ten sharp that morning,
the way she always does. She's an early riser, also a faithful side-
kick. I can be in Port Chester or Port-au-Prince, but when the big
hand is on the twelve and the little hand is on the ten, Sara's hand
is on the doorknob.

Sara came to me two years ago after working a while for a dentist
on Park Avenue. Although she's not exactly a showstopper in
looks, with freckles, a turned-up nose, bobbed hair, and a face
that's a bit too round, she's no mirror-breaker either. She appealed
to the dentist enough to attract his amorous attention.

This aging D.D.S. paid Sara Park Avenue wages, a lot higher than
mine, but after a few weeks of having him insist on certain after-
hours' activities of a nondental nature, she complained. She's not
that kind of girl. But the dentist chuckled and kept on insisting.
She gave up complaining, kneed him once when he charged,
tromped hard on his foot, and chucked the job.

"Morning, Sara," I said, entering the gray confines of World-
Wide's fly-specked office. It was a few minutes before noon. I
stopped at her desk, caressed her arm in my fatherly way, quoted a
line from Swinburne, and blew the dust from the top of her Under-
wood. "Any calls?"

She gave me that little-girl beam of hers, all feigned naivete, and
her freckles danced. "Melva Dominic phoned a few minutes ago.
She said she'll phone again at three."

"Melva Dominic?"

"Not Little Red Riding Hood," Sara said sweetly. "And you got some mail this morning. Two letters, both special delivery. One from Melva Dominic in Boston. The other from Melva Dominic in Thatcher, Arizona. The envelope from Boston is doused in Chanel Number 19."

"The vultures are flying," I said. "I wonder how they got the scent of carrion?"

Sara tapped a copy of the *Evening Standard* lying on her desk. The paper was two days old.

"Martha Talis, the syndicated columnist, that's how." Sara pointed to the column. "She must have found out about your search and put two and two together. Or else that creaky lawyer who was in here spilled it to her. Anyway, half the country knows about the missing Melva Dominic and how she stands to inherit all those buckets of ducats."

"Private eye goes public," I growled, heading for my glassed-in cubicle.

I got halfway there.

The office door opened and in walked a dream. She was tall and slim and cool and elegant, with upswept black hair and gray eyes flecked with gold. Her outfit had the look of Lord & Taylor and her walk had the grace of a Monocan princess.

She glanced at me as if I might have an outside shot at being her footman if I'd agree to shave once a day and give up the horses and the hooch.

Sara, good secretary that she was, kept her head on straight and asked this shining vision its name.

"Melva Dominic," came the melodic reply. "From Roselle Park, New Jersey. I'm looking for a gentleman who calls himself Matt Coleridge."

"I'm Coleridge," I said. "From Hunger, out of Bensonhurst. Let's float into my private office." I motioned toward the gap in the frosted-glass wall.

She swung her fashionable hips past me, lowered herself into a straightback chair, extracted a mile-long cigarette from a gold case, put it in her face, and set fire to it. She blew a fan of smoke into the charged air, watched the smoke plume toward a cluster of cobwebs on the ceiling.

My swivel chair creaked as I lifted a handy bottle of spirits from the bottom drawer. "Drink?"

"A Morning Glory Fizz, please. Light on the absinthe."

I grunted something in Anglo-Saxon and poured out two nips of bourbon neat.

"Now, Miss Dominic," I said in what I thought was a business-like tone, "let's be honest with each other. I'm Matt Coleridge, as my shingle says. I can prove it. You're Melva Dominic, so you say. I'm pretty sure you can't prove it."

With solemn deliberation she dipped into her Gucci handbag and fished out a bundle of plastic cards, official-looking papers, and glossy photos. She handed them to me.

I bent studiously over this batch of undistilled proof. Melva feathered smoke through her nostrils.

After five minutes I broke the silence. "It's inspiring what a good forger can do," I gave my opinion. "Especially when he's teamed up with a top photographer and a first-class con artist. This assort-ment of junk you're carrying is practically perfect. If I didn't know better, I'd swear on a stack of Maltese Falcons that you really *are* Melva Dominic."

"Would you like to see me dance?" she asked seductively, cross-ing her legs and showing a lot of thigh. "The way I used to at the Maximilian Club in Tijuana?"

"You bet I would," I said. I never lie when I'm asked a question like that. "But it won't convince me of anything." I went up against the hooch again. "Listen, sweetheart, you're no more Melva Domi-nic than I'm Rudy Nureyev. The real Melva is on the shadow side of forty. She's only about five-foot-two. Also—"

The telephone jangled. We stopped parrying. A few seconds later Sara poked her turned-up nose into the cubicle and said, "I have Melva Dominic on the line." She looked from me to the raven-haired knockout and back again. She didn't smile, or scowl, or anything. "The Melva Dominic from Boston."

"I'll take it," I said, grabbing the horn. "Hello, Miss Dominic."

A shy voice said, "Hello, Mr. Coleridge. I believe you've been looking for me."

"No, not you. I'm after the bona-fide Melva Dominic."

Her reply was a light lilting laugh. "Your secretary must have misunderstood, Mr. Coleridge. My name is Melva Dominic. It really is."

"Can you prove it?"

"Of course."

"Papers? A driver's license? A Social Security card? That sort of thing?"

"Yes."

"Okay. I believe it. You've found the Instant Identity Factory too. Can you buzz down to New York?"

"Yes. I live just a few minutes from Logan Airport . . . wait . . ."

"Wait?"

"Who are you? . . . why are you . . . stay away!"

"Miss Dominic?"

No answer. Then:

"Please . . . it's all a mistake . . ."

"Melva!"

"It's got to be . . . a terrible—"

Four loud reports.

In 22 years of running the affairs of World-Wide, I'd never heard pistol shots on a telephone wire. I was pretty sure I was hearing them now. Four shots, evenly spaced. Professional.

"Melva?"

The line went dead.

I slammed down the receiver. "Come on, Dreamboat," I said to the Roselle Park version of Melva Dominic. "We're catching the next shuttle to Boston. I think your namesake up there has come to dust."

To my surprise she put up no struggle. Hand in hand we dashed toward the elevator. On our way past Sara's desk I scooped up the Chanel No. 19 letter from Boston. I needed the address.

Sara gave Roselle Park a look of open envy.

The elevator stopped at every floor going down, which it always does when time is pressing. Finally it thumped to ground level at 47th Street. Roselle Park and I skittered for the front entrance.

Sunlight filtered down through the perpetual midtown smog and grime. It painted little patches of gold on the pavement. The street had its usual midday traffic, yellow cabs vying with Uncle Sol to bring a touch of color to the pervading drabness.

I saw a black Cadillac limousine illegally parked at the curb directly in front of us. For an instant the significance of the limo failed to register. Then I saw a glint of sun on steel. I saw a shaft of light fall on a familiar yellow mustache. That did it. I jerked Roselle Park suddenly back toward the World-Wide building. She yelped. I shouted.

Too late.

A burst of gunfire erupted from a side window of the Caddy. I dove for the pavement. So did she.

I was bruised and breathless, but otherwise okay.

Roselle Park was dead before she hit the concrete.

It was an execution, a rub-out, a murder in the course of business. I had seen gang-style executions before, but never at such close range. It was a murder without emotion, without amenities. A murder without icing.

I canceled the trip to Boston.

Eyewitnesses are usually about as valuable as slag in a steel mill, but this time half a dozen bystanders gave the police the license number of the Caddy. A young black kid even chased the limo for two blocks on foot, finally losing it west of Ninth Avenue when he was tackled by an alert patrolman. The kid was frisked, questioned, and released.

The car was recovered on Eleventh Avenue a few minutes later. It had been stolen an hour back from an East Side parking lot.

After telling my story to a sleepy-eyed detective sergeant from Homicide, I rode the elevator back to World-Wide. I felt washed-out, depressed.

The fourth floor hadn't changed much. It was still in need of demolition.

Sara knew nothing about the shooting below, but she didn't act too concerned. She yawned when I told her about it, and went back to her reading. Since there hadn't been much filing or typing to do the last few months, she'd been leafing her way through a pile of Agatha Christie novels. An avid fan of the Great Dame, she pored over Agatha's urbane puzzles, she said, to escape the harsh realities of 47th Street.

Back in my office I wearily traced down the telephone number for an address on Hennissy Street, Thatcher, Arizona, where the third Melva Dominic claimed to live.

I guess she did live there, because the noise I got when I called the number was a lot of anguished wailing at the other end of the line. Something about a Louise Sprague—"poor dear Louise!"—who had just been gunned down at the Tucson airport while waiting for a flight to New York.

I hung up and told Sara the latest casualty count.

Three Melva Dominics.

All dead.

Then it hit me like a bolo punch. The killings might not be over yet. There might be another murder to go. There was at least one more Melva Dominic on the loose—the one who had phoned this morning and talked to Sara. She was supposed to call back at three.

I checked my Timex. 2:59. A minute passed. The phone rang.

"Mr. Coleridge?" It was a throaty feminine voice, the kind that can cozen hardheaded businessmen out of yachts and sables, diamonds and negotiables. The South oozed out of that voice like juice oozing from chitlins.

"Melva?"

"Why, Mr. Coleridge, how wonderful of you! Did you recognize my voice? I'll bet you caught my act in Cal City or Reno! Am I right?"

"No, Melva. This is the first time I've caught your act. And listen, doll, you'd better drop that act pretty quick if you want to keep your lungs vacuuming air. It's open season on Melva Dominics."

Her laugh had the same carefree trill as one I'd heard that morning—from a lady whose corpse was now on its way to the Boston city morgue.

"Where do you live, Melva?"

"Why, Mr. Coleridge, you shameless shamus, you! I don't give out my address. Not like that, not at the drop of a hint!"

"I'm not trying to date you, doll. 'Love is not all,' as the green-eyed poet says. Besides, my bulletproof vest is at the cleaners, and with you in sight I'd need it. I'm trying to protect you."

"How *sweet!* Mr. Coleridge, you sound like such a strong chivalrous man. I can hardly resist you. A brave detective, and tough."

Tough, I thought. That's me. Coleridge is tough. Tough as a three-dollar steak, but with a heart as big as a wheel of cheddar cheese and as soft as a wedge of brie.

I took notice to the bourbon, lowering the glass carefully toward one of the 200 or more rings of brown stain that decorate the gray enamel of my desk.

"Listen, Melva. Tell me where I can find you. Tell me quick, because you're in big trouble. This is rub-out day for Melva Dominics."

She hesitated.

"Don't hesitate, doll."

"I'm at the Port Authority Bus Terminal," she said, a note of pique in her voice. "On Eighth Avenue, I think. I got in from Winston-Salem a few minutes ago."

"Stay there," I said, "and light up a butt. There's a Hoffritz store on the street level. Wait for me at the jackknife counter. I'll meet you there in ten minutes."

I chug-a-lugged the last four ounces of bourbon, filed the empty in my wastebasket, and told Sara where I was going. She blew me a kiss, then went back to *Murder in Mesopotamia*.

The Port Authority Bus Terminal, where I park my four-year-old Plymouth, is a massive building of tan brick and concrete completely surrounded by urban horrors. The more respectable social causes are represented inside by wandering missionaries and stern-faced fanatics who sit behind bannered card tables and hope against hope.

I pushed my way through the pre-rush-hour crowd at the Eighth Avenue entrance, vaguely aware that I had picked up a tail. I paused at the newsstand and tried to get a clear make on my shadow. It was easy. He was thin and pockmarked, yellow-mustached, and outfitted like a rhinestone cowboy. Harry Handlebars.

No introductions were called for. I walked up to him, yanked a hot-rod magazine off his beak, and said, "I take it there's a contract out on little Melva."

"You take it right, Coleridge," he drawled. "Fifty thousand boffos riding on her head."

"For what?"

Harry glanced around casually. "What the hell," he said. "I don't see it can hurt much to tell you."

"It'll make you feel all warm inside."

"Sure it will." He drew a hairy paw across the craters of his chin.

"It goes back fifteen years. It's an old contract. Melva Dominic was working The Fortinbras in Vegas. She got close and cosy with Mr. Eff, the boss there. Too cosy, if you know what I mean."

"Spell it out."

"What I mean is, one thing led to another. She learned a lot about the operation. Learned about the skim. Learned where the mob's cash was kept, how it got delivered. She always had a weakness for cash, according to Mr. Eff. Didn't go in for jewels or fancy clothes, but loved that green stuff. One morning she up and—"

"Lifted it."

"Yeah. A heist. Did it by herself. A whole week's skim, which is one hell of a lot of cash."

"She disappeared."

"Like Jimmy Hoffa, only alive. She had her moves planned like a pro."

"Mr. Eff was unhappy."

"Unhappy? He was purple like a turnip. The mob was likewise unhappy. Mr. Eff was lucky not to end up the way Bugsy did, looking like a bloody Chinese checkerboard. Finally Mr. Eff had to dig into his own pocket to square himself with—well, you know."

"Mr. Eff didn't like that."

"He barked more than usual. He snarled and foamed. Mr. Eff, he's the wrong guy to cross. He put a price on Melva's head. Fifty thousand. It's still there, or was until today. As of now Mr. Eff owes a nice even two hundred G's on the contract—unless he can straighten out the whole mess better'n I think he can."

"Meaning what?"

"Meaning Melva Dominics are turning up under every rock from here to Frisco."

"Hey, wait a minute. Didn't you say two hundred G's? That means four dead Melvas. My count is three."

"There's a chilled Melva down in Aruba," he said. "She probably ain't on your scratch sheet yet. Miami Max hit her about three hours ago. He's claiming his fifty G's down there."

"And you're claiming it in New York."

"Come on, Coleridge. I'm too modest to brag."

"You're not modest, you're greedy."

"Well, fifty grand ain't penny ante. I'm not knocking it. But a hundred grand would be my kind of day. Which is why I'm tailing you again."

So here he was, Harry Handlebars, the torpedo who had iced Miss Roselle Park. Here he was, itching to cool off Miss Winston-Salem.

It was time for the refrigeration to stop. It was time to warm things up.

I threw a straight left jab to set him up, classical style, the way Sugar Ray Robinson would have thrown it. I used to work out in Stillman's gym, and 20 years ago I had a punch. But I'm not in Sugar Ray's class. Never was.

Before I could jolt him with a short right hook, he got inside me and butted the top of his yellow skull into my chest. I grunted and staggered back.

He reached inside his plaid jacket and came out with a shiny .32 automatic.

Enough with the boxing. I aimed my right foot at him, kicked his neat little .32 over the newsstand for a field goal. A well-dressed gent snatched it up off the floor, no hesitation, and ran away with it. So much for well-dressed gents at the Port Authority Bus Terminal.

Then Harry Handlebars parted company with his senses. He rushed me. He ran into a stiff solid left that I'd launched in the other direction. I heard something crack, and when I looked down at him, his eyes had rolled up toward the ceiling. He didn't move.

I did. Before the cops got the hang of things.

Thirty seconds later I was inside the Hoffritz emporium, examining an assortment of jackknives and hunting knives. I was breathing hard. There was a well-stacked little brunette standing next to me, also engrossed in knives.

"Hi," I said. "You must be the fifth Melva Dominic."

She smiled without warmth. "No. I'm Elsa Schlotterbach. But I can take you to Melva Dominic if you want me to."

I stared hard at her. She was about 45, in fine repair, with wide violet eyes, a pointed chin, and a look of quiet competence. She stood maybe five-two. Her voice was the sexy Southern drawl I had heard on the phone.

"I'd swear you were Melva Dominic."

"I thought about being Melva Dominic," she said levelly. "Until a few minutes ago. But then this nice man behind the counter"—she pointed toward a bearded Hoffritz clerk—"began filling me in on some of the recent obits."

"And you decided to pull out of the Dominic sweepstakes?"

"I decided to tell you my real name. Elsa Schlotterbach. I think I'd rather be Elsa than Melva."

"It's safer. But not as profitable. You lose a legacy of eighty million that way."

"Win some, lose some. I know where Melva Dominic is."

"Uh huh. That's what I'm supposed to be finding out. How did you happen to find out?"

"I used to room with her. Twelve years ago."

That stopped me for a minute. "In North Carolina?"

"In New Jersey. Parsippany. She called herself Mary Hedstrom in those days. Do you have a car, Mr. Coleridge?"

"You're very fast with the non sequiturs, Elsa. As a matter of fact I do. It's parked on top of this brick-pile."

"Would you like to visit Melva?"

"What do you think?"

A few minutes later we were under the Hudson River, wheeling west. The tunnel stretched out ahead of us like a hollow, illuminated snake.

Escaping into the spring sunshine, we drove through the Secaucus marshland, past the gleaming new Sports Complex, under fluffy clouds that lay piled above Route 3 like pink cotton candy. Traffic was light, and before long the garish commercial glut of Route 46 began reeling past us like technicolor scenes from a bad movie.

Miss Schlotterbach said nothing for the first fifteen miles, just sitting over against the door and watching the mileposts loom up and disappear.

After a while she started to inch her way closer to me, and all at once she wanted to talk. The words flowed out like Southern Comfort at a three-day convention of Sun Belt politicos.

"When Melva and I first met," she said, "we both had studio apartments in Parsippany. Nobody knew much about anybody else in Parsippany in those days. It was like an old-fashioned boom town. Houses and apartments were springing up everywhere. I worked for a small ad agency, and she worked for a five-and-dime store. We got acquainted at a bar in Lake Hiawatha. We compared the wages we were making and decided we'd be better off sharing a two-bedroom apartment."

"I'm listening," I said. Her voice had a kind of dreamy quality to it, as if she was making up the story as she went along.

"Everything worked out fine. No serious arguments. No jealous boy friends. She lived her life, I lived mine."

"An idyll."

"Idylls went out with lances and chain mail, Coleridge. We got along."

"Until when?"

"Until '65. Early June."

"What happened then?"

She shuddered a little, and I reached out a hand to comfort her. It fell on her knee, and she responded with a karate chop.

"Do you know anything about Parsippany?" she asked.

"Only what I read in the travel brochures."

"Well, the main street of Parsippany is Route 46. There aren't any sidewalks on Route 46. No crosswalks. But you've got to cross that damn road every now and then, either to catch a bus or to get to your parked car."

"Yeah. So?"

"So Melva was crossing Route 46 one night. It was after nine o'clock, but it was barely dark. A sports car screamed out of a liquor store parking lot and slammed into her. It dragged her about two hundred feet on the pavement. Turned the left side of her into raw hamburger. The driver didn't brake, didn't stop."

"An accident?"

"It's hard to say. The police thought so. I wasn't so sure."

"Melva? DOA?"

"No. She was rushed to the hospital in critical condition. She lived for three days. Mostly unconscious. But she woke up long enough to make a last request."

"With you sitting conveniently by her bedside?"

Elsa looked at me sideways. "She didn't have any relatives."

I took that in and nodded. I figured it had to be a pretty handy coincidence, this deathbed request.

Elsa said, "Turn right."

I turned right. The newly paved blacktop under us was called

Putnam Road, and it skirted a cemetery. Elsa pointed toward the stone fence surrounding it. We drove in at the main gate.

"I never knew her as Melva Dominic, you know. I knew her as Mary Hedstrom. But as she was dying, she asked me to do her a favor. Asked me to buy her a headstone. She died as Mary Hedstrom. That's what her death certificate says. But she didn't want the marker over her grave to say that. It was a lie, she said. A stonecarver will carve whatever you tell him to. And the caretaker of the cemetery couldn't care less. Stop here."

We stopped, got out of the car, and walked across a green blanket of grass. And there it was, neatly chiseled proof, a flat little planchet of granite standing off by itself. It said: "Melva Dominic, 1929-1965."

"Poor Melva," I said. "But no. She wasn't poor, was she? Little Melva wasn't poor, in spite of her rent-sharing roommate and her job in a five-and-dime. Little Melva had money."

Elsa looked up at me, coloring. "That's right. She had quite a bundle in her savings account. She left it to me."

"Six figures?"

Elsa frowned, laid a finger to her lips. "Let's say it was more than enough to pay for the headstone. Quite a bit more. I guess Melva must have earned big money somewhere."

"Uh huh," I said. "Somewhere."

We climbed back into the car. The Plymouth's tires spewed gravel as I whipped the wheel back toward the Big Apple, once Bright and Golden, now Cored and Peeled.

For a long time neither of us spoke. I was thinking of four dead imposters with their silly but expensive sets of forged identification. Maybe she was thinking of them, too.

On Route 3 eastbound you can see the New York skyline rise up in front of you like a paper cutout. It seems to sit there on the horizon, gray and fantastic, with no more reality than a carved-to-order gravestone in a Parsippany boneyard.

As far as Mrs. Bootsie Foote Dominic Olmsted would know, the case was closed. Melva Dominic had turned up. She was no heiress-to-be, though. She was just another slab of meat, the fifth slab to bear the name.

But I knew better.

I've been tracking wandering daughters for a long time.

I gazed across the seat. The demure-looking brunette beside me had introduced herself on the phone as Melva Dominic. And why not? That's who she was. No wild kid any more, but then neither am I.

I pulled two dog-eared photos from my shirt pocket and examined them under the rim of the steering wheel. The wide eyes, the straight nose, the pointed chin, the high cheekbones—thirty years later, but there was no question about it.

The lady sitting next to me was Charlie Corkscrew's natural daughter, Melva Dominic.

"Six figures," I said thoughtfully, aiming the picture side of the old photos her way. "It's a better wad than you can make dealing blackjack. But it's a digit or two away from eighty million bucks."

"Those things happen."

"There may be an angle. I figure you're entitled to the eighty million."

She looked at me, soft and interested. "You're a sweet guy. But what would I do with the eighty million? Buy myself a diamond-studded casket?"

"You've got a point there, Melva."

"Please don't call me Melva. Not now, not ever again. Mama can keep her money."

I dropped my palm lightly to her knee. This time she didn't club it away.

I said, "Who's actually buried under that tombstone?"

She moved closer. "If I tell you, Coleridge . . . if I tell you the truth, what will you tell Mama?"

"I'll tell Mrs. Olmsted exactly what that piece of Parsippany granite tells her. No more, no less."

Her lips played across the stubble of my chin. "Thanks, Coleridge. You're a prince."

"I try," I said. "Even without my lance and chain mail, I try. Let me guess who's buried back there."

"One guess."

"Well, I figure that Mary Hedstrom alias of yours gave you pretty good cover. It kept the mob away for three years. But it was still a phony identity, with forged papers. Maybe you wanted a real identity, with real papers."

"You're brilliant," she breathed.

"You needed something bona fide. Something that would stand up against any search by Mr. Eff and his goons."

Her head rested against my shoulder.

I said, "I'd guess that Elsa Schlotterbach is the dame who's buried back there in Parsippany. Not little Melva, but little Elsa. The pretzel who died crossing Route 46."

Melva looked up at me. Her violet eyes shone. "That's right, Coleridge. I didn't inherit any money from Elsa. She was broke. Mary Hedstrom was the one with money in the bank. My money. Vegas money. What I inherited from Elsa Schlotterbach was her identity. I've been using it ever since."

I shook my head admiringly. "You're a shrewd damsel all right. First you bury Elsa under the Mary Hedstrom alias. Then you put a Melva Dominic marker over her grave, just in case. You turned out to be one fast-shuffling roommate."

"Was I wrong, Coleridge? Was I wrong to do it?"

"You were right, sweetheart. Right as Rilke."

She nodded. "Elsa didn't seem to mind."

I chewed on that for a while, couldn't digest it. I floored the accelerator of the Plymouth, shuddered past a slow-moving truck that claimed to be paying $4000 a year in road-use taxes. Four thousand bucks—a nice round amount, just about the fee I figured Bootsie Olmsted owed me for the caper now concluded. Not a bad fee either, but a little short of Melva's lost inheritance of $80,000,000.

Four thousand bucks. Chicken feed to the nabobs, but to me it was T-bone steak, with plenty of hooch to wash it down. The fee wouldn't buy much at Cartier's, but it represented a lot more cash then I'd had on the World-Wide books since—when? Since a couple of years back, I guess, when Pick-Up-Sticks came in at Aqueduct at 300-to-1.

THE DARK GAMBLE: END OF THE TRAIL

HUGH PENTECOST

Jason Dark had known fear many times in his life. In 22 years as a tough cop he had faced many situations in which he had known fear. In five years as a private investigator there had been some very bad moments, like the night when two men had hacked off his right hand and left him to bleed to death in New York's Central Park. The violence of that moment had been too great for him to be aware of fear. That had come the next day, lying in a hospital bed, his life saved by a Park policeman. How could he live and function with only one hand? That produced fear. How could a cripple hunt down his cripplers? Those questions produced a cold sweat of fear as he lay there, staring up at the whitewashed ceiling.

He had known fear, pinned down in a back alley by a sniper on the roof of an overhanging building. He had known fear in a locked room with a time bomb ticking away in a safe that he couldn't open with his uneducated left hand. He had known fear driving down a narrow mountain road, careening from side to side, aware that someone had tampered with his brakes.

Jason Dark had never felt that fear and courage were incompatible. You knew fear, but you had the courage to cope with it. A man without fear was a man without imagination. Dark knew when there was danger around him, when you had to be afraid of it. He also knew exactly what his capabilities were for facing that danger.

Never, until this morning, had he felt that the odds were worse than fifty-fifty against his surviving.

This morning Dark was afraid of Youth.

Jason Dark, in his early fifties, was a short square little man whose deceptively mild eyes stared at the world through slightly tinted wire-rimmed glasses. He looked more like a retired school-teacher than a man who had dedicated his life to fighting the violence that man inflicts upon man.

This morning he sat with his back to the windows of the living room in his East 40th Street duplex apartment, his plastic right hand covered by a black glove buried in his jacket pocket. He was studying his visitor—and he knew fear.

Alex Clement had been sent to him by a trusted friend as a foreign correspondent for *Network News* who "may be able to lead you to a path you've been trying to find." From the moment Clement had walked into the apartment, however, Dark had felt a jolt of fear induced by a situation he knew he wasn't equipped to battle.

He couldn't fight Youth. He couldn't fight what he had to de-scribe as a kind of male beauty. He couldn't fight a sparkling charm. The instant contact this young man made with the girl who opened the front door to him was like the excitement of the hunter who spots game—the response of youth to youth without any words being spoken. These were dangers Jason Dark knew he couldn't evade and wasn't equipped to fight.

All his life until a year ago Jason Dark had been a loner. There had been women in his life, but none who mattered. And then Sharon Evans, blonde, lovely, in her mid-twenties, had found her-self in the middle of one of Dark's adventures—and found herself in love with this gentle-tough older man. He wanted her so much and yet he argued fiercely against any sort of permanent relation-ship. "I'm old enough to be your father! My life is no kind of life for you."

But she had replied, "Life without you is no kind of life for me."

One night he came home and there she was. She had moved into his apartment, bag and baggage. His life was turned around. There were things in this relationship he hadn't imagined existed. Two people seemed to become one. Deep inside him Dark knew it couldn't last forever. Some day someone more nearly the right age for Sharon, with her kind of glorious vitality, would appear on the

scene and that would be that. He should be thankful for all he had
had, he told himself, but the thought of losing her was the most
excruciating fear he had ever known.

When Alex Clement stepped into the apartment this morning,
Dark felt his heart jam against his ribs. With nothing tangible to
base it on, instinct told him that this was it.

Clement, knowing nothing of the relationship, assumed that
Sharon was a daughter, or a secretary. The thought that she might
be an old man's love, an old man's world, never occurred to him.
That was the way Dark saw it. Twenty-five or twenty-six, Dark
thought—just about Sharon's age.

"Thank you for seeing me," Clement said to Dark, but his eyes
were on Sharon as she brought coffee from the kitchen.

"Bob Maclyn is an old friend," Dark said. It was Maclyn, in the
State Department in Washington, who had suggested he see Clement. *He may be able to lead you to a path you've been trying to find.*

He may be able to turn my life into something bitter and empty,
Dark thought.

"I have been stationed in the Middle East for *Network News* for
the last ten months," Clement said. He watched Sharon move over
to the window seat just to the right of Dark. She was smiling at
Clement. Was it the polite smile of a hostess, or was something
electric passing between them?

"You and I, unaware of each other, have been working along the
same line, so Maclyn tells me," Clement said. "Quadrant International."

Quadrant International was one of the biggest of the multina-
tional corporations, bigger than any three Middle East countries
put together—dealers in tanks, guns, planes, pharmaceuticals,
computers, suppliers of technical experts and expertise. Jason
Dark, on a case unrelated to Quadrant, had come across an informer who talked of the bribery of foreign government officials,
the corruption of local politicians by Quadrant.

Dark had made tapes of the informer's stories and stored them
away for future use. Then he had been trapped in the kitchen of a
restaurant in the city where his informer had set him up. Two men
in ski masks had strapped his hand to the butcher's block, de-
manding the tapes. They had crushed and then chopped his hand
to pieces. He had managed, in his agony, to keep the hiding place

of the tapes secret, because he knew he would die if he revealed it. Since then Dark's one goal was to find the man who had ordered his torture and to destroy his empire, Quadrant International.

"Maclyn told me the story of your hand," Clement went on. His eyes moved toward the pocket where Dark's black-gloved plastic hand was buried. There was curiosity, not sympathy, in the look. "You have reason to believe that the men who did this to you were hired by Quadrant. Maclyn says you had some documents or tapes they wanted."

Dark nodded. Maclyn had done a lot of talking to this young man. The State Department man must trust him completely to have told him so much.

"You couldn't identify those men if you confronted them again?"

"They wore ski masks and gloves," Dark said. "No uncovered flesh."

"My assignment in the Middle East was an in-depth study of terror and terrorists," Clement continued. He seemed to be addressing what he had to say to Sharon, not Dark. Trying to impress her, Dark thought. "We are living in a time when hijacking, kidnaping, the mass murder of innocent people—like the slaughter of Israel's Olympic team at Munich—is a way of life. Holding hostages for political gain is move one between governments, between governments and corporate entities. An endless battle for power with human life having little or no value. Your friends in the ski masks didn't kill you because they think your terror will be so great the next time that you'll give them what they want."

"The next time!" Sharon's voice was a frightened whisper.

"There will be a next time," Clement said. "The name of the game is to get what you want—by any means."

Dark produced a cigarette with his left hand, put it between his lips, lit it with a lighter held in his left hand. He had become expert with that left hand over the months.

"I have been aware of that," Dark said. "I have been trying to get to them before they get to me."

"But why have they waited eighteen months to strike at you again, Jason?" Sharon asked.

"May I guess at the answer?" Clement asked, giving her his brightest smile. "Whatever Mr. Dark has is not dangerous to them right now. It probably will be dangerous to them when they make some move in the future. They tried to get it early. Failing, they attracted attention to themselves. Too many people know about Mr. Dark's war against Quadrant. To destroy him now would result in too many questions being asked. But sometime—maybe tomorrow, maybe six months from now—they will have to get what they want or risk a failure they can't afford."

"You haven't told me anything I don't know, Mr. Clement," Dark said. "I have been living on borrowed time." He glanced at Sharon. "I know that. Maclyn indicated you could give me some concrete help. Lead me to a path I've been looking for—that's the way he put it."

Clement took a little cigarette-sized cigar from a flat box in his pocket and tapped it on the back of his hand. "Trademarks, Mr. Dark," he said, "I kept thinking about what has happened to you while I was talking to Bob Maclyn. Terrorists in the Third World have a way of dealing with their enemies—and their own people who turn to private crime. A murderer is murdered in exactly the same fashion that he did his own killing—a bullet if he shot someone, a knife if he knifed someone, a garroting if he strangled someone. A thief—his hand is cut off."

Clement held a lighter to his little cigar. "In their eyes you are a thief, Mr. Dark. You stole information from them. I can think of a dozen better ways to make you talk than hacking off your hand. But if I were controlled by ancient traditions I would automatically think of the accepted way my ancestors had for dealing with a thief."

"But Jason was attacked here, in New York City, in America!" Sharon said.

"The assassins, the hijackers, the torturers and kidnapers come from all over the world," Clement said. "You want a man wiped out in the airport at Jerusalem, you hire a hit man from Japan. You want a British diplomat eliminated in London, you import your killer from Spain. If the killer is caught he has no record, no traceable connections in the country where he's working. An outfit like Quadrant can reach out to find a hit man anywhere in the world. They chose men from the Middle East to work on you here in New York, Mr. Dark. What they did to your hand proves that to me— the Third World punishment for a thief."

Dark fought with impatience. He wanted to put an end to what he sensed was a special exchange between this handsome young man and Sharon. "It's an interesting theory," he said, "but it isn't any real help to me."

"But if you knew where to look?" Clement smiled at Sharon. He was, Dark thought with a touch of anger, showing Sharon how clever he was. "Three days ago," Clement went on, "I was strolling down Fifth Avenue when I saw a man I knew from another time, another place. This man, a Palestinian, had performed some violent acts for Quadrant in the Middle East. He is a murderer, a torturer, an expert at sophisticated violence."

"So you went to the police?" Sharon asked.

Clement shook his head. "No proof, no solid evidence. If I went to the police I'd probably be murdered in my bed before the next sunrise. But I was curious, so I followed this man."

"He has a name?" Dark asked.

"He probably has a dozen names," Clement said. "In the Middle East I heard him referred to simply as The Man. A genius in the art of violence. As I say, I followed him. He went to a small renovated brownstone on East 63rd Street. I saw other dark-skinned Moslem types come and go from that house. Not strange there, you understand. That part of the city has stopped being curious about foreign types. The United Nations. But here, I thought, is a little nest of violent men."

"With no reason to think they had anything to do with this," Dark said. For the first time he took the black-gloved plastic hand out of his pocket and rested it on the table.

"I made some discreet inquiries," Clement said. "I learned that the owner of that brownstone is Richard Harkness of Harkness Chemical."

Dark felt his stomach muscles tighten. Harkness Chemical, he knew, was a subsidiary of Quadrant International. Clement might have something.

"I still don't understand why you haven't gone to the police," Sharon said.

Clement gave her a charming if slightly patronizing smile. "In my business you keep alive on tips, on secret sources of information. Let it become known that you will pass what you know to the police or other law-enforcement agencies and you are done for. I badly want to know what cooks in that house on 63rd Street, but I can't go to the police. It occurred to me that Mr. Dark might run risks I can't afford to run. It occurred to me that by doing him a favor he might, in turn, do me a favor."

"Such as?"

"An exclusive account of what you discover at 63rd Street," Clement said.

"And if I refuse?"

Clement shrugged, smiling. "A gamble I'm taking," he said.

Dark looked down at his black-gloved hand. The man responsible for it might now be within reach. He would owe something if that turned out to be true.

"I can reach you, I suppose, at the offices of *Network News,*" he said.

"I'm staying in a friend's apartment," Clement said. "Trying to put ten months of work into some kind of readable order. I can give you a phone number in case you need to call me."

Clement wrote down a number on a slip of paper Sharon supplied. He also wrote down the exact address of the house on 63rd Street. At the door he smiled down at Sharon who had followed him there.

"May I call you sometime?" he asked.

"If you think it's worthwhile," she said.

Dark sat still, staring down at his hand, as the door closed on his visitor. And then she was beside him, her arms around him, her cheek pressed against his.

"You idiot!" she said. She laughed. "Do you really think I could be interested in that brash young clown? Oh, Jason, my darling, you surprise me. I had thought you were quite grown up."

He held her close, and his world started to come together again.

There is a vast difference between a routine, fact-gathering, note-taking detective and the genuinely great crime hunters and crime breakers. The difference, Jason Dark knew, was an intangible thing, an instinct, a built-in alarm system, a kind of personal radar. He remembered as a child reading about some hero whose faithful horse refused, even when subjected to whip and spur, to cross a bridge. Seconds later the bridge collapsed into a raging torrent that would have killed both rider and mount. Instinct? Some kind of psychic alarm system? Once in his career Dark had ignored the warning that came to him from his own special instinct for danger. It had cost him his right hand.

Dark had heard men say they had "a hunch" about a situation. They were, he thought, the kind of men who draw to an inside straight at poker and go broke. It wasn't just a hunch he had about the house on 63rd Street. He was inundated by private warnings.

There was nothing noteworthy about the house, an old-fashioned brownstone, except something lifeless about it that Dark couldn't quite define. Venetian blinds were drawn over the windows facing the street, presumably to guard against the bright afternoon winter sun. Clement had seen men come and go from the house, but after two hours of watching, Dark had seen no one. If the people who lived there were involved with the United Nations, the place could be deserted until the afternoon sessions at the world organization were finished. It would be an ideal time to let himself into the house and have a look around, but the inner warnings against such a move were almost physically painful. Years ago, until he had learned to trust those feelings, Dark had thought he was afraid. He knew better now. Something was wrong.

New York City is a repository for millions of tons of records, files, special information. If you knew the right place to go, the right person to ask, you could find out almost anything that was important to you. After watching the house from various places along the block, after going around to the rear and coming up a back alley without seeing any signs of life, Dark decided to make sure of his facts. He called a friend who worked in one of the offices that handled city records.

Clement had been right. The house on 63rd Street belonged to Richard Harkness of Harkness Chemical. The connection with Quadrant International was there—it was real. He had mistrusted Clement because he was jealous of his youth, his handsome face. For once he had allowed his instinct to be fouled up by the fear of losing Sharon. She was right. He'd reacted like an adolescent.

But something more than instinct was involved in his reluctance to proceed. Experience told him that things that came easy must be examined closely. Clement had pointed out a place to him which was almost certainly used by terrorists hired by Quadrant. All he had to do was choose the right moment to walk in and catch them red-handed, perhaps the very men who had maimed him a year and a half ago. He wanted so urgently to square that account; he could taste the moment of revenge. And yet both instinct and common sense warned him off. Wait—wait for some sign of life!

Almost directly across the street from the house was a little fruit and grocery store. *GARDELLA'S,* the sign read. He had seen school children and workmen enter and leave. Gardella's made sandwiches and sold fruit, cheese, and pasta products. Dark went into the store. A dark-skinned little man, probably Gardella, smiled at him. Dark selected a McIntosh apple and asked for a piece of Vermont cheese he saw displayed.

"That house across the way, number 123, is it occupied?" Dark asked.

Gardella shrugged. "Sometimes," he said. "I think people from the U.N. use it. Years ago a family lived there, but no more."

"I wondered if it might be for rent or sale," Dark said.

"I don't know," Gardella said. He scowled at the building. "I see people come and go, but they don't shop in the neighborhood."

"Recently?" Dark asked.

"How's that?"

"You've seen people come and go recently?"

"Sure. Last night I see men—three or four—go in."

"And you saw them come out?"

Gardella shook his head. "But I don't watch all the time when I'm busy."

Dark reached in his left-hand jacket pocket for a cigarette. "Damn!" he said. "I forgot that my lighter is empty. I'll buy a tin of lighter fluid from you, Mr. Gardella. Might as well make it a large one. I'll be taking it home."

Winter darkness came a little after five. There were lights everywhere except in the Harkness house. Jason, his topcoat collar turned up, went around the block and came up the alley in the rear. On his first trip he had seen two large metal trash cans filled with torn papers. He had noted there was no food garbage, only paper. He took out of his pocket the can of lighter fluid he'd bought at Gardella's and doused the contents of both cans. His lighter, working perfectly, started two fires. He hurried down the alley and to a phone booth on the corner. He called in a fire alarm, then walked quickly around to the front again. Others had seen the flames and smoke and people were gathering outside the house. If there was anyone inside they would surely emerge now.

Fire equipment came barreling down the street. People shouted at the firemen, indicating that the fire was in the back yard. Jason waited for someone to come out of the house. No one did.

A fireman came out of the alley. "Seems to be in the garbage cans," he said. "But we'll have a look inside, just to be sure."

The words were hardly out of the man's mouth when there was a thunderous explosion from the back of the house, the sound of shattering glass, and someone screaming.

A fireman, his face cut and bleeding from broken glass, came staggering up the alley.

"Whole damn place blew up when we got the back door open," he said. "Couple of guys blown to hell and gone. Oh, God! Must have been a gas leak or something."

Jason Dark walked away, his blood like ice in his veins. His instinct had been correct. The place had been booby trapped for him. Two men had died in his place.

It was a little after midnight, hours after the explosion on 63rd Street. Jason Dark stood outside the door of an apartment on the tenth floor of a modern residence building in midtown. He had rung the doorbell and was waiting, his hands jammed deep in his overcoat pockets.

The apartment door opened and handsome young Alex Clement faced his visitor, a look of almost comic surprise on his face. Clement was wearing an overcoat, and Dark saw a suitcase standing just inside the door. It appeared the young man was just leaving.

"Man, am I glad to see you!" Clement said.

"Glad?" Dark stood quite still, his face an expressionless mask.

"It's been all over TV and radio," Clement said. "The house on 63rd Street. There's been an explosion of some sort. Did you know? Two firemen were killed."

"I know. I was there," Dark said.

"Well, come in, for God's sake," Clement said, opening the door wide. "I was concerned. I was afraid you might have been in the building. I half expected to hear they'd found a third body. They say it may have been a gas leak, set off by a fire that started in some trash cans outside the building. Come in."

Dark stepped through the doorway into a small undistinguished apartment. His hands were still in his pockets.

"They 'say' it may have been a gas leak, but they know it wasn't. It was a carefully planted booby trap. Two of them. Anyone who opened the front or back door was a dead man."

"Good lord!" Clement said.

"You were going somewhere?" Dark said.

"My friend, whose apartment this is, is coming home unexpectedly. I was about to find myself a hotel room somewhere. I have the makings of a drink if you'd like one."

"Thanks, no," Dark said. "But make one for yourself. It may be a long time before you have another one."

Clement's eyes narrowed. "I don't follow."

"I'm about to take you in on a murder charge," Dark said, "or at least as an accessory to the murder of two firemen."

"You have to be kidding!" Clement said.

Dark took his left hand out of his pocket. In it he held a small photograph. It was of a dark young man standing by a fountain in some foreign city. "Recognize this man?" Dark asked.

Clement frowned and shook his head. "I don't know him," he said. Then the corners of his mouth moved in a small bitter smile. "Maybe I can guess, though."

"Who better than you?" Dark said. "The man in the picture is, of course, Alex Clement of *Network News*. The photo was taken in Beirut last month."

The handsome young man turned away toward a portable bar in the corner of the room. It seemed he needed that drink.

Dark returned the picture to his pocket. "It took me some time to track it all down," he said. "After the explosion I knew you'd set me up. It was totally out of key for Alex Clement, an established and reputable reporter. Oh, I realized Clement might have been bought by Quadrant, but I had to be sure. I checked with *Network News* and this snapshot was the result. I checked with my friend Maclyn in the State Department. It turned out he didn't know Clement personally. When you called him on the phone and told him you were Clement, he passed you on to me. All you had to do was to persuade me to go into that house on 63rd Street to look for

my torturers and you would have done the job you were paid to do
—set me up for death."

The young man at the bar poured himself a drink. "Why didn't
you go into the house?" He didn't seem at all concerned, only
curious.

"Something smelled suspicious about it," Dark said. "Some instinct warned me. I thought your terrorists might be waiting inside
for me. So I set the fires in the trash cans, thinking I'd smoke them
out. I called the fire department and, indirectly, caused the death of
two men. You're going to pay the price for that, my friend."

"I rather doubt it," the young man said. He swallowed half of the
drink he'd poured.

Dark's left hand came out of his pocket again and this time it
held an efficient-looking handgun. "I'd like nothing better than to
have the excuse to spatter your brains right here on the carpet," he
said.

"That could be the greatest mistake of your life," the young man
said, and finished his drink. He was suddenly quite businesslike.
"Things don't always work the way we plan them," he said. "But
Quadrant always covers its people. I think I'm going to walk out of
here and that you'll make no attempt to stop me."

"Try," Dark said, his voice flat.

"First, I suggest you call your apartment and talk to your Miss
Sharon Evans," the young man said. "Or rather, try to talk to her.
She isn't there, you see."

Dark didn't speak. His finger was dangerously tight on the gun's
trigger.

"Some hours ago, just in case," the young man said, "your
Sharon Evans was taken into custody. If you have any hope of
seeing her again, you will stand aside and let me go. In a couple of
days, when I am safely away, you will receive instructions as to
how you may be able to get her back." The bright smile that he was
afraid had charmed Sharon lit up the young man's face again. "I do
hope, for her sake, your instinct tells you I'm not bluffing."

"If she has been harmed—" Dark said, his voice unsteady.

The young man walked calmly over to his suitcase and picked it
up. "A piece of advice, Mr. Dark, because I suspect you are, at
heart, a decent guy and I know you are a better than good investigator. You have been working for months to find the man at the

top at Quadrant who gave orders to have you crippled. That's horse-and-buggy thinking. There is no one man at Quadrant who controls the show. Knock off one top man and another slips immediately into his place. You're fighting a system, Mr. Dark, not a man. You haven't got a chance, you know. But you just might get your girl back if you do what they want you to do." The young man made for the door. "See you around," he said.

Dark aimed his gun steadily, then slowly lowered it. They had him, he knew. They had him cold.

Months ago, when what Jason Dark called "the miracle of Sharon" took place, he had become aware that a new vulnerability had been added to his situation. For 22 years as a cop and more than five years as a private investigator, Dark had been a loner. It was an advantage for a man who insisted on projecting himself into the center of a violent world. He could remember wondering about other cops when he was on the force. He could recall tense moments he had shared with another man, a partner who was married and had a couple of kids. Would that man hesitate in a crisis, concerned about the future of his family without him?

Any judgments, any decisions that Jason Dark made down the years, had involved no one but himself. Risks were his to run without concern for anyone else. Then Sharon Evans had come into his life, a girl half his age. How could this lovely blonde girl love a short stocky little man in his fifties who peered at the world through slightly tinted, wire-rimmed glasses? It was a miracle. It had made over his life. He was loved and he loved. Now this thing that was so precious to him was being used against him, could destroy him.

He didn't care about himself. It was the terrible danger to Sharon that left him immobilized, sick with anxiety. In what Dark had thought of as a moment of triumph, the capture of a Quadrant terrorist, the blow had fallen.

"Call your apartment and talk to your Miss Sharon Evans," the Quadrant terrorist had said. "Or rather, try to talk to her. She isn't there, you see. If you have any hope of seeing her alive again, you will stand aside and let me go. In a couple of days when I am safely away, you will receive instructions on how you may be able to get her back."

Dark, gun in hand, had stood aside and let the terrorist go. He had no choice. Sharon, in the hands of Quadrant's people, was a weapon he couldn't match.

Or could he? . . .

"I have lost the ability to think straight," Dark said to his friend.

The friend was sitting behind a Florentine desk in a plush office on the second floor of the Hotel Beaumont, New York City's top luxury hotel. His name was Pierre Chambrun, and he was the legendary manager of The Beaumont. He was perhaps a year or two older than Jason, elegantly tailored, with very bright black eyes almost buried in deep pouches.

An original Picasso of the Blue Period was on the wall opposite his desk; the oriental rug on the floor was a gift from a Middle Eastern potentate. Pierre Chambrun dealt in luxury and he lived in luxury. There were people who had known him 35 years ago in a different frame of reference. As a young man Chambrun had been a flamboyant hero in the French Resistance, fighting the Nazis who occupied his beloved Paris.

Chambrun knew the worlds of luxury and violence equally well. He saw people from both worlds pass through his hotel every day. The Beaumont was the home-away-from-home for politicians, diplomats, and lobbyists whose center of interest was the United Nations.

Chambrun listened to Dark's story, the smoke from one of his flat-shaped Egyptian cigarettes curling around his head.

"You have two choices," he said to Dark. "You give in to their demands, which will certainly be that you turn over to them the tapes and notes you have. You can hope that for that they will return your lady unharmed."

"Hope?"

Chambrun shrugged. "Why should they return Miss Evans? They can keep you out of business forever by holding onto her. Further than that, once they have your tapes and notes you no longer have any life insurance for yourself. You are alive, Jason, because you have something they need. Once you turn it over to them they can safely do away with the nuisance that is Jason Dark forever. They may turn your lady loose, but she will have no one to come back to."

Dark moistened dry lips. "And my second choice?"

"Fight," Chambrun said, his voice harsh and hard.

"And risk Sharon's life?"

"Whatever you do, that's a risk you have to run."

Dark was silent for a few moments, and he was aware of compassion in his friend's eyes. "I have dreamed for a long time," he said, "that I—all alone—could somehow smash Quadrant International. I have nit-picked at them, I have snapped at their heels like an aggressive fox terrier. But the dream of total victory was infantile —I realize that now."

Chambrun put out his cigarette in the brass ashtray on his desk. "Perhaps not," he said. "Not unless you are squeamish about fighting criminals in a criminal fashion."

"An eye for an eye?" Dark asked.

"A blackmail for a blackmail," Chambrun said. "How good is the evidence you have—these tapes, these notes?"

"Enough to embarrass them," Dark said. "Not good enough to sink them."

"Then we will have to find something that will sink them."

"We?"

Chambrun smiled at his friend. "You came to me for help, didn't you, Jason?"

Chambrun had poured two cups of Turkish coffee which he brewed in a samovar on the sideboard in a corner of his office. He sipped his with relish. Dark tasted and put his cup aside.

"To win a fight with a powerful enemy you have to know every detail of what makes him tick," Chambrun said. "Every habit, every technique, every move and countermove he will make automatically. At the same time you must make that enemy think you are capable of things of which you may not be."

"For example."

"Would you kill a man to get Sharon Evans back?" Chambrun asked.

"Yes," Dark said without hesitation. "If I was sure it would get her back."

Chambrun shook his head. "You must convince them that there are no 'ifs'."

"And whom do I kill?" Dark asked.

"You make them think you will kill a man," Chambrun said, "but what you really mean to kill is a system. The system that is called Quadrant International."

"In two days?"

"In two days—if you have the guts for it," Chambrun said. "The world is sick with violence and treachery and blackmail and terror. There are the fanatics who will die for a cause, like the Kamakazi pilots of Japan who dove into the smokestack of a battleship to sink it, destroying themselves at the same time. Fanatics are hard to fight. The Nazis found that out in Paris long ago. But your Quadrant International people are not fanatics in the true sense. Their aims are money and power. They won't die to get them. They want to live to enjoy them. That is how they differ from the fanatic."

"So what good does it do me to know that?" Dark asked.

Chambrun sipped his coffee. "If you were tortured to reveal secrets that would endanger your country, would you talk?" Chambrun glanced at Dark's black-gloved hand. "I think we know you wouldn't. But if all you had to save was money, would you give up your life for it? After all, you wouldn't be able to spend it then, would you?" Chambrun's smile was wry. "You might also be afraid to die because you would have to face your God with all your guilts."

"It's an interesting lecture," Dark said, "but where does it get me?"

"You are fighting men who will not willingly die for what they want," Chambrun said. "That gives you an advantage because we know that you would die for what you want, the safety of your woman. That gives you a slight edge over your opponent as you face each other."

Chambrun raised his hand to silence an interruption. "Yes, an edge—no matter how big and powerful and rich he may be, you have the edge of the fanatic. You will go all the way—which means giving up your life—to win. He will spend all the money necessary, corrupt all the decent men necessary, put his competition out of business, bribe, steal, betray to win. But he will not give up his life,

Jason, because that would make his victory meaningless. So I repeat, to start with you have an edge."

"That's comforting to know," Dark said. He sounded bitter. "But do you have any idea how I can use that edge?"

Chambrun grinned at him, an almost boyish grin. "Of course I do, or why would I bring it up?"

Guests of the Beaumont Hotel might have been disturbed if they knew how much the management knew about them when they signed in for a stay. Every morning a card passed across Chambrun's desk on which was the name of a newly registered guest. On it were letter symbols like A for alcoholic, WC for woman chaser, XX for a man double-crossing his wife, and WXX for a woman double-crossing her husband. There would also be a credit reference. At the Beaumont's prices they had to be sure a guest could pay for what he was contracting for. Hotel Security referred to these cards, preparing themselves for any intervention that might be necessary.

There was another symbol which was simply PC. That meant that Pierre Chambrun had special information about the guest which he kept to himself. If Chambrun had been a criminal, he could have run the greatest blackmail factory in the United States. He knew more about many of his guests than the State Department, the F.B.I., or the C.I.A. might have been expected to know. He used what he had to protect the hotel from scandal, from violence, from anything that would disrupt its Swiss-watch efficiency. The Beaumont was Chambrun's world, and he guarded it jealously.

On this day he did an unheard-of thing, something he had never done before in his long career as manager of the Beaumont. He made available to an outsider some secret PC information about a guest. After all, a girl's life was at stake.

"There is a man staying in my hotel who may be the key to your problem," Chambrun said. He had gone to the wall safe and taken from it a card, an ordinary filing card. It rested on the desk in front of him. "He is an Egyptian citizen, but in truth he belongs to no country unless you think of Quadrant International as a nation. This man's father was an important political figure in Egypt in the days of the late king. The father married a famous British actress named Lois Dexter.

"Your man, my guest, chooses to call himself Dexter Fahid. He's about thirty-five years old. He has bank accounts in New York, London, Cairo, and almost certainly in Switzerland. Secret-numbered accounts in Switzerland. He has a Rolls-Royce at his disposal here in New York, another in London, a third in Cairo. He has his own private jet plane. And yet, Jason, this man inherited nothing from his father or his mother but his wits.

"He has amassed his enormous fortune as a special emissary for Quadrant. He is the man who buys and sells kings and presidents, prime ministers, senators and congressmen, bankers and supposed patriots for Quadrant. He is the master of the treacherous payoff. This man knows enough to turn the whole political world upside-down. He is a genius at skulduggery. This man knows enough to blow Quadrant International out of the water for a long time."

"And I go to him and say, 'Please, Mr. Fahid, tell me something that will help me get my girl back?'" Dark sounded bitter. "He would laugh himself sick."

"Not if he was too frightened to laugh," Chambrun said.

"And what could frighten him that much?" Dark asked.

"The presence of a believable fanatic," Chambrun said.

Mr. Dexter Fahid, trim and athletic-looking, his black hair and black mustache trimmed by a stylist—nothing so ordinary as a barber for Fahid—had concluded a most satisfactory evening. There had been a dinner at Twenty-One with a carefully chosen lady. The lady was chosen for a kind of elegance that would attract attention to her escort. Dexter Fahid enjoyed the spotlight. He enjoyed being stared at like a Hollywood star, and it was also good for his business, which was buying and selling people. He had to look—and smell, he thought—like money.

After Twenty-One there was an intimate night club with an enchanting girl singer. Dexter Fahid regretted, briefly, that he wasn't spending the evening with the entertainer. Ali, his cousin and bodyguard, had tried to arrange that for him without success on another occasion. Fahid accepted little defeats, like the girl singer, without too much regret because he never suffered big defeats.

That was why he squired his lady of the evening around town in a Rolls-Royce driven by Ali, and why he could have supplied her with the same kind of transportation in London and Cairo, and could have flown her to those places in his own jet.

Tonight his impressive suite at the Beaumont—the daily rate for it would have staggered most people—was perfect for the occasion. Champagne in an ice bucket awaited him and the lady. They talked a little about fun places in different parts of the world. In the end the lady provided the delights for which Fahid had paid so handsomely.

But unlike a man who had conquered through courtship, Dexter Fahid did not take the lady home. He thanked her with courtesy and charm but Ali was given the job of transporting the lady. Ali had given his cousin and employer a slight smile just as he left.

"You mind if I take my time about this?" he asked.

Fahid didn't mind. He glanced at his watch. It was almost three o'clock in the morning. Ali wouldn't be back till breakfast time at the earliest, he told himself. Wearing an elegant silk dressing gown, Fahid stretched out on the couch in his living room, armed with a nightcap of Spanish brandy on the rocks, and picked up some papers that had to do with tomorrow's luncheon with a Syrian diplomat. He could almost taste the man's greed. There would be no problem persuading the Syrian to use his influence on behalf of Quadrant International. Fahid was just glancing at a column of figures when all the lights in his suite went out.

Now a man living in his own home is usually prepared for such emergencies. He has a flashlight hidden away somewhere, or candles. In the Beaumont where nothing ever went wrong Fahid was unprepared. He found his cigarette lighter on the coffee table beside the couch and flicked it on. It was absurdly inadequate in the high-ceilinged room but it showed him the telephone. He picked it up and was promptly answered by the switchboard operator.

"This is Dexter Fahid," he said. "All the lights seem to have gone out in 12C. Is it a general power failure?"

"No, Mr. Fahid. I'll have a maintenance man there at once. So sorry for the inconvenience."

Fahid, with the aid of his lighter, found the little vestibule at the entrance to his suite and opened the door into the hall. Bright lights everywhere. The door had an automatic closing spring and

Fahid propped a small straight-back chair against it to keep it open. Enough light filtered through into the living room to let him see the portable bar in the corner where he refreshed his drink.

Dexter Fahid expected efficiency at the Beaumont, but he was surprised at how quickly the repairman arrived. Fahid was still pouring brandy when he was aware that the front door had closed. An extremely bright electric torch partially blinded Fahid as it was aimed straight at him.

"Thanks for coming so quickly," Fahid said.

"Sorry you've been inconvenienced," the repairman said. Behind the torch he was only a shape. "We'll just have a look at things."

Fahid could see a large black bag or tool kit put down on the table behind the couch. He saw the repairman's hand move in and out of the bag, placing objects on the table which he couldn't identify. The repairman's torch was suddenly aimed again at Fahid's half-blinded eyes.

"It is now time to start playing the game," the repairman said.

"I don't understand. Game?"

"The game of life or death, Mr. Fahid," the repairman said. There was something about the deadly calmness of his voice that raised the small hairs on the back of Fahid's neck. He thought of Ali, his protector, now far away.

The light moved out of Fahid's eyes and focused on an object on the table. "Do you see what this is, Mr. Fahid?"

"You've blinded me with your torch," Fahid said, "but it looks like—it looks like a hand grenade."

"Quite correct. It is a hand grenade. You will do exactly what I ask of you, Mr. Fahid, or I will blow you, and me, and this whole wing of the hotel to hell and gone."

"You're joking, of course!" Fahid's laugh was forced and hollow-sounding.

"Would you be joking if your loved ones were dead or being tortured? Would you be joking if you had been subjected to torture yourself? No, Mr. Fahid, I'm not joking. You are the only person who can supply me with the ammunition to destroy my enemy. If you don't choose to give it to me I have no reason to go on living, and I certainly have no reason to preserve your life." A hand lifted the grenade from the table and out of the circle of light. "When I pull the firing pin on this grenade we will have less than five seconds, not even time for you to get to the front door, even if you could get past me."

"But what have I to do with you—or your enemy?" Fahid, of course, knew the answer to that. Quadrant International. Associating murder or torture with them was not inconceivable.

"Let's not waste time, Mr. Fahid." The repairman's torch focused on the table again. "This is a tape recorder. You will talk into that small microphone. You will identify yourself and then you will tell me what I need to know."

"But I have no idea what you need to know!"

"Names of people you have bribed for Quadrant. Names of diplomats who have betrayed their countries and under what circumstances. I need enough for the State Department and the C.I.A. to involve Quadrant in a worldwide scandal."

"How will you know if I am telling the truth?" Fahid asked, fencing for time—time to think.

"Because I already know much of the truth. I only need you to confirm it," the repairman said.

"It might be easier to be blown to pieces than to be punished for betraying my employers," Fahid said.

"You will certainly die if you refuse me," the repairman said. "You must have prepared for such a moment, Mr. Fahid, with your secret bank accounts and your private plane. Sooner or later someone was certain to double-cross you." A hand reached out and lifted the grenade out of sight again. "Your decision has to be now. Time is running out."

Dexter Fahid was sweating. "I will be dead whatever I do," he said, in a shaken voice.

"You will certainly be dead if you don't give me what I ask for," the repairman said. "But I'll give you a chance to beat the other rap, Mr. Fahid. I'll give you one full day before I make the tapes public. In a day you can reach any safe place on earth you have prepared for yourself. Now, Mr. Fahid—or never."

Fahid moistened dry lips, and then he reached for the little microphone. "My name," he began, "is Dexter Fahid. I am—or have been—a contact man, a dealer, for Quadrant International. Let me begin with the oil-producing countries in the Middle East—"

The cold was bone-chilling. The location was a little wooded area surrounding the fourth tee of a golf course in Westchester, some miles out of the city. Jason Dark stood beside a bench on which he had placed a black leather suitcase. He was warmly enough dressed for this winter night, and it occurred to him that what chilled him to the core was not the weather but fear that his plan, his and Pierre Chambrun's, would fail.

It was nine o'clock at night, a moonlit night. It was almost 14 hours since Dexter Fahid had finished talking into Dark's tape recorder in suite 12C at the Beaumont. It had taken three hours for Dark to have copies of the tapes made and to dispose of the copies in a satisfactory fashion. Then he had gone home to his duplex apartment on East 40th Street to wait. This was the day when Sharon's kidnapers had said they would contact him.

He had had no sleep, but he couldn't sleep. Sleep would be filled with nightmares, he told himself. Once, shortly after noon, the phone rang.

"This is not the call you are waiting for, Jason," Pierre Chambrun's cool voice said. "But I thought you should know that our friend, Mr. Fahid, has taken off. He checked out of the hotel shortly after nine o'clock. He'd asked for his bill earlier, but he apparently had to wait for his cousin and bodyguard to return from somewhere. His private jet took off from Kennedy a little after eleven, heading for Argentina according to the control tower. He didn't keep a luncheon appointment with a Syrian diplomat, nor did he leave any excuse or explanation for that gentleman. I think that is important for you to keep in mind."

"Why?" Dark asked in a flat dull voice.

"To give you hope," Chambrun said. "If Fahid wasn't in full flight he would have left some word for the Syrian gentleman. He was to have been a customer. It tells me that what is on the tapes is genuine."

Hope, God knows, he needed. But the day wore on and twilight came and there was no word from Sharon's kidnapers. Then there was darkness. Then there was the call.

There were instructions on how to reach the fourth tee of a certain golf course. Dark was to bring with him the evidence they had tried to get from him once before during the brutal destruction of his hand. He was to be at the designated place at nine o'clock.

"How do I know that Sharon Evans is alive and that you will turn her over to me unharmed?"

The caller allowed himself a brief chuckle. "You will have to take my word for it, friend."

Now Dark waited on that wintry golf course. It was a few minutes past nine, and Dark's anxiety mounted. Perhaps they had learned, since their call, about Fahid. Perhaps they wouldn't come. If they didn't he knew he would never see Sharon again. The gamble he and Chambrun had taken would be lost.

"Dark!" It was a muffled voice.

A man walked out of the woods, his face covered with a ski mask. Months ago two men wearing ski masks had destroyed Dark's right hand. This could be one of those men. Dark felt a pulse beating at his throat.

"The evidence is in that bag?" the man asked.

Dark bent down and opened the bag. All that was in it was a cassette tape player. "Before I turn this over to you I would like you to listen to something," he said. He turned on the player which was already loaded.

" 'My name is Dexter Fahid,' " a tinny-sounding voice said. " 'I am—or have been—a contact man, a dealer for Quadrant International. Let me begin with the oil-producing countries in the Middle East—' "

The voice went on, naming names, quoting sums of money. The man in the ski mask stood motionless, listening. After a while Dark switched off the machine in mid-sentence.

"There are four full tapes of this information," he said. "I apologize for the quality of the recording, but of course this is a copy. The original tapes are in the hands of friends. If they don't hear from me by nine thirty—which is exactly twenty-two minutes from now—they will be turned over to the State Department and the C.I.A."

"Your price?" the man asked, quite calmly.

"Sharon Evans, safe and unharmed."

"And if we deliver her?"

"Then the tapes will stay where they are," Dark said.

"Can we depend on it?"

Dark gave the man a thin smile. "You will have to take my word for it, friend."

Ski-mask was still motionless. "I cannot produce Miss Evans in twenty-two minutes."

"Twenty minutes and thirty seconds now," Dark said.

"How long will it take you to get back to your apartment?" the man asked.

"Fifty minutes."

"Go, then. Miss Evans will be waiting for you when you arrive. But I must have those tapes. My superiors must know why I have made a deal with you—if I am to survive."

"Help yourself," Dark said. "There are several copies. You may even have the player."

Forty-eight minutes later Dark unlocked the door of his apartment on East 40th Street and Sharon came running across the room and into his arms. They clung to each other like children who had been lost.

She told her story. She had been held in a private house only a few blocks away by men in ski masks. She had been well treated. They had brought her here only a few moments ago and told her to expect Dark.

"Oh, Jason, you gave up the evidence you suffered so much to keep!" She pressed her cheek against his black-gloved hand.

"On the contrary," he said. "I got even better evidence against them." He told her of Chambrun's scheme and how he had persuaded Dexter Fahid that he was a dangerous fanatic. He told her about his meeting on the golf course. "Tomorrow," he said, "an international scandal will break that will make Watergate look like a kindergarten exercise."

"You double-crossed them!" she said, almost laughing. "You told them the tapes would stay where they were if I was produced."

"The exact truth," Dark said. "Because the tapes have been at the State Department and the C.I.A. since early this afternoon." He held her close, touched her soft blonde hair with the fingers of his left hand. "Chambrun persuaded me to play the role of a fanatic," he said. "It worked. But then I discovered I really was a fanatic—on the subject of your safety. Nothing could persuade me to refrain from punishing them—for having dared to touch you, love."

He reached for the telephone on the table behind the couch on which they were sitting. "Time to let the boys in Washington know that you're safe and they can go ahead and lower the boom."

HARD LUCK STORY

RICHARD A. MOORE

He was seated at the bar, one hand loosely clutching in a forgotten sort of way a watery Scotch and soda. His suit had that rumpled appearance that could be from two hours or two days of summer driving. His glance, when I took the stool beside him, indicated I wasn't so pretty myself.

Conversationalists are rare in the imitation wood-and-leather barrooms of interstate motels, when the most recent memories are of service stations, chain restaurants, and a close call near Cincinnati. But this guy was a born talker.

"Traveling on business, eh? So am I, in a way." Pausing for a moment, twisting his glass, he continued, "Traveling *from* business is more like it. Mine has gone down the tube. Zip, gone, despite everything I could do to hold it together. That's why I'm on the road."

When the bartender took my order, the guy waved a renewal at his glass and then forced a humorless chuckle. "Luckily there's no crime in leaving the scene of a disaster."

I waited for my drink, debating whether or not to hear out his personal version of failure. It had been a long day of many miles and I hate business-trip conversations. It's either the pushy egotism of the salesman with a brain saturated with phony confidence or it's his dark brother, the suicidal hulk that remains after the confidence is gone.

I've heard many versions of both types in my time. But there is always that chance of learning something from those who admit their failures. I guess I'm just a sucker for a hard-luck story.

I turned slightly toward him. "There's no disgrace in bankruptcy. Certainly not these days."

"It's not the failure I'm running from. It's the end result of my last frantic attempts to hold the business together."

He turned to gaze at me, and I noticed how haggard he looked. "You have no idea how easy it is to let yourself be dragged into something dangerous and despicable when all your other options are gone. If I had just let it fail naturally a year ago, everything would be all right by now. But when I thought of my wife and daughter and how they would detest the pity and hidden smugness of their friends, I just couldn't let it go without a fight."

A touch of the old fire blazed for a moment in his eyes, feeding on my sympathy. I knew he must have been a tough man in negotiations, back when he was king of the mountain.

"Who can blame you for that? The problems come with losing, not with fighting."

He paused to strip a cigar of its cellophane wrapper and accept my light. "That isn't always the case. No, sir, I found a way to make a business failure seem like a minor detail.

"I don't know how familiar you are with business these days, but a man can present all the appearances of being well-to-do one day and be broke the next. All it takes is one panicky bank calling a note, and millions in investments can collapse like a house of cards because of one hundred thousand dollars in cash.

"Oh, it's happened to better men than me. You see, this world floats on confidence. I've had a bit of luck in the past, and since then have had no trouble raising money for projects. People will invest, banks will lend more on the basis of your reputation than on a stack of projections and balance sheets.

"But you can't afford to fail. One flop and everyone gets antsy. It's no longer the brag of being in a deal with the guy with the touch of gold. You're only as good as your last deal."

He bellowed out a huge puff of smoke and accepted another drink from the bartender. "I stretched myself too thin. Four or five deals going at once, all begun in the time when raising money was the simplest part of an operation. A bank where I had a hundred-grand note was hurt in the foreign-money market and really roughed up by the collapse in real-estate development. They needed cash and called some notes, mine among them.

"On paper I looked great. A millionaire. But in fact I couldn't scrape together one-tenth of the note: undeveloped real estate was worthless for raising cash. You couldn't move it. What cash I did have was taken in a fight for control of a New Orleans business. The minority interest there had a brother-in-law on the bank board and in a pressure deal to get us to sell out cheap, the bank cut my line of credit—anyway, for all practical purposes, I was broke."

He combed his fingers through plastered-down black hair, while I lighted another cigarette and waited.

"Every bank in town turned me down on terms both long and short. I wasn't really worried. There's money out there if you can shake it loose. A couple deals almost came off, but one guy turned out to be nothing but talk, and another was hit with a crisis of his own that dried up his ready money. The deadline was put off several times, but the day of reckoning finally came.

"I was almost out of hope when a guy I had hit with the deal called me with an idea. I knew him fairly well and he was sympathetic. If he had the spare money, I believe he would have bailed me out himself. I offered him one-half of a six-hundred-grand proposition for one hundred upfront G's.

"He had been in a similar bind once and knew a way to get money if all else failed. He himself had not had to use it because at the last minute something else had always come through for him."

The man hesitated, then waved to the bartender for another drink. I waited until the stillness stretched into more than a minute. "Well, what was the deal?"

"He introduced me to some people. People with connections. They could get me a loan from a certain New York bank in a day's time. With their okay the bank would mysteriously grant the loan immediately. I would pay the bank the usual rates and pay the local connections two percent every month."

I whistled under my breath. "Two percent a month is twenty-four percent a year. On top of the bank rates you would be paying about thirty-five percent a year."

His face broke into a rueful grin. "Oh, it was robbery, no doubt about it. But like an idiot I figured to swing another deal in a month's time and get out from under this one. But I needed the time to operate, which this would give me.

"My friend warned me. He told me to take the deal if I must but never miss those monthly two percent payments. 'These boys don't fool around,' he said. And he was so right.

"The hundred G's went into the business and then I faced the new problems of coming up with the monthly payments to both the bank and under the table. It was the same thing all over again. In smaller doses for sure, but every damn month.

"I put my house into hock, my summer place, everything. Month by month it all went toward the same thing until I had nothing left. Hell, I couldn't even pay my utility bills. Finally the day came when I just didn't have it."

I let him sit staring into his drink for a minute. The noise from the jukebox swelled over us.

"They worked me over pretty good. I was never so frightened in my life. My wife, my daughter—they threatened them both. I now had two payments to raise plus the late penalty of another two percent. I couldn't do it. There just was no way."

He lapsed again into one of his pauses, beginning to show the effects of the Scotch. "What did they do?"

He smiled. "Nothing, so far. I figured if I beat it, there would be no percentage for them to mess with my family. My wife and kid know nothing about the deal. I wrote a note threatening to go to the D.A. if they bothered my family. So I figure I'm the only one in danger. And that's why I'm here. Another thousand miles and I'll find a quiet place to start all over. After the dust settles, my wife should have enough to put the kid through school, if I don't send for them first."

He drained his drink and slid off the stool, clutching the bar for support.

"Why didn't you go to the police? They would give you protection. You could put the locals behind bars and a smart D.A. might be able to trace it all the way to New York."

"I thought of that. Frankly I haven't ruled it out. Right now, however, I just need to get away and think it through. I don't want to do anything that might endanger the wife and kid."

He clapped a hand on my shoulder. "Thanks for listening to me and my problems. Maybe you can profit from it. I'm sure there are a dozen morals in the story somewhere."

He staggered and I caught him. "Are you going to be able to make it to your room?"

"Yeah. Just give me a hand out the door."

I helped him out of the bar and along the narrow concrete walk back to the motel and his room. His was a sad story, and I've heard plenty in my time.

I got him onto the bed and he was asleep almost immediately. I put the pistol near his left ear and it spit a quick death. With the silencer it sounded like a popped light bulb.

There would be hell to pay for this one. Hell to pay for whoever had approved the deal. Anybody could have spotted him for a bad risk.

SMALL TALK

TERRY COURTNEY

Frankie Ice slid into the rear booth across from Bellinger. "Ready for a taste, lieutenant?"

Bellinger held up his glass to show Frankie that it was almost full. He would not have recognized Frankie on the street. The once lean, handsome Mediterranean face was jowly, the trim body running to bloat. His hair had turned a dirty gray.

Frankie called to the waitress. "Double V.O. water, honey."

Bellinger said, "Why the meet, Frankie?"

"Nothing special, lieutenant. Just a couple of old players getting together for some small talk. You know, old times."

Bellinger knew. It was Frankie's meet, and men like Frankie had a near obsessive compulsion to indulge in some verbal broken field running before they could come to the point of a conversation. That's the way it was, that's the way it had always been. Bellinger would be patient. Sometimes it paid off, sometimes it did not, but he had to know.

The waitress slid Frankie's drink onto the table and left. Bellinger said, "How's it going, Frankie? Jewelry still your specialty? Climbing through windows that don't belong to you?"

Frankie shrugged. "I gave that up. I got a few things going for me. Nothing important, but I'm comfortable, thank you."

Bellinger knew exactly what Frankie had going for him. "But they still call you Frankie Ice."

"You know a name, lieutenant. It stays with a guy forever."

"Like Tony Bags."

"Sure, like that. Tony ain't stuffed pieces of anybody in plastic in fifteen years, but he's still Tony Bags."

"Until the day he gets stuffed into something."

Frankie waved away the thought. "Tony Bags is retired in Arizona. Nobody wants him for anything. He'll die in bed."

"One of the chosen few."

"See, you understand the way it is, lieutenant. You and me, we're old-time players. We know what's happening. I said that just the other day. I said that Lieutenant Bellinger goes way back and knows how the game is played, you know?"

"What game is that, Frankie?" Bellinger asked, his creased, well used face without expression. He looked exactly like what he was: a cop who had seen and heard too much during his twenty-seven years on the force. His hair was more salt than pepper these days. The job did that to a man.

"The game," Frankie said. "Come on, you know what I mean. My people and your people. We do certain things to try to make some money. Your people don't approve of some of the things we do to make money and try to catch us at it. If you don't catch us, we make money. If you do catch us, you give us free vacations downstate at the granite hotel. It's a simple game. And you know one thing that has always been true? How the game is played. When we make money, your people never take it personal, and when we get vacations, we never take it personal. It's a rule of the game. You get my drift?"

Bellinger nodded. Frankie was getting there.

Frankie sipped his bourbon. "Because if people, mine or yours, was to take it personal, then the game would get nasty, sloppy, and my people would not like that to happen. I don't think your people would like it, either."

"You mean Carmine Anzalone wouldn't like it," Bellinger said.

"You know names ain't cool, lieutenant."

Bellinger ignored the reproach. "Somebody taking something personal, Frankie?"

Frankie made a face. "Once in a while you get a guy with a bad case of dumb. It happens."

Bellinger waited while Frankie signaled the waitress for a refill.

Frankie was silent until he had his fresh drink and they were alone again. He sipped and Bellinger waited.

Finally Frankie sighed loudly, his glass thunking on the table. "You remember a player named Salvatore Minella, lieutenant?"

Bellinger mentally sorted through the felon file in his memory, and the name dropped into place. "Three or four years ago. Extortion of a building contractor."

"It was five years ago. Sal got caught by a wire, and that bought him a nickel downstate."

"I remember. He made a rookie mistake."

"Nobody's perfect. Sal got the vacation, and word comes back that he is doing hard time. Very hard time. And that worried my people."

"I'll bet it did."

"Right, because when a guy is doing hard time, your people are always visiting him, offering him Christmas candy if he will tell them stories. You know?"

Bellinger's eyebrows rose and fell. "It's part of the game," he said with the hint of a smile.

"So my people send people to see Sal all the time, just to make sure he understands that he shouldn't be telling no stories to nobody. And these people come back saying how bad Sal is doing down there."

"I never heard of Minella dealing." Bellinger realized that Frankie was not quite there yet.

"That's the point. He didn't deal. No stories, no candy. He stayed together, which makes what happened so unreal. He didn't do the whole nickel. Four years and change. He got out two weeks ago and came home for his benefits."

"What benefits?" This was new to Bellinger.

"Maybe you don't know about that. It ain't a thing we talk about. See, when a player goes away there are two benefits. First, his family is taken care of, in Sal's case a wife and kid."

"I know about the family thing. Did it happen?"

"For about two years. Then Sal's wife divorced him and married some upright dude who works for the phone company. They moved to a far suburb, and she said she didn't want anything any more, to leave her alone. Sal told somebody it was all right, he was glad to get rid of her."

"And the other benefit?"

"A guy who goes on vacation and is cool has ten grand a year waiting for him when he gets out."

"For not telling stories."

"That and a stake. So Sal comes home, and even though he didn't do the full five, they gave him fifty large."

Bellinger snorted. "I was him I'd be in the Bahamas."

Frankie's grin had no mirth in it. "He just might be at that."

"What do you mean?"

"Lieutenant, we got a problem with Sal right now. When Sal got his money, my people told him to take a month off. Get an apartment, a car, clothes, visit some ladies, get back in the life. Come back in a month, he can go back to work. So he got all those things, except I wouldn't know about the ladies. And he went around seeing all his old friends, one of which is Louie Guarino, who is a player I know you definitely know."

"Once upon a time I arranged a vacation for him."

"I know about that. So, Sal and Louie are tight. Partners. And Sal tells Louie that the time in the joint is so bad it is a thing he can't forget and won't forgive. Sal's words. And he is going to do something about it, like a solo number. He is going to off the man who did it to him." Frankie's voice went quiet. "That would be Kerwin."

Bellinger did not fully grasp the meaning of what Frankie had said for a moment, then his eyes blinked rapidly. "Adam Kerwin? Detective Sergeant Adam Kerwin?"

"The same."

"Sweet Jesus! Is Minella insane? Doesn't he realize what he could start?"

"Maybe, maybe not, but he don't seem to care. But my people know, and they care very much. Louie Guarino told somebody who told somebody else who told another party, and it got back. You know what small talk can be. So word is sent to Sal that he will not do anything that stupid and that is an order. And Sal sends word back which is in fact two words and they are not Happy Easter."

"That must have shocked the bile out of Carmine . . . your people."

"Definitely. So a couple of guys were called in."

"Hitters?" Bellinger asked.

"A couple of guys to convince Sal of the error of his thinking."

"Hitters," Bellinger declared.

"Only Sal got word maybe, or maybe just figured, and he disappeared. And that's where we are now, lieutenant. My people have looked everywhere they could think of; family, friends, every hidey hole we know of. He's gone, vanished. But he's out there carrying a very large hate for one of your people."

"What do you want from me, Frankie? Specifically."

"Look, you got the whole police force and that national computer and that all points thing and all. Maybe you could find Sal where we can't. All we want you to do is try. You get him picked up for something and make sure he's held wherever it is until our couple of guys can get there, then let him go. You make a phone call, tell us where he is, we tell you how long to hold him, and that's all. We take it from there and you don't know how it happened. Nobody wants him to ruin the game. This is just as important to us as it is to you."

"I see where you're coming from, but I'm not sure we can do that. It will have to work through the captain. I'll do my best."

"Do better than that, lieutenant. We're talking one of your friends got a target on his back."

"Minella must have the I.Q. of a turnip."

"The joint does different things to different guys. And you should maybe talk Kerwin into taking a vacation until we find Sal. It could save his life."

"I know Adam Kerwin. He runs from no man."

Frankie made a noise with his mouth and slowly shook his head. "That attitude ain't always smart. You know how Sal got connected in the first place: a judge put him in the army for two years. In there they discovered he was a natural with a rifle. Two years and all he did was shoot on some kind of army rifle team. Contests or whatever. He said if he had stayed in the army he could have been in the Olympics. But he came out and was doing odd jobs for my people. Strictly errand boy stuff. Then a matter came up that needed a guy good with a rifle. A long-range thing. Somebody remembered Sal, and they gave him the work. He did a nice, clean job, and that got him a little action of his own. There were two more rifle jobs after that. Each time Sal did good work and got a little more of the pie. Then he went away."

"An expert rifleman. I didn't know. Lordy."

"You see what I'm getting at? Sal could hit Kerwin from half a block away, and Kerwin would be dead before the sound got to him. Listen, with the guns they make now, Sal could do it from two blocks away with one of those scope things. And remember, Sal's got all the cash he needs to buy any kind of rifle he wants."

Bellinger slid out of the booth. "Thanks, Frankie. I owe you one. We'll keep in touch."

Frankie Ice did not reply. Instead he handed Bellinger a folded piece of paper with a telephone number printed on it.

Captain Wexler's round, ruddy face constantly changed expression as he listened to Bellinger. When the lieutenant finished his recital, Wexler said, "We must locate Kerwin right away, and that could be a big problem."

"I've got that working, captain. I called dispatch on the way in. Adam is out on an investigation. I impressed upon them the urgency of the situation, and they will try to contact him every ten minutes and tell him to check in with you or me. The question is, can we go all out to find Minella?"

"We have no choice. He is urgently wanted for questioning in a homicide case. Please hold and notify."

"I'll get it out, local and national." Bellinger started to stand up.

"Stay a minute, lieutenant. I think I had better fill you in on the entire situation, like why locating Kerwin quickly could be a problem. Also, the real reason Carmine A. did us this favor."

Bellinger's expression reflected his puzzlement.

"What I say doesn't leave this room." The captain picked up a pencil and rolled it between his palms. "For the past three-plus months Adam Kerwin has been on Carmine A.'s payroll."

Bellinger jerked forward. "Adam Kerwin on the pad? I don't believe it. There isn't a more honest man alive than Adam."

"It took us almost a year to set it up, but it worked to perfection." The captain's mouth turned down at the corners. "Until now."

"You mean it's a sting?"

"Exactly. We picked Kerwin because he's single, so no family would be hurt. In addition, his partner had applied for a transfer to

Homicide over a year ago, so we sent him over there and he believed it was routine. We didn't give Kerwin another partner. He went through a typical scenario. Gambling heavier and heavier, got in debt to the bookies, went to a loan shark and then couldn't make the payments. It was inevitable that Carmine A. would make him an offer he couldn't refuse."

"What was Adam doing to earn his keep?"

"For the first two or three weeks it was simple things. Tip them off in advance of raids. We had to set up raids we normally would never have conducted just so Kerwin could pass the word. Then it got more complicated. They had Kerwin arrange that none of our cars were in a certain area on a particular night at specified times. Keep the coast clear so they could pull off high dollar burglaries. Exclusive jewelry stores, appliance warehouses, like that. And when that went well, they got greedy and had him clearing out areas for big-volume drug deliveries. Truckloads."

"You know my next question. What do we get in return?"

"Video tapes. We set up hidden surveillance units on loan from the FBI, equipped with camcorders. They get the drug busts. We've got tapes of every job they did. That scum will go into shock when they find out how many of them are movie stars."

"How long were you going to play it?"

"We were day to day. When we felt it had run its course, we planned a cattle call. Wholesale arrests, with the tapes to guarantee the cases would hold up in court. We already have enough to burn twenty-five or thirty of those dirtbags."

"I see what you mean about the favor."

"Of course. They certainly don't want Minella to kill Kerwin, but not primarily because of the trouble it would start, although that is a consideration. No, their main concern is Minella's cutting off their pipeline to the department. Their protection."

"Even so, we still have to find Kerwin and get him out of sight until somebody finds Minella, and finding him is our first priority."

The captain got up and walked around to perch on the corner of his desk. "I agree, Minella is our prime target. But as I said, locating Kerwin could be difficult. He only checks in every three or four days. Right now he's supposed to be investigating that warehouse burglary on Reeve Avenue. That's a cover for the department. He knows who did that job. We have it on tape. So off he goes for days, supposedly investigating, only I don't know where he actually goes. The track, the movies, to see his girl, to see Carmine A. I know that one time he went to the country for a few days. But there is one positive aspect to that. If we don't know where he is, then neither does Minella." The captain stood and steered Bellinger out the door. "Get the word out on Minella. Each and every source and agency, especially the FBI. And keep after dispatch."

As Bellinger turned to leave, a sergeant approached, his face a twisted, frozen mask. "Captain."

"Yes?"

"Captain."

"What is it, Bill? Speak up."

The sergeant passed a hand across his forehead. "It's Sergeant Kerwin. A . . . a sniper . . . dear God. The sergeant was shot through the head as he came out of an apartment building on Fifty-second street. He's dead."

The captain seemed to grow smaller, shrivel up inside himself. "That's where his mother lives." He wheeled around and rushed inside his office, slamming the door.

Bellinger realized he had stopped breathing and slowly exhaled. He shook himself, patted the sergeant on the arm, and headed for the communication section. His mourning and rage would have to wait.

Frankie Ice took a long drink of the best bourbon dishonest money could buy, made a contented sound, and grinned. "I'm telling you, I should get one of them Oscars. I was great."

Across from Frankie, seated behind an ornate, handcarved teakwood desk, Carmine A. nodded his leonine head. He was sixty-nine years old and looked fifty, his facial skin as tight as the plastic surgeon could pull it without turning his head inside out.

Frankie said, "Bellinger bit like a starving carp. About now there is one huge manhunt out for Sal. But they believe he acted on his own, and they won't lay it at your doorstep. They think we want him as bad as they do."

Carmine A. had a laugh like dry sticks breaking. "You think they're ever going to find Sal?" He laughed again.

Frankie laughed with him. "They might. All they got to do is dig up a hunk of the new freeway."

"Every time I ride over that part, I'm going to say a prayer for good old Sal."

"This is the best thing he ever done for us."

"The Kerwin hit went well?"

"Smooth as a pool table."

Carmine A. scowled. "That Kerwin was a rat bastard. He fooled me, and that's what hurts the most. I'm not supposed to be easy to fool. You got any idea how many good people have to leave town because of him and his video tapes? Who would have figured? Movies of every job. All those people with their faces on film. Rat bastard."

"So now he's a dead rat bastard, and that's something. Also, it could have been worse. It could have gone on a lot longer. The important thing is nobody is going to blame you."

Carmine A. stood up, dismissing Ice. "Stop and see Gino on the way out. He's got something for you."

Bellinger looked around the restaurant and spotted Tony Guarino sitting at a rear table. Tony the Blimp was doing what he did best: eating with both hands. The lieutenant snaked his way among the tables and sat down.

Tony looked up and said, "Please, lieutenant, not while I'm eating."

Bellinger stared at him.

Through a mouthful of linguini with clam sauce Tony said, "What do you want? Can't I eat in peace?"

"Don't sweat, if that's possible. I'm not looking for you. You hear about Sergeant Kerwin?"

"Who hasn't?"

"I'm looking for your brother."

"What do you want Louie for?"

"Actually, I'm not looking for him, either."

"You got a funny way of not looking for people."

"Louie's not in trouble, so tell me where he is. I just want to talk to him. It's Minella I'm after."

"Louie don't know where Sal is. I can tell you that."

"I would rather he told me himself."

"I'll tell you the truth, lieutenant. I ain't seen my brother in days. As long as you're not looking for him, why don't you try his house?"

"I did. He hasn't been home in five days. His wife doesn't know where he is, and she's worried. He's just gone."

"Him and a lot of other guys. Why do you think Louie knows where Sal is?"

"Louie was the last person I know of who saw Minella. Minella told him he was going to kill Kerwin. Maybe he also told Louie where he was going to run."

Tony slowly and deliberately propped his fork and spoon on either side of his plate, laced his fat fingers on his round stomach, and looked Bellinger in the eyes. "None of what you just said is true, lieutenant. Louie never saw Sal after he came home. Sal never told him anything about no killing, so don't lay that on Louie."

"Minella and your brother got together a few days after Minella was released from prison. Minella told him things."

"That never happened. It was supposed to, but it didn't. Louie told me Sal called him up and wanted a get-together. They were supposed to meet right here. Louie showed up, but Sal never did. Louie said he waited almost three hours. And he ain't seen or heard from Sal since."

"Maybe Louie lied to you."

Tony's eyelids drooped for a moment. "Listen to yourself, lieutenant. Why would Louie lie? He knows I don't care one way or the other if he meets or don't meet Sal. Why would he lie to me?"

He wouldn't, Bellinger thought. But Frankie Ice had definitely said it was Louie Guarino who had started the word about Minella's intention to kill Kerwin. A sudden thought caused Bellinger to catch his breath. He nurtured it, coaxed it, probed it. Could it be? Yes, it was possible. And if that was the way of it, who designed it for you, Carmine A.? You're as subtle as a dog with gas. The longer Bellinger explored the possibility, the more outraged he became. Why me? Why think you could use me? They must have some fine opinion of my intelligence. And they were almost right.

He turned to Tony the Blimp. "What did you mean, Louie and a lot of other people are missing?"

"Just guys who are around all the time suddenly aren't. All of a sudden I don't see them around, and people are looking for them."

"Like who?"

"Like Davey Cohn and that lunatic he runs with."

"Izzy the rabbi?"

"That's him. They're always around together, almost every night, and I ain't seen them in as long as I ain't seen my brother. And the Santoni brothers. Stan and Ollie. Their sister has been calling all over for them. Their father is real sick, and she can't find them."

And your brother, Bellinger thought, and he was certain. He saw it in all its flawed symmetry. And he was supposed to be a key player. He fought back his anger. "Stay put, Tony. I need the phone. I'll be back."

"My linguini got cold," Tony complained, showcasing his priorities.

"Order more on me." Bellinger went to the telephone and called headquarters. Several transfers reached the captain. "Captain, do you know exactly who you have on those tapes? Which players got filmed in the act?"

"I think I can remember most of them. Why?"

"It's important. Were two of them Davey Cohn and Izzy the rabbi?"

"Three times."

"And the Santoni brothers? They're called Stan and Ollie."

"That was the jewelry store on Pinson Boulevard. The big job."

"What about Louie Guarino?"

"Yes."

Bellinger laid his arm across the top of the telephone box and rested his forehead on it. He was tired. So very tired. Of so many things. "Minella is dead, captain. He's been dead almost since the time he got out of prison. I can't prove it yet, but I know it. Somehow they got wise to Kerwin and wanted him dead. Minella was smoke so we wouldn't come back on Carmine A. when Kerwin got hit. They even used a sniper with a rifle, Minella's specialty. We're supposed to spend eternity looking for Minella, and we won't even find his body. The people I just named have probably left town. Make your arrests now, tonight. They know about the tapes and what jobs Kerwin cushioned. The men who pulled those jobs have been warned. Trust me on this. And captain, you could have a leak in the department. Or maybe in the fed film crews."

"Those rotten . . . what are you going to do?"

"I'm going to see a man about two murders. Ice said something about taking things personal. They tried to use me and almost made it work. I take that very personally. I'm going to fire on Fort Sumpter."

"You're what?"

"I'm about to declare war." Bellinger hung up before the captain could reply, walked back to Tony Guarino, and stood staring down at him.

Tony said, "What?"

"You know what you are, Tony? You and your brother."

"Yes, lieutenant," Tony said, quietly and perhaps sadly. "We know exactly what we are, and that gives us a leg up on a lot of people."

"I'll tell you what you are. You're loose ends that somebody forgot all about. And loose ends always unravel."

"I don't understand."

"But you will, probably the hardest way. So long. And Tony, thanks for the small talk."

THE 730 CLUB

ALAN GORDON

The greatest thing that ever happened to Downtown Louie was when the New York state legislature raised the minimum on grand larceny from two hundred fifty dollars to a thousand. Downtown Louie was a small-time grifter who took great pains that his various scams, swindles, and out-and-out thefts remained strictly petty. It became a game to see how far he could push it, and he developed into such an expert misdemeanant that he regularly achieved hauls of two forty-nine.

Downtown Louie had done felony time once, a one-to-three bid in a frigid rural county near the Canadian border, and it was enough to make him appreciate as an occupational hazard the shorter spans that he periodically served in the various city jails. While inside, he had also become something of a legal expert, availing himself of his constitutionally mandated access to the prison law libraries. He soon found work assisting other prisoners in futile longhand writs of habeas corpus and mandamus, motions to relieve their court-appointed lawyers in favor of other court-appointed lawyers, and carefully worded letters to spouses and girlfriends that begged them to drop charges while stopping just short of violating the orders of protection issued by judges who didn't appreciate just how rough true love could be.

It was during his last stay, over a silly misunderstanding concerning a long-distance phone access number that wasn't techni-cally his, that Louie read the updated amendment to the Penal Law that effectively quadrupled his potential income. His mind churned with scams he had only fantasized about before: the safety deposit key switch, the rigged bingo games in the abandoned church on 115th Street, the fake drug factory that heat-sealed tea leaves and baking soda into baggies. With an entrepreneurial zeal that rivaled the best of the junk-bond traders during those go-go years of the mid-eighties (the Golden Age of Scams as far as Louie was concerned), Louie patiently plotted and waited for his sentence to end, staying especially model-prisonerish so he wouldn't lose his good time.

Spring was in the air and in Louie's step as he got off the bus from the prison. The mid-town traffic jam's noise was a welcome relief from living on the Rock, directly under the final approach to LaGuardia Airport, and Louie breathed deep the familiar stench of the city that was to become once again his plaything. He marched west until he reached a decrepit tenement in a part of the city that would always be Hell's Kitchen despite the best efforts of the gentrifiers to transform it into a yuppie purgatory. He entered and climbed the stairs to the third floor. He noticed some burly men carrying furniture past him going down but didn't think much of it until he saw which apartment they were coming from. A short, balding, rotund man stood despondently by the doorway.

"Hey, Sid," said Louie. "What gives?"

Sid looked up without expression. "Hello, Louie. Didn't know you were coming out today. Would've baked you a cake."

"Skip it. Where goes the furniture?"

"Into the street. I'm being evicted. Lack of payment of rent. You get only eight months behind, and they start getting antsy. Go figure."

"I'm sorry, Sid," said Louie. "Okay if I pick up my stuff?"

Sid shrugged. "There's only a little bit left. You remember my nephew? The junkie? He stole most of your stuff. Lotta mine, too. The rest is in a box in the kitchen."

Louie cursed under his breath and went inside. The box was half full. Or half empty, as it had been full when he last saw it and he was feeling increasingly pessimistic. His good suit, the businessman costume, was gone. His marked decks, his fake IDs, his counterfeit gold jewelry, gone. He was grateful that he was wearing his winter coat the last time he was arrested—they were hard to replace, and his still looked clean enough for him to be somewhat presentable. He started to take his belongings out of the box, then, ever-thrifty, took the box itself. It might be useful for running a shell game.

He didn't bother asking Sid for a loan as he left. It would have been pointless, and there were better sources of money, or so he thought. There was a crowbar that had been left by the eviction crew while they were carting Sid's belongings outside. Waste not, want not, he thought as he slid it inside his coat. But as he made the rounds of the neighborhood, he found that the old crew had vanished, forced to emigrate to different parts of the city or ending up guests of the Department of Corrections. His fences had folded their tents and vamoosed, and the only pawn shop left on Eighth Avenue had become scrupulously legit when a search warrant executed after long surveillance had placed the owner in jeopardy of losing everything he had.

After hours of searching, Louie was beginning to get worried. He had no qualms about his abilities, but he needed some kind of grubstake to get started, not to mention a place to stay. He briefly considered collecting bottles and cans, but at a nickel a shot it wasn't worth the effort. The crowbar was an asset he wasn't sure about using. His self-imposed felony injunction forbade forcing any building locks. He scanned the cars parked locally but, given the neighborhood, the "No Radio" signs were likely to be accurate, especially since a large percentage of them already had broken windows and popped trunks. He wandered through the bus terminal, eyed closely by the uniforms on duty, and walked down the steps to the subway entrance. A Chinese guy was slumped in one corner, snoring ostentatiously with a dollar peeping out of one pocket. Downtown Louie grinned to himself and surreptitiously scouted the area until he made the other undercovers watching from nearby newsstands and snackbars. Never scam a scammer, he thought.

He moved on to the subway, using a slug from his dwindling supply. There was a line of commuters waiting to purchase tokens. A young black man sidled over to some of them and sold a few below cost. A token-sucker, thought Louie as he got on the train. The lowest. Put your mouth on a turnstile slot, who knows what you're picking up? Not worth it for just a few bucks. These guys don't think big enough. And he leaned back against the seat and felt the crowbar press into his side.

Newton had a similar experience when the apple hit him. It's the combination of unrelated events that trigger ideas in the great. Downtown Louie took a petty theft—token-sucking—and applied to it his appreciation of technology and the big picture. He left the subway at a stop where he knew police activity was normally sporadic, went upstairs, and hid his box of belongings. Then he reentered the station with the crowbar held inside his right sleeve.

The timing was crucial. You hit the turnstile just after the rush hour surge, but before the clerk has had a chance to leave the booth to collect the tokens. Louie eyed the turnstile briefly, then slid the business end of the crowbar into the slot where the side panel ended, and easily forced it open. Inside was a bucket containing several hundred tokens. Paydirt.

Louie grabbed the bucket and started to run. That's when he found out exactly how heavy several hundred tokens could be. He loped awkwardly towards the exit, the metal handle cutting painfully into his left hand, banging the bucket against his kneecap. Suddenly there was a shout from behind him. A uniform had been lurking behind a pillar, watching for farebeaters. Louie ran, limping, but before he could reach the steps he was grabbed from behind. He loosed the bucket, which went clattering off to the left. The cop, sensing a struggle, slammed him into the wall. Reeling in pain, Louie made his last mistake. Even as his mind screamed, "Give it up! Don't do it," he swung the crowbar blindly behind him. There was a crunch and a scream from the cop, and Louie was free. Cursing himself, he forced his way up the stairs in time to see two other uniforms drawing their guns. He dropped the crowbar before they could justify shooting him, put his hands behind his head, and dropped prone before them. One of them picked up the crowbar, stuck his gun in Louie's back, and froze. Louie closed his eyes and stayed very still.

"Stand up," said the cop. Louie stood up.

"Put your hands behind your back," said the cop. Louie did so, and felt the familiar loss of circulation as the cuffs bit into his wrists.

"You're under arrest," said the cop, and then he took his nightstick with two hands and drove the end of it into Louie's left kidney. By the time he recovered, he was in the paddy wagon heading towards the precinct, bouncing painfully against several other prisoners.

Think, Louie, think. He went over what he had done. Assault on a cop, that's second degree, D felony, minimum two-to-four, max of three-and-a-half-to-seven. Assault with a dangerous instrument, same degree. Serious physical injury? Did he break the guy's arm? Same degree, but if you add that with one of the other factors, is it first degree? That's a C felony, three-to-six minimum, top of . . . He had to visualize the sentencing chart, tracing columns against rows. Seven-and-a-half-to-fifteen. God, no.

And then he remembered with a sickening feeling what he had been doing just before he hit the cop. Stealing tokens. A nice, stupid little misdemeanor, and then he lost his cool and hit a cop. Using a dangerous instrument in the theft or flight therefrom, or something like that. Robbery One, thought Louie. A Class B felony. Four-and-a-half-to-nine minimum, and the max was so high that he didn't want to even think about it.

Louie remembered how cold the winters were upstate and then and there made up his mind to launch his desperation plan. The one he devised while shooting the breeze with the other jailhouse lawyers at their weekly study session. He was dead on the case, he was too much of a realist to think otherwise. So the only question left was where he would spend the time.

When they hauled him out of the precinct lockup to take his pedigree, he was drooling and flopping from side to side. When they asked his name, he stuttered, "J—J—J—Jim," and started crying. They slapped him around some, got nowhere, and gave up in disgust. One of them took his prints, and Louie rotated each digit slightly as the marks were made. The officer faxed them off to Albany, and Louie crossed his ink-blackened fingers and prayed.

He was transported through Central Booking to the holding pens behind the arraignment court. A day later, an earnest-looking young woman tapped on the interview booth, saying, "You the John Doe?"

He entered the booth warily, trying to view his court file. Even upside-down, he could pick out the Robbery One charge. But the rap sheet looked much too thin to be his.

"How you doing?" said the lady. "My name is Belinda Pressman, and I'm your Legal Aid lawyer."

She slid him a card saying that she was indeed who she said she was. He put it in his pocket. She skimmed through the file.

"First arrest?" she asked, and he gave silent thanks to the gods of scamming. The fingerprints had smeared just enough so that the computers in Albany couldn't match them with his record. He had been reborn. Sooner or later, however, he would either have to cop a plea or get convicted at trial. They would reprint him then, and he couldn't count on the same trick's working again. He decided to stick with his plan.

She had been talking about the charges against him, and he started paying attention to her. "So," she concluded, "we're talking about a minimum of two-to-six for a first arrest, unless I can talk the D.A. down a count. Not likely—he's got a strong case and a cop with a broken arm. You'll be lucky to get the minimum. So tell me what *you* say happened."

He looked her directly in the eye and started to giggle. She leaned back, startled. Encouraged, he started giggling more and more until he sounded like a baboon being tickled. She stared at him suspiciously.

"Look, Mister Whatever-your-name-is," she said, "you've got to talk to me." He kept on giggling. "Otherwise, I'm going to have to have you examined by a court shrink to determine if you're capable of assisting in your own defense." He started howling with laughter, and an officer came over to make sure Pressman was all right. She waved him off, stood up, and walked out.

Louie kept giggling as they brought him before the judge. Pressman, standing a safe distance away, stated, "Your honor, pursuant to Criminal Procedure Law 730, I would like to have this defendant examined as to his competency. I have been unable to communicate the nature of his charges to him, or get any response from him whatsoever."

"So be it," ordered the judge, and, after searching for the appropriate rubber stamp among the two dozen or so before him, he duly sent Downtown Louie off to be examined.

The court shrinks saw him a week later. "Who is your lawyer?" they asked. Louie giggled.

"What is the function of a judge?" they asked. Louie giggled.

"Do you understand the nature of the charges against you?" they asked. Louie giggled. The best answer, he knew, was no answer. Sure enough, he was dubbed wacko. And since you have a right to be mentally competent before they try you, they sent him off to the Farm in Orange County to rest and be medicated until they could make him sane enough to send to prison.

Which was precisely what Louie wanted them to do.

Meanwhile, in the expensive office of an expensive lawyer ten blocks south of the courthouse, a powerful and nasty fellow was reluctantly coming to the same conclusion that Downtown Louie had reached without benefit of counsel.

"There's no way you could get the time in federal prison?" asked Theo the Nut. "I liked the one in Allenwood best. Good arts and crafts program."

"It's a state crime," replied the lawyer. "It's state charges, state cops, state prosecutors using state wiretaps authorized by state judges. So, either you go to state prison . . ."

"Or I go to the loony bin and relax for awhile," finished Theo. He leaned back in the Moroccan leather chair. He was under-dressed for such a fancy office. In fact, he was barely dressed at all, wearing only a shabby pair of pajamas that didn't effectively cover a flabby, hairy body.

"Look," said the lawyer. "We've been setting this up as a defense for years. You've been wandering around in pajamas just so we could send you to the Farm instead of prison if you ever got caught. You got caught. You go to prison, we can't guarantee your safety. There are a lot of guys upstate who'd like a piece of you."

"How many of them are there 'cause they had you for a lawyer?" growled Theo.

The lawyer flushed with anger but didn't say anything. He was getting paid too much money to talk back to his client. Plus, Theo had been known to break the heads of people he didn't like.

"I'll be safe at the Farm?" asked Theo.

"Guaranteed," said the lawyer. "You'll be surrounded by nut cases, but they're all heavily medicated. We have enough control over the staff to get you treated right. And in the meantime, we'll find out more about your case. It may take awhile, but it beats the twenty years they want you to do."

"Yeah," mused Theo. "A lot of their witnesses could disappear very quickly while I'm in. Okay, I'll take the vacation. You stay in touch with Larry. Where do I sign?"

The next day, amidst the hoopla of the tabloid reporters, well-known mobster Theo the Nut shambled up the steps of the Criminal Court to surrender himself on an impressive variety of charges. He had put on a pair of new pajamas for the occasion, and had added a robe and slippers to make it more formal. A 730 exam was arranged, and since he had been carefully coached on what to say, his nickname was made formal and he was sent to the Farm.

As it happened, Downtown Louie, now known officially as Jim Doe, arrived about a week before Theo the Nut. After being checked in, he was examined in two different offices by the two resident shrinks. He giggled at each of them in turn. The first declared him a paranoid schizophrenic and prescribed for him some pills that would make him happy. The second decided that he was a manic depressive psychotic and prescribed pills that would keep him from getting too happy. Both watched him carefully place the pills on his tongue, drink a glass of water, and open his mouth to show he had swallowed everything. Both of them then sent him away and missed seeing him slip the pills he had palmed into his pocket.

The day orderly, a small, wiry Puerto Rican named Ramon, walked him through a series of doors that he unlocked with keys drawn from the bunch chained to his waist. Once he arrived at the main dormitory, he started giving Louie the tour.

"Showers over there. This wing is for the dangerous guys, the not guilty by reason of insanities. We keep them segregated from the incompetents like you. Cafeteria, you'll like the food. Tastes good, and it's good for you. Gym, classrooms are down that way. You like painting? Most of the guys here paint, art therapy they call it. You paint, then the headshrinkers analyze what you do. Every year they have a show, and people come to see what's what. Rorschach City. Okay, here's your new home away from home."

He unlocked another door and showed Louie into a large, sunny room with several cots set up barracks style. They were made up with army blankets and looked a little firmer than the bunk beds he was used to on the Rock. There were two at the end of the row that were unoccupied. Ramon guided him to the one farther from the wall and sat him down.

"Okay, Mr. Jim Doe," he said. "This is your bed. You are in Dorm A, Room 3, Bed 9. Remember that, A-3-9. The others should be back from the playground soon. Dinner's at five, medication at nine, lights out at ten, wakeup at seven. You'll get used to it. See you around." He left.

Louie stretched out on the cot and stared at the ceiling, then examined his surroundings. There was a cabinet made from sheet metal next to the bed. He placed his prison-issue clothing inside, then looked for a place where he could stash the pills. He finally opted for the obvious hiding place—inside a leg of the bed. He wrapped the pills in tissue first, thinking he might experiment with them a little when he got the chance, or else sell them once he determined where the black market was.

Just as he moved the cot back into position, the others returned, sounding like nothing so much as a group of schoolboys chattering and screaming on their way back from a field trip, only an octave lower. They stopped abruptly when confronted with Louie, staring suspiciously at the new face. Louie, staying in character, giggled at them. Four of them giggled back, three frowned, and a very young looking man burst into tears.

"Okay, okay," said the man who brought them in. "This is the new guy, he doesn't know his real name, so we call him Jim. Say 'Hello, Jim,' campers." The gigglers kept giggling, the frowners stuttered over their hellos, and the young man kept crying. The orderly went over to where Louie was standing.

"So, Jim, I guess Ramon gave you the shpiel," he said. "My name is Arnold. I'm the night orderly for this wing. Get yourself cleaned up, it's dinnertime." He held out his hand. Louie shook it, and Arnold abruptly pulled him forward until Louie's face was inches away from his own.

"Now, Jim," he said softly, "I don't expect you to be any trouble, and even if you wanted to be trouble, I don't think you'll be any. You behave, because I've got no problem with disciplining people. You see Jerry over there?" He indicated the crying man, who by this time was listening intently through his tears. "Jerry tried to give me trouble. Now he mostly cries. Don't be like Jerry if you want to get along with me. And you do, don't you?" Louie nodded, and Arnold let him go.

"Okay, campers, inspection time," he barked, clapping his hands twice. The inmates shambled into a semblance of a straight line and held out their hands. Arnold moved down the line. "Okay, Dwayne. Good, Curtis. Marcus, get those nails better. Very good, Jerry." Jerry beamed like a puppy allowed back in the house. Inspection was completed, and the nine of them were led to the cafeteria.

The food was surprisingly good, certainly better than the usual prison fare. The room was filled with the din of insanity, with the normal dysfunctional chatter interrupted by the odd shriek or howl. When it was over, Arnold led them back into the room and switched on *The Cosby Show*. Louie noticed that his fellow inmates laughed at all the jokes. They also laughed at the straight lines, the commercials, the news bulletin, and sometimes at nothing at all.

At nine o'clock a nurse came by with a tray of small paper cups and a pitcher of water. She inspected the name at the foot of each bed, handed the occupant the appropriate pills and a cup of water, and watched until she was sure the pills had been swallowed. Louie did his sleight-of-hand bit again and lay back and watched *Cheers* while his companions conked out. Arnold peeked in at ten. Louie feigned sleep while he turned out the lights but soon fell asleep for real.

The daily routine turned out to be not too bad. The Farm, although secure, lacked the feel of a prison, containing as it did large swathes of greenery that the inmates could roam at will. Louie quickly worked his way into the gardening class and spent many happy hours planting and weeding while enjoying the sunshine and the fresh air. Once a week, he was taken in to giggle at the shrinks but otherwise he found himself left largely alone.

Yet the loneliness was getting to him. He hadn't counted on the fact that maintaining his charade would mean absolutely no human contact on any intelligible level. He found himself eavesdropping on the staff just to remind himself what conversations sounded like. He missed the raucous give and take of the prison lawyers' rap sessions, as well as the day to day support of a really tight cellblock. But he knew that one slip-up in his act would tip them off that he was a malingerer, and he would be zipped back into the city where judges frowned upon people who tried to evade justice by defrauding the courts.

So it was with a great deal of curiosity that he examined the new guy who took the last empty bunk a week after he arrived. A large, powerfully built man who wore pajamas and a bathrobe instead of clothes. Louie sent a test giggle in his direction, which was received with a growl. Okay, thought Louie. This guy wants to be left alone, and he's big enough to have his own way. Looks like he could take Arnold if he wanted to, he concluded, and he sat and waited for the inevitable confrontation between the two.

But Arnold, to Louie's surprise, treated the large man with deference. He omitted the introductory threats, spoke gently and with respect, and three days later slipped him a pack of cigarettes. Louie's scam detector went off with a loud clang, and he kept a very close watch on his neighbor.

This turned out to be an easy matter, as the large man turned out to be a fellow garden enthusiast. He worked the same section as Louie and went into frequent reveries while staring at the newly-grown sage and basil plants in his care. The herbs and the good weather seemed to improve his spirits, and one day he actually plucked some oregano and handed it to Louie.

"Smell," he commanded, and Louie inhaled appreciately.

"What a sauce I could make with the fresh stuff," continued the man. "You'd love it. Look, you seem like a quiet, friendly guy." He looked around to make sure they were not being overheard. "I'm going crazy here." He laughed suddenly. "I know, I was supposed to be crazy to get sent here. But that's the point. I faked it. I've been faking it for years. Smart lawyer suggested it, only now I'm not so crazy about the idea any more. Crazy. That word again. I'm hanging out in this cozy place with a bunch of nut jobs, and I can't talk to no one. I didn't count on that. So if you don't mind listening, I'm gonna talk to you."

Louie thought for a second, then said, "Okay by me. I know the feeling, believe me. But keep looking at the plants. We don't want anyone in on this who shouldn't be."

The large man stared, then started chuckling. "Jesus Christ. You're doing it, too. I'm Theo the Nut."

Louie grinned and stuck out his hand. "I've heard about you.

Pleased to meet you. I'm Louie DeSalvo. I knew your nephew Leo from when he was a corrections guy at the Tombs."

"Not Downtown Louie?" Theo shook his head in amazement. "I've been hearing stories about you for years. Everybody's got a Downtown Louie story at the social club. I figured if even half of them are true you gotta be the craziest grifter working the streets. They say you only do misdemeanor weight. What are you doing here?"

Louie was going to give him a short version, but Theo pointed out the absolute absence of any time pressures, so he gave him the full story. Theo shook his head when he got to the end.

"Bad luck with the cop," he commented. "Too bad you weren't working for me, we coulda fixed things. So, what lawyer figured this one out for you? I never figured Legal Aid for perpetrating fraud."

"No lawyer. I figured this one out for myself. I was reading the Criminal Procedure Law and finally got to section 730 and said, hey, I could use this if push ever comes to shove. And it did."

"Lawyers," spat Theo. "I'm paying this Wall Street WASP three hundred G's just to have him on retainer, and a petty scammer figures out the same thing in the joint. You should be a lawyer, Louie."

"Don't think I could get by the Ethics Committee interview."

"Ethics got nothing to do with it. They do the same thing we do, only they got a license. So tell me, did you really pull the Murphy game on the captain at the 117th?"

"My finest moment," said Louie, and he launched into a compli- cated tale that carried them up to the dinner hour.

So the last of Louie's problems was solved. The two of them spent the summer absorbing rays and trading stories, Louie of scams past and Theo of the old days on the loading docks. Some- times at night, after the lights went out and Arnold had finished bed check and was busy pursuing the night nurse, the two of them would whisper back and forth like childhood friends, paying no heed to the occasional whimpers and howls of their roommates when the medication failed to still their nightmares. Friendships are made in the darkness when there is no one else but the two of you, cut off from the world.

As the summer progressed, Louie noticed that Theo was looking more and more worried. He waited, because you don't press guys like Theo. Sure enough, he opened up.

"It's that lawyer of mine," he explained as they picked some fresh mint for the kitchen. "I think he and my brother are putting a move on, and I can't do nothing to control it. I can only get visits from my family and the lawyer; I need to get to one of my boys."

"Can you get to one of the staff here?" wondered Louie. "Somebody's gotta be buyable."

"Maybe. Ramon is too straight, he'd tip off the administration. Arnold's working for my brother already. I don't know anyone else here well enough to take the chance."

Louie thought, "Maybe we could sneak in to where there's a phone. Hey, I saw one in the kitchen staff room one time when we were dropping off the oregano. Maybe you could get in there."

Theo brightened. "Sounds good. I'll need a distraction."

Louie smiled. "My stock in trade."

Ramon came to collect them, and they followed him to the kitchen where three women and a man were busy preparing dinner. Ramon was walking two feet ahead of Louie and chatting up one of the women when Louie suddenly screamed and pointed to a blank spot on the wall. He lurched back into a woman who was carrying a large metal container of salad. She dropped it, screaming along with him, and he grabbed handful after handful of lettuce and started throwing it at the wall, pointing and yelling, "Buh, buh, buh . . ." The women huddled against the oven while Ramon and the man tried to restrain him. He kept breaking free and throwing salad at the wall, then abruptly burst into tears and collapsed amidst the wilted lettuce and the ruined tomatoes.

Ramon knelt down and almost tenderly put his arm around Louie. "It's okay, man," he murmured. "Whatever you saw, it's gone now, and it won't come back. Easy, easy." He sat with Louie and rocked him back and forth. Louie's sobs slowly subsided. Finally he looked around, then looked ashamed and started picking up the pieces of salad and putting them back into the container. As he did so, he saw Theo quietly emerge from the staff room.

"You okay now?" said Ramon, standing up. Louie nodded, and Ramon escorted them to their dorm. As they washed up, Louie saw Ramon talking quietly to Arnold, who had just arrived for the evening shift. He towelled off his hands and readied himself for inspection. Arnold entered the room.

"Good, Marcus. Dwayne. Anthony, okay. Jerry, Jerry, Jerry, how many times do I have to tell you about scrubbing hard when you've been playing in the garden?" He cuffed Jerry lightly in the face, and Jerry, cringing, scuttled back to the sink. Then Arnold came to Louie, who steeled himself for the punch. But he was surprised.

"Jim, Jimbo, my boy," beamed Arnold. "Ramon says you went a little crazy in the kitchen. Now, the docs have gone home for the night, so we've made an appointment for you first thing in the morning. In the meantime, Nurse Brown will give you an extra sleeping pill, so relax, okay? No more problems. Okay, boys, let's all go to dinner."

"Whattayaknow," Louie muttered. "The guy isn't always a jerk."

"He gave you a break for good behavior," Theo muttered back. "Besides, it didn't happen on his watch. By the way, I want to talk to you later."

Dinner proceeded without incident. When they got back to the dorm, Arnold sat in the room and watched TV with them. Nurse Brown arrived at nine o'clock with her rolling cart and doled out pills and paper cups of water to each of them. When she got to Louie's cot, Arnold came over to observe.

"Hello, Jim," she said with a big smile. "We got an extra-special sleeping pill for you tonight. Now, be a good boy and make it go bye-bye."

With Arnold watching him like a hawk, Louie didn't risk palming the pill. It was large and blue, and went down with difficulty. They left the room, and she shrieked with laughter at something Arnold said.

Theo chuckled, "You had to swallow it for real this time, didn't you?"

"Yeah," Louie said ruefully. "I should be out like a light in a few minutes, so tell me how the call went."

"I got hold of my boy Tony, who runs the docks for me. He confirmed what I thought was going down with my brother and the shyster, so I gave him a few orders. Things are happening fast, and this is a delicate situation, what with family being involved and all. We'll see how it goes." He paused and looked over at Louie. "There's something I want to tell you before we both conk out here. I owe you big-time, Louie. You're a helluva smart guy. If I get out of this cuckoo house and come out on top back home, I'm gonna make sure there's a spot for you. I could use a guy with your smarts. Nothing that will get you sent up, just good advice for good pay. You game?"

Louie put out a hand, and Theo clasped it in his bear's paw. The drug was kicking in, and Louie felt a sense of calm and happiness he'd never felt before. His years of scamming were about to pay off, he had the friendship and respect of a major gangster who was going to set him up for life. He turned over sleepily and cast a fond glance at Theo, who by then was snoring heavily.

He heard Arnold come in and turn off the lights and started to let himself succumb to the sedative. But something alerted him. Arnold hadn't left the room. He was walking towards him. Arnold stopped at the foot of Louie's bed. Louie peeped at him through almost closed eyes. Arnold continued between his bed and Theo's and leaned over and removed the pillow from under the comatose giant's head. As Louie stared groggily, Arnold placed the pillow over Theo the Nut's face and pressed down.

Theo's struggles, hindered by his medication, were feeble and brief.

As he finished the job, Arnold abruptly looked behind him and saw that Louie was still awake. He smiled reassuringly. "It's okay, Jimbo, you're just having another bad dream. You'll see the doctor in the morning." He reached over, patted Louie on the shoulder, and tossed the pillow onto Louie's bed. Louie wanted to kick it off but could do nothing more than whimper helplessly as the room faded around him.

He woke to find sunlight streaming into the room and Ramon shaking him. "Jim, get up, we have to move you into another room for a few minutes." Louie shook his head with confusion, then saw that there was already a team of cops snapping shots of Theo the Nut, a still life. One of the cops said, "Where's his pillow?," then noticed the extra one on Louie's bed. He picked it up and sniffed at it suspiciously, carefully placed it into a large plastic bag, and sealed it.

Louie, still groggy, put on his clothes and followed Ramon and his fellow inmates into the cafeteria. Breakfast was a quiet affair for a change and was followed by their being led into the gym where Ramon told them to sit quietly.

A few minutes later, a cop, one of the doctors, and a guy in a grey suit with a red power tie came in and looked at the group. The suit turned out to be a local prosecutor, who seemed apprehensive about his surroundings. He whispered to the doctor, who pointed at Louie. The D.A. went over and stared at him from a safe distance.

"Mr. Doe?" he said. Louie giggled, and the D.A. walked back, disgusted. "What am I supposed to do?" he said. "If one of them did it, and they all could have done it, then he could have done it in plain view of everybody in the room and I couldn't do a damned thing about it. They're nut cases. No way in hell I put any of them on the stand, they could say anything. Or nothing. Or just giggle."

"But we found the pillow on that guy's bed," objected the cop. "And we know he's been violent in the past. Look at what he did to that transit cop."

"Yes," agreed the doctor. "And he apparently had a little episode yesterday, something involving salad. Isn't that right, Ramon?"

"Yeah, but that was nothing," said Ramon reluctantly. "I really don't believe Jimbo did it. He was a model inmate except for yesterday, and I think he really liked the Nut. They always hung together. I don't think it was him."

"Well, it doesn't matter who it was," concluded the D.A. "Without witnesses, all we've got is a weak circumstantial case against Mr. Doe over there, and anybody could have dumped the pillow on his bed. Imagine, committing a murder in a room full of people, and none of them is competent enough to be a witness under the law. It's the perfect crime." He looked over the survivors of Dorm A, Room 3 as they giggled, frowned, and stared. "All I needed was one sane guy," he commented. "Oh, well." And they left the room.

Ramon turned to the group. "Okay, dudes. Let's play some volleyball."

Louie considered his options. He thought about volunteering his information. Cut a deal: his testimony for his freedom. But there were major problems. If they didn't deal, he would have blown his cover. Goodbye, Farm; hello, Canadian border. And even if they did deal, it wouldn't necessarily work. He could hear Arnold's defense lawyer now: "And isn't it true, Mr. De Salvo, if that is indeed your real name, that you have built your entire existence on deceit, fraud, and chicanery?" Yes, it is. "And you're conning us now, aren't you, Louie?" And Arnold goes free.

That was the part that rubbed him the most. Arnold had walked past him in the night and murdered his best friend, the only guy who made life bearable. And he did it knowing Louie saw him, and didn't care that Louie saw him. And to top it off, he threw what suspicion the authorities had on Louie. This was intolerable. This was a situation that cried out for justice.

The moment he thought about justice, Downtown Louie knew there was just one thing he could do. Avenge the death of his friend. And with a flash he realized he had one advantage over Arnold, and that was that Arnold didn't know he wasn't crazy. Arnold thought he had committed the perfect crime, a murder in a roomful of crazy people. It would be appropriate, thought Louie, for Arnold to die the same way. Only this time, it would be perfect.

He spent the day spying out the landscape for some sharp or blunt instrument with which he could do the job. Unfortunately, it was raining, so he couldn't go out and filch one of the gardening implements. Nor was he allowed back in the kitchen after the previous day's events. It wasn't until he got back to his room that he saw what he needed. One of the metal bars on Theo's cot was loose at one end. With a little coaxing, Louie managed to detach it. He slipped it under his mattress. It seemed fitting, he thought. Get Theo's murderer with part of the last place Theo had been while alive.

Arnold came in and took them to dinner, taking his usual slaps at Jerry and smirking at Louie. Louie bided his time. He figured that Arnold would come in at ten o'clock after harassing the night nurse to turn off the lights as he usually did. That would be the time to strike.

They went back from dinner and watched television. Nurse Brown came in at the stroke of nine and passed out their pills. Louie managed to palm his successfully, then leaned back and stared at the ceiling, too keyed up to watch any more tube. He reached under the mattress and was starting to remove the bar when Arnold suddenly strode into the room and marched straight to the foot of Louie's bed and sat down, smiling at him.

"So, Jim, how's everything tonight? Or should I call you Louie?" said Arnold, smiling even more broadly. Louie's blood froze.

"Louie De Salvo, Downtown Louie. Am I right? You see, Theo made two mistakes. He called the wrong boy, and he mentioned you in passing. Tony had already gone over to his brother. So when Theo called Tony, Tony called Larry, and Larry moved up the execution date. But Tony forgot to tell Larry about you until today. So we all have a problem. There are too many people in this room who aren't crazy." Louie tightened his grip on the bar. Arnold chatted on. "You did a good job fooling everyone, Louie. So good that nobody's gonna care much when you die. You'll be in a grave, and nobody will ever know who's really buried there. And you're just as sane as me." Arnold stood up and walked slowly towards the head of the bed. "Saner, in fact," he said. "Because I like to kill people, and you don't."

"There's always a first time," responded Louie, and with that, he swung the bar as hard as he could.

And missed.

Arnold had ducked the blow easily and with a quick movement twisted Louie's arm and sent the bar clattering off under the bed. Louie butted him in the chin and tried to get away but found himself overwhelmed as Arnold used his bulk to force him down onto the bed. He tried to scream, but Arnold belted him across the jaw, then reached under him and pulled out his pillow. The last thing Louie saw before it blotted out his vision was the same jovial smile that Arnold had worn when he killed Theo.

Louie writhed under the pillow, trying to shift his head to the side, but Arnold had one hand gripping his hair, preventing him. He was starting to black out when the pressure abruptly ceased. He flung the pillow aside and sucked in as much air as his lungs could hold, then focused on what was in front of him.

Arnold had stopped smiling. His mouth hung open, and his eyes slowly rolled up into his head. He sagged to the floor, and Louie could see a crudely made knife sticking into his back. Louie looked up.

"Boy, I've been wanting to do that for a long time," said Jerry. Louie gaped. Jerry? Crying, meek little Jerry?

"Keep your voice down," whispered Marcus, who was standing by him. "Dwayne, how's it look?"

"Coast is clear," said Dwayne, who was peering cautiously out the door. "No alarm." The others gathered around Arnold and hoisted him onto their shoulders, Marcus barking out orders. Louie watched, dumbfounded.

"Here," said Jerry, handing him a cup of water. He swallowed it gratefully.

"Shoes off, everybody?" Marcus called out. "Good. Okay, the guard doesn't hit this section until five past ten, so we got ten minutes. Who's got the lockpick?"

"Yo," said Curtis, waving it.

"Doesn't Arnold have keys?" pointed out Louie. The others looked at him, then laughed.

"You're gonna do just fine," commented Marcus as he removed the late orderly's keyring. "Okay, quick march, go."

They scampered out into the hallway and dashed silently past the gym to where the not-guilty-by-reason-of-insanity guys were sleeping. Marcus thumbed through the keys until he found the right one and opened a door.

"Okay, heave ho," he whispered, and the rest of the crew flung Arnold into the room. Marcus threw the keys in after him, and closed the door. They ran back the way they had come and closed the door of Dorm A, Room 3, behind them.

Louie looked at them. They looked calmly back at him.

"None of you?" he said.

They chuckled softly. "None of us," said Marcus. "Well, maybe Dwayne, a little, but only around the holidays. We weren't sure about you, though. You did a good job of fooling everybody. We also didn't figure on Arnold being that gonzo, so he caught us by surprise when he killed Theo. We didn't even know it was happening until it was too late. I'm sorry, Jim."

"Louie," corrected Jerry. A bell started clanging in the distance.

"I believe the animals have escaped from the zoo," observed Marcus. "That should keep the guards busy and shift the focus away from us. Dwayne, cups for everybody." Dwayne quickly distributed the cups while Curtis poured water. Louie watched as they each produced their sedatives from an impressive variety of hiding places. Jerry glanced at him.

"You better get yours," he advised him. "We should all be sound asleep when they come looking. If they can't wake us up, they won't suspect us."

"Good idea," said Louie, and he took two from his cache of drugs. They climbed into their beds, and Marcus held his pills and cup aloft.

"Gentlemen, it gives me great pleasure to propose a new member. The legendary Downtown Louie, scammer supreme. All in favor?" There was a muted chorus of "ayes." "Sounds unanimous to me."

"Get on with it," growled Curtis.

"Pills," commanded Marcus, and they popped them into their mouths. Louie followed suit. Marcus saluted him with a mock toast. "Gentlemen," he intoned, raising his Dixie cup. "I give you the 730 Club!" To a man they drank, and then crushed the cups and threw them in the general direction of the wastebasket. Louie lay back as the extra dosage kicked in quickly, and soon found himself happily dreaming of innocent sheep just waiting to be fleeced.

The uproar over Arnold's death and the breakdown in security in the really crazy wing lasted for some weeks. The investigation of the murder subsided, however, when Arnold's bank accounts were found to have some deposits unjustified by the paltry salary paid to him by the State of New York. Checks were traced, and a very expensive lawyer in the Wall Street area was found in a parking lot in a very expensive car with a bullet in his head that probably came from a very expensive gun. The power struggles in Theo the Nut's old mob played out in their usual violent manner, and the few who remembered about Downtown Louie forgot or took that knowledge with them to unexpectedly early graves.

Meanwhile, the 730 Club continued in its clandestine way. Scamming techniques were exchanged like recipes, and their overt behavior was so good that Ramon was eventually given a promotion for his expertise in overseeing them. Louie was happy for Ramon. In fact, he was generally happy. The Club was the best group he had ever hung out with, and as he watched the foliage change, he realized that the Farm was as close to paradise as he would ever come, certainly in this world.

And so he puttered happily along in his garden, stopping only to remember his friend Theo when the scent of freshly cut rosemary wafted towards him. But Theo had been avenged.

About a year later, Ramon dropped by the garden with a letter. "Hey, Jimbo. Someone actually wrote you. Go figure, huh?" Louie took the letter with trepidation. He didn't know anyone who knew he was here. But he had forgotten about his Legal Aid lawyer.

"Dear Jim Doe," it began. "I thought you might be interested to know that the police officer who was the complainant in your case decided to move to New Zealand. He is not coming back. I mention this because they can't prosecute you without him. I hope you feel better. Belinda Pressman, Esq." The word "better" was underlined several times.

Louie chuckled to himself. She had figured him out. Maybe from the beginning. Smart cookie, very smart. He got up, brushed himself off, and walked to the chief psychiatrist's office.

The shrink was startled when he walked in and sat down. "Mr. Doe," he stammered, "your appointment isn't until tomorrow."

"Doc," said Louie. "The most amazing thing has happened. I'm cured." He wanted to laugh at the expression on the shrink's face, but that would have blown the image.

It actually took a couple of weeks to clear out all of the red tape between him and the outside world, but once it was determined that there was going to be no criminal case against him, the Farm gave up and kicked him loose. As he packed his things, the Club gathered around and cheered.

"Don't forget us," said Marcus, shaking his hand.

"Impossible. Even if I tried." Louie turned to Jerry, who was on the verge of real tears. Louie, to his surprise, was crying, too. They embraced.

"You saved my life, man," he said. "I owe you forever. Let me know when you get out."

Jerry wiped his nose. "I don't think I'm getting out. I never liked it much out there. This place suits me just fine."

"Yeah," said Dwayne. "It has its drawbacks, but it beats all hell outta the Bronx."

"Come on," said Louie. "What about those great scams we came up with? I can't do them without you guys."

"Well," said Curtis. "I'm getting too old for that stuff. Maybe you are, too. See you when I see you."

Ramon came in to escort him through the doors to the bus that would take him back to the city. "You fooled those doctors pretty good, Jimbo," he said. "It was fun seeing them look like idiots. Good luck." He shook Louie's hand and pressed a ten dollar bill into it.

Louie watched the scenery roll by and counted his assets. They weren't much. A couple of changes of clothes, ten dollars, and a pass to a city shelter. He felt extraordinarily tired. Maybe Curtis was right, he was getting too old for scamming.

He got off in Times Square, stunned by how many of his old haunts had been torn down to make room for the new skyscrapers. He recognized nobody. The weather was good, so he walked along Broadway thirty blocks to Union Square. The bums had been moved out, and a farmer's market was doing major business with the yuppies. He bought a can of Coke and drank it slowly, savoring the taste.

You caught a lot of breaks, Louie, he thought. You coulda been in prison for robbery. You coulda been dead under a pillow. Maybe you should consider making an honest living. He tossed the can into a trash basket, then, reconsidering, retrieved it. He found four more soda cans that had been abandoned by the subway entrance. He took them across the street to a supermarket that had a re-cycling machine. One by one, he placed the cans in the receptacle, closed it, and heard the satisfying crunch. Then he pushed the button on the right, and a bright, shiny quarter rolled onto his waiting palm. He held it up and contemplated it.

What the hell, it was a start.

CHARLIE'S VIGORISH

BRIAN GARFIELD

When I saw the phone's red message-light flashing I had a premonition—it had to be Rice; no one else knew I was in New York.

I rang the switchboard. "This is Mr. Dark in 1511. There's a message light." I tossed the folded Playbill on the coffee table and jerked my tie loose.

"Yes, sir, here it is. Please call Mr. Rice. He didn't leave a number, sir."

"That's all right, I know the number. Thanks." I cradled it before I emitted an oath. Childishly I found ways to postpone making the call: stripped, showered, counted my travelers' cheques, switched the television on and went around the dial, and switched it off. Finally I made a face and rang through to Rice's home number in Georgetown.

"Charlie?"

I said, "I'm on vacation. I didn't want to hear from you."

"How was the play?"

"Dreary. Why don't they write plays with real people in them any more?"

"Charlie, those *are* real people. You're out of touch."

"Thank God. What do you want?" I made it cold and rude.

"Oh, I just thought you might be lonesome for my voice."

"Has hell frozen over?" He's my boss but I will not call him my superior; I loathe him as much as he does me. I said, "If it's an assignment you can shove it somewhere with a hot poker. You've already postponed my vacation once this year."

"Actually I've been thinking of posting you to Reykjavik to spend a few years monitoring Russian submarine signals. You're designed for the climate—all that blubber insulation."

"The difference between us," I told him, "my blubber's not between my ears. You called me in the middle of my vacation to throw stale insults at me?"

"Actually I wish there were some terrible crisis because it might give me the pleasure of shipping you off to some Godforsaken desert to get stung by sandflies and machine-gun slugs, but the fact is I'm only passing on a message out of the kindness of my heart. Your sister-in-law telephoned the company this afternoon. Something's happened to your brother. It sounded a bit urgent. I said I'd pass the word to you."

"All right." Then I added grudgingly, "Thanks." And rang off. I looked at the time—short of midnight—and because of the time zones it was only about nine in Arizona, so I looked up the number and rang it.

When Margaret came on the line her voice seemed calm enough. "Hi, Charlie, thanks for calling."

"What's happened?"

"Eddie's hurt."

"How bad?"

She cleared her throat. "He was on the critical list earlier but they've taken him off. Demoted him to 'serious.'" Her abrupt laugh was off-key. I suspected they might have doped her with something to calm her down. She said, "He was beaten. Deliberately. Nearly beaten to death."

Eddie isn't as fat as I am, or as old—by six years—but he's a big man with chins and a belly; his hair, unlike mine, is still cordovan but then unlike me he's going bald on top. The last time I'd seen him—a quick airport drink four years earlier, between planes—the capillaries in his nose had given evidence of his increasing devotion to Kentucky bourbon. His predilection was for booze while mine was for cuisine.

This time his nose and part of his skull were concealed under neat white bandages and both his legs were in plaster casts. He was breathing in short bursts because they'd taped him tight to protect the cracked ribs. They were still running tests to find out if any of his internal organs had been injured.

He looked a sorry sight on the hospital bed and did not attempt to smile. Margaret, plump and worried, hovered by him. He seemed more angry than pained—his eyes flashed bitterly. His voice was stuffed up as if he had a terrible head cold; that was the result of the broken nose.

He said, "Been a long time since I asked you for anything."

"Ask away."

"I want you to get the guy who did this."

"What's wrong with the cops?"

"They can't touch him."

The hospital room had a nice view of the Santa Catalina mountains and the desert foothills. There was only one chair; Margaret seemed disinclined to use it, so I sat down. "Who did it?"

"Three guys. Border toughs. The cops have them—they were stupid enough to let me see their car when they cornered me and I had the presence of mind to get the license number. They don't matter—they've been arraigned and I'll testify. They're just buttons."

"Hired?"

"Ten-cent toughs. You can rent them by the hour. Somebody briefed them on my habits—they knew I'd stop at Paco's bar on my way home. They were waiting for me in the parking lot."

Margaret said, "They're in custody but of course they claim they don't know who hired them."

"They probably don't," Eddie said. "A voice on the phone, a few hundred dollars in cash in an unmarked envelope. That's the way it's usually done. It makes certain the cops can't trace back to the guy who hired them."

I said, "The Mob."

"Sure."

"You know who he is, then?"

"Sure. I know." Then his lids drooped.

Margaret said, "You're a sort of cop, Charlie. We thought you might tell us how to handle it."

"I'm not a cop." Around the fourth floor in Langley they call us loose stringers, meaning we're nomadic troubleshooters—no fixed territorial station—but I'm by no means any kind of cop. Margaret and Eddie didn't know my actual occupation; they knew I worked for the government and they assumed I was with the C.I.A. but for all they knew I was a message clerk. I found their faith touching but misplaced.

Eddie said, "If you were a cop you couldn't do me any good. I don't want somebody to read the scum his rights—I want somebody to nail him."

"I'm not a hit man, Eddie. I don't kill people."

"I don't want him killed. He didn't kill me, did he?" His eyes glittered. "I just want him to hurt."

"Who is he?"

"Calls himself Clay Foran. I doubt it's the name he was born with. What he does, he lends money to people who can't get it from the bank."

"Loan shark."

"Yeah."

"Eddie, Eddie." I shook my head at him. "You haven't grown up at all."

"Okay, I can't move, I'm a captive audience if you want to deliver yourself of a lecture."

"No lecture. What happened?"

"An apartment-house construction deal. I ran into cost overrides —rising prices on building materials. I had to come up with another fifty thousand or forfeit to the bank that holds the construction mortgage. I figured to clear a four hundred kay profit if I could complete the job and sell it for the capital gain, and of course there's a whopping tax-shelter deduction in that kind of construction. So I figured I could afford to borrow the fifty thousand even if the interest rate was exorbitant."

"Vigorish."

"Yeah. Usury. Whatever. Trouble is, I was already stretched past my limit with the banks and the building-and-loans. Hell, I was kiting checks over the weekend as it was, but I was in too deep to quit. I had to get the building completed so I could sell it. Otherwise the bank was set to foreclose. So I asked around. Sooner or later somebody steered me to Clay Foran."

"And?"

"Very respectable businessman, Foran. Calls himself an investment broker. Of course he's connected with the Mob. Arizona's crawling with them nowadays, they all moved out here. For their health," he added drily.

"How big is he?"

"Compared to what?"

"Nickel and dime, or million-dollar loans?"

"In the middle. It didn't pinch his coffers to come up with my fifty kay but he only did it after I offered him a little extra vigorish on the side. Mostly I imagine he spreads it around, five thousand here, ten thousand there—you know, minimize the risks. But hell, those guys get five percent a week; he's rich enough."

"Two hundred and sixty percent annual interest?"

"You got it. I know, I know. But I was in a bind, Charlie, I had nowhere else to turn. And I figured to sell the project inside of a month. I figured I could handle it—ten grand interest."

"But?"

"You see what they did to me. Obviously I came up short. It wasn't my fault. The building next door caught fire. My building didn't burn but the heat set off the automatic sprinkler system and it ruined the place. Seventy thousand damage—carpets, paint, doors, the works. The insurance barely covered half of it, and the damage set me back more than two months behind schedule. I had to bail out, Charlie. What choice did I have? My construction company went into Chapter Eleven.

"It's not my first bankruptcy and maybe it won't be my last— you know me—but I'd have paid them back. I tried to keep up the payments. I was a few days late a couple of times and we got threatening phone calls, so forth—you know how it goes. Then it wasn't a week any more, it was three weeks, and you see what happened. They took out their vigorish in blood. I guess they wrote me off as a bad debt but they figure to leave me crippled as an example to other borrowers who think about welshing. Nothing personal, you understand." His lip curled.

Margaret took his hand between hers. Margaret was always there to cushion Eddie's falls: good-humored, fun-loving, careless of her appearance. She had endured all his failures; she loved the real Eddie, not the man he ought to have been. If I ever find a woman like Margaret I'll have won the grand prize.

Eddie said, "I know the ropes, I had my eyes open. I'm not naive. But they've crippled me for life, Charlie. Both kneecaps. They'll be replaced with plastic prosthetics but I'll spend the rest of my life walking like a marionette. Two canes. I almost died. Maybe I still will. We don't know what's bleeding inside me."

"You knew those guys played rough, Eddie. You knew it going in."

It sounded lame and self-righteous even as I said it. Eddie's eyes only smiled at me. He knew I'd pick up the baton.

My long-distance call to Rice was lengthy and exasperating. He kept coming back to the same sore point. "You're asking me to commit Agency facilities to your private vengeance scheme. I can't do it."

"The Agency's got no use for it. Never will have. The press blew its cover in 1969 and it's been sitting there ever since, gathering dust. They're carrying it on the books as a dead loss—they'll be tickled to unload and get some money out of it. From your end it's a legitimate transaction and the profit ought to look pretty good on your efficiency report.

"And one other thing. If you don't authorize it I'll have to apply for a leave of absence to help my brother out. The Agency will grant it with pleasure—you know how eager they are to get rid of me. And of course that would leave you without anybody to pull your chestnuts out. You haven't got anybody else in the division who can handle the dirty jobs. You'd get fired, you know."

"You damn fat—" I didn't hear the rest.

Foran was slight and neat. The word dapper is out of fashion but it fits. He had wavy black hair and a swimming-pool tan and the look of a night-club maitré-d' who'd made good.

It took me a week to get the appointment with him, a week of meeting people and letting a word drop here and a hint there, softly and with discretion. I'm good at establishing the bona fides of a phony-cover identity and in this case it was dead easy because the only untruth in the cover story was my name: I didn't want him to know I had any family relationship with Eddie.

His office on the top floor of a nine-story high-rise had a lot of expensive wood, chrome, and leather. The picture windows gave views of the city like aerial postcard photographs. It was cool inside —the air-conditioning thrummed gently—but you could see heat waves shimmering in the thin smog above the flat sprawling city: the stuff thinned out the view of the towering mountain ranges to the north and east. I felt a bit wilted, having come in from that.

Foran had a polished desk a bit smaller than the deck of an escort carrier; it had a litter of papers and an assortment of gew-gaws made of ebony and petrified wood. He stood up and came affably around this display to shake my hand. His smile was cool, professional; behind it was a ruthlessness he didn't bother to conceal.

He had a deep confident voice. "Tell me about the proposition."

"I'm looking to borrow some money. I'm not offering a prospectus."

"If my firm authorizes a loan we have to know what it's being used for." He settled into his swivel chair and waited.

"What you want to know," I said, "is whether you'll get your money back and whether I'll make the interest payments on time."

"I don't know you, Mr. Ballantyne. Why should I lend you money?"

"I'm not being cute," I said. "If I lay out the details to you, what's to keep you from buying into the deal in my place while I'm still out scrounging for capital?"

"That's a risk you have to take. You'd take the same chance with anybody else, unless you've got a rich uncle. At least give me the outlines of the deal—it'll give us a basis for discussion."

I brooded at him as if making up my mind. I gave it a little time before I spoke. "All right. Let's assume the government owns a small private company with certain tangible assets that are of limited value to any domestic buyer, but might be of enormous value to certain foreign buyers to whom the present owner is not empowered to sell. You get my drift?"

"An arms deal?"

"In a way. Not guns, nothing that bald. The way this is set up, I'll be breaking no laws."

"Go on."

"You've had a few days to check me out," I said. "I assume you know I work for the government?"

"Yes."

"I'm about to retire. This deal will set me up for it. I need money to swing it, and it's got to come from somebody like you. But let me make it clear that if you try any odd footwork on me you'll find yourself in more trouble than you want to deal with."

His smile was as cold as Rice's. "Did you come here to threaten me or to borrow money?"

I sat back. "The C.I.A. founded, or bought, a number of private aviation companies fifteen or twenty years ago. They were used for various purposes. Cover fronts for all sorts of operations. They used some of them to supply revolutionary forces, some of them to run bombing missions against unfriendly countries, some of them to train Cuban exiles, and that sort of thing. It was broken by the press several years ago, so you know the story."

"Yes."

"All right. A few of those companies happened to be here in Arizona. I'm interested in one of those. Ostensibly it was a private air service, one of those shoestring jobs that did everything from private executive charters to cropdusting. After the C.I.A. bought it the facilities were expanded to accommodate air-crew training for student pilots and gunners from Cuba, Haiti, South Vietnam, and a couple of African countries. Then the lid blew off and the Agency got a black eye because we're not supposed to run covert operations inside the United States. After the publicity we were forced to close down the operation."

"Go on." He was interested.

I said, "The facility's still there. Planes, ammunition, bombs, radar, Link Trainers, the whole battery of military training equipment."

"And?"

"And it's on the market. Been on the market for seven or eight years. So far, no buyers. Because the only people who have a use for those facilities are governments that we can't be seen dealing with. Some of those governments would pay through the nose for the equipment—far above its actual value."

"You figure to be a go-between?"

"I know those countries. I've got the contacts. And I've recently chartered a little shell corporation in Nassau that I set up for this deal. The way it goes, I buy the Arizona Charter Air Company and its assets from the government. I turn around and sell it to the Nassau shell corporation. The shell corporation sells the stuff wherever it wants—it's in the Bahamas, it's outside the jurisdiction of American laws.

"When we make the sale, the shell corporation crates up the assets in Arizona and ships them out of the country on a Bahamian bill of lading, and then they're re-shipped out of Nassau on a new ticket so that there's no evidence in this country of the final destination. As I said, the buyers are lined up—they'll be bidding against one another and I'll take the high bid."

He was flicking his upper lip with his fingernail. He looked deceptively sleepy. With quiet brevity he said, "How much?"

"To buy the aviation company and pay the packing and shipping and incidental costs I figure one million nine hundred thousand. I'd rather call it two million in case I run into a snag somewhere—it's better to have a cushion. It's a bargain actually—the government paid upwards of fifteen million for that stuff."

"Maybe. But what condition is it in now? It could be rusty or obsolete or both."

"Obsolete for the U.S. Air Force, maybe, but not for a South American country. And it's all serviceable. It needs a good dusting, that's all. I've had it checked out."

"How much profit do you expect to realize?"

"That's classified. Let's just say I intend to put a floor under the bidding of three million five."

"Suppose you can't get that much? Suppose you don't get any bids at all?"

"I'm not going into this as a speculation. I've already made the contacts. The deal's ready to go down. All I have to do is name the time and place for the auction—but I've got to own the facilities before I can deliver them."

"Suppose we made you a loan, Mr. Ballantyne. And suppose you put the money in your pocket and skipped out to Tahiti."

"All right. Suppose we draw up contracts. If I don't pay the interest and principal you foreclose the company. The assets will remain right here in Arizona until I've sold them and received the cash down-payment, which will be enough to repay your loan. If I skip out with the money you'll have the assets—and with them a list of the interested governments. Fair enough?"

"We'll see. Two million is a great deal of money."

"Did I ask you for two million? I've got my own sources of private capital who want to buy in for small shares. I've raised six hundred thousand on my own. The loan I need is for one million four." That was elementary psychology: scare him with a big amount, then reduce it attractively.

Then I dropped the clincher on him. I said, "I'll need the money for no more than six weeks. I'll pay one percent a day, no holidays, for six weeks. That works out to just short of six hundred thousand dollars interest. You lend me one million four, you get back two million."

"I'll have to check this out first."

I knew I had him.

Margaret looked tired but she covered the strain with her smile. She set out cheese and biscuits in the living room while I mixed the drinks.

She said, "They haven't found any internal bleeding. He's going to be all right." She cut me a wedge of cheddar. "He's a foolish man sometimes but he didn't deserve this. Money's only money. Eddie —he's like a kid playing games. The money's just a counter, it's the way you keep score. If you lose a game you don't kill your opponent—you just set up the board and start another game."

"Foran doesn't play by those rules, Margaret. Eddie knew that."

She drank; I heard the ice cubes click against her teeth. "Did Foran go for it?"

"I won't know for a while. He's checking things out. But I think he'll buy it. He's too greedy to pass it up. The easiest mark for a con man is another crook."

"If he's checking things out, is there anything for him to find?"

"I doubt it. Most of what I told him was true. My boss set up the Nassau shell corporation for me. It'll be there when Foran looks for it. The Arizona Charter Air Company exists, it's on the government's books just as I told him it was, and the assets and facilities are exactly as I described them to him."

"If you pull it off, Charlie, they'll come after you."

"I don't think they'll find me. And I don't think I'll lose any sleep over it." I smiled to reassure her. People have been trying to kill me for more than 30 years and many of them are far more adept at it than the brand of thugs that Foran and his kind employ.

I knew one thing. If Foran didn't fall for this scam I'd just get at him another way. In any case Foran was finished. Eddie and Margaret didn't know it, but they had pitted the most formidable antagonist of all against Foran. I'm Charlie Dark. I'm the best there is.

The results of his investigations seemed to satisfy Foran. His lawyers drew up the most ironclad contracts I'd ever seen. Not a single item of Arizona Charter Air Company equipment was to be moved off its present airfield location until every penny of the loan had been paid back. The only thing the contract didn't include was the vigorish—the actual usurious interest rate; on paper we had an aboveboard agreement at 12% annual interest with a foreclosure date six weeks from the date of signatures.

The money was in the form of a bank cashier's check and I endorsed it over to the government in exchange for the deed to all outstanding stock in the Arizona Charter Air Company. I flew back from Washington to Tucson with the deed and stock certificates in an attaché case chained to my wrist. Twelve hours later they were in a safe-deposit box to which Foran had the second key, so that if I skipped out without paying, he would have possession of the documents and stock certificates. If I didn't repay him within 42 days he would be the legal owner of the company and all its assets.

We shook hands at the bank and I departed for the airport, whence I flew to Phoenix and rented a car. By midnight I was on the desert airfield that belonged to me. I dismissed the night watchman and took over the premises. As soon as I was alone I began setting the demolition charges.

There was nobody to prevent my destroying the equipment. I had canceled all the insurance policies the day before, so that I was perpetrating no fraud. It was my own property; I was free to do whatever I pleased with it.

The explosions would have thrilled any 12-year-old war movie fan. When the debris settled I drove to the hospital to say goodbye to Eddie and Margaret.

Eddie's eyes twinkled. "Mainly I regret he'll never know I had anything to do with it."

"Keep it that way. If he ever found out he'd finish you."

"I know. I'm not that much of a twit—not any more."

Margaret said, "What will happen to Foran?"

"Nothing pleasant," I said. "It can't have been his own money, not all of it. He's not that rich. He must have laid off a good part of the loan on his Mob associates. At least a million dollars, I'd guess. When he doesn't pay them back they'll go after Foran the way he went after Eddie."

Then I smiled. "And that, you know, is what they call justice."

PHILIP MARLOWE'S LAST CASE

RAYMOND CHANDLER

He was a slightly fat man with a dishonest smile that pulled the corners of his mouth out half an inch leaving the thick lips tight and his eyes bleak. For a fattish man he had a slow walk. Most fat men are brisk and light on their feet. He wore a gray herringbone suit and a handpainted tie with part of a diving girl visible on it. His shirt was clean, which comforted me, and his brown loafers, as wrong as the tie for his suit, shone from a recent polishing.

He sidled past me as I held the door between the waiting room and my thinking parlor. Once inside, he took a quick look around. I'd have placed him as a mobster, second grade, if I had been asked. For once I was right. If he carried a gun, it was inside his pants. His coat was too tight to hide the bulge of an underarm holster.

He sat down carefully and I sat opposite and we looked at each other. His face had a sort of foxy eagerness. He was sweating a little. The expression on my face was meant to be interested but not clubby. I reached for a pipe and the leather humidor in which I kept my Pearce's tobacco. I pushed the cigarettes at him.

"I don't smoke." He had a rusty voice. I didn't like it any more than I liked his clothes, or his face. While I filled the pipe he reached inside his coat, prowled in a pocket, came out with a bill, glanced at it, and dropped it across the desk in front of me. It was a nice bill and clean and new. One thousand dollars.

"Ever save a guy's life?"

"Once in a while, maybe."

"Save mine."

"What goes?"

"I heard you leveled with the customers, Marlowe."

"That's why I stay poor."

"I still got two friends. You make it three and you'll be out of the red. You got five grand coming if you pry me loose."

"From what?"

"You're talkative as hell this morning. Don't you pipe who I am?"

"Nope."

"Never been east, huh?"

"Sure—but I wasn't in your set."

"What set would that be?"

I was getting tired of it. "Stop being so damn cagey or pick up your grand and be missing."

"I'm Ikky Rossen. I'll be missing but good unless you can figure some out. Guess."

"I've already guessed. You tell me and tell me quick. I don't have all day to watch you feeding me with an eye-dropper."

"I ran out on the Outfit. The high boys don't go for that. To them it means you got info you figure you can peddle, or you got independent ideas, or you lost your moxie. Me, I lost my moxie. I had it up to here." He touched his Adam's apple with the forefinger of a stretched hand. "I done bad things. I scared and hurt guys. I never killed nobody. That's nothing to the Outfit. I'm out of line. So they pick up the pencil and they draw a line. I got the word. The operators are on the way. I made a bad mistake. I tried to hole up in Vegas. I figured they'd never expect me to lie up in their own joint. They outfigured me. What I did's been done before, but I didn't know it. When I took the plane to L.A. there must have been somebody on it. They know where I live."

"Move."

"No good now. I'm covered."

I knew he was right.

"Why haven't they taken care of you already?"

"They don't do it that way. Always specialists. Don't you know how it works?"

"More or less. A guy with a nice hardware store in Buffalo. A guy with a small dairy in K.C. Always a good front. They report back to New York or somewhere. When they mount the plane west or wherever they're going, they have guns in their brief cases. They're quiet and well-dressed and they don't sit together. They could be a couple of lawyers or income tax sharpies—anything at all that's well-mannered and inconspicuous. All sorts of people carry brief cases. Including women."

"Correct as hell. And when they land they'll be steered to me, but not from the airfield. They got ways. If I go to the cops, somebody will know about me. They could have a couple Mafia boys right on the City Council for all I know. The cops will give me twenty-fours to leave town. No use. Mexico? Worse than here. Canada? Better but still no good. Connections there too."

"Australia?"

"Can't get a passport. I been here twenty-five years—illegal. They can't deport me unless they can prove a crime on me. The Outfit would see they didn't. Suppose I got tossed into the freezer. I'm out on a writ in twenty-four hours. And my nice friends got a car waiting to take me home—only not home."

I had my pipe lit and going well. I frowned down at the one-grand note. I could use it very nicely. My checking account could kiss the sidewalk without stooping.

"Let's stop horsing," I said. "Suppose—just suppose—I could figure an out for you. What's your next move?"

"I know a place—if I could get there without bein' tailed. I'd leave my car here and take a rent car. I'd turn it in just short of the county line and buy a secondhand job. Halfway to where I'm going I trade it on a new last-year's model, a leftover—this is just the right time of year. Good discount, new models out soon. Not to save money—less show off. Where I'd go is a good-sized place but still pretty clean."

"Uh-huh," I said. "Wichita, last I heard. But it might have changed."

He scowled at me. "Get smart, Marlowe, but not too damn smart."

"I'll get as smart as I want to. Don't try to make rules for me. If I take this on, there aren't any rules. I take it for this grand and the rest if I bring it off. Don't cross me. I might leak information. If I get knocked off, put just one red rose on my grave. I don't like cut flowers. I like to see them growing. But I could take one, because you're such a sweet character. When's the plane in?"

"Sometime today. It's nine hours from New York. Probably come in about 5:30 p.m."

"Might come by San Diego and switch or by San Francisco and switch. A lot of planes from both places. I need a helper."

"Damn you, Marlowe—"

"Hold it. I know a girl. Daughter of a Chief of Police who got broken for honesty. She wouldn't leak under torture."

"You got no right to risk her," Ikky said angrily.

I was so astonished my jaw hung halfway to my waist. I closed it slowly and swallowed.

"Good God, the man's got a heart."

"Women ain't built for the rough stuff," he said grudgingly.

I picked up the thousand-dollar note and snapped it. "Sorry. No receipt," I said. "I can't have my name in your pocket. And there won't be any rough stuff if I'm lucky. They'd have me outclassed. There's only one way to work it. Now give me your address and all the dope you can think of—names, descriptions of any operators you have ever seen in the flesh."

He did. He was a pretty good observer. Trouble was, the Outfit would know what he had seen. The operators would be strangers to him.

He got up silently and put his hand out. I had to shake it, but what he had said about women made it easier. His hand was moist. Mine would have been in his spot. He nodded and went out silently.

It was a quiet street in Bay City, if there are any quiet streets in this beatnik generation when you can't get through a meal without some male or female stomach-singer belching out a kind of love that is as old-fashioned as a bustle or some Hammond organ jazzing it up in the customer's soup.

The little one-story house was as neat as a fresh pinafore. The front lawn was cut lovingly and very green. The smooth composition driveway was free of grease spots from standing cars, and the hedge that bordered it looked as though the barber came every day.

The white door had a knocker with a tiger's head, a go-to-hell window, and a dingus that let someone inside talk to someone outside without even opening the little window.

I'd have given a mortgage on my left leg to live in a house like that. I didn't think I ever would.

The bell chimed inside and after a while she opened the door in a pale-blue sports shirt and white shorts that were short enough to be friendly. She had gray-blue eyes, dark red hair, and fine bones in her face. There was usually a trace of bitterness in the gray-blue eyes. She couldn't forget that her father's life had been destroyed by the crooked power of a gambling-ship mobster, that her mother had died too.

She was able to suppress the bitterness when she wrote nonsense about young love for the shiny magazines, but this wasn't her life. She didn't really have a life. She had an existence without much pain and enough money to make it safe. But in a tight spot she was as cool and resourceful as a good cop. Her name was Anne Riordan.

She stood to one side and I passed her pretty close. But I have rules too. She shut the door and parked herself on a sofa and went through the cigarette routine, and here was one doll who had the strength to light her own cigarette.

I stood looking around. There were a few changes, not many.

"I need your help," I said.

"The only time I ever see you."

"I've got a client who is an ex-hood used to be a troubleshooter for the Outfit, the Syndicate, the big mob, or whatever name you want to use for it. You know damn well it exists and is as rich as Midas. You can't beat it because not enough people want to, especially the million-a-year lawyers who work for it."

"My God, are you running for office somewhere? I never heard you sound so pure."

She moved her legs around, not provocatively—she wasn't the type—but it made it difficult for me to think straight just the same.

"Stop moving your legs around," I said. "Or put a pair of slacks on."

"Damn you, Marlowe. Can't you think of anything else?"

"I'll try. I like to think that I know at least one pretty and charming female who doesn't have round heels." I swallowed and went on. "The man's name is Ikky Rossen." He's not beautiful and he's not anything that I like—except one thing. He got mad when I said I needed a girl helper. He said women were not made for the rough stuff. That's why I took the job. To a real mobster, a woman means no more than a sack of flour. They use women in the usual way, but if it's advisable to get rid of them they do it without a second thought."

"So far you've told me a whole lot of nothing. Perhaps you need a cup of coffee or a drink."

"You're sweet but I don't in the morning—except sometimes, and this isn't one of them. Coffee later. Ikky has been penciled."

"Now what's that?"

"You have a list. You draw a line through a name with a pencil. The guy is as good as dead. The Outfit has reasons. They don't do it just for kicks any more. They don't get any kick. It's just book-keeping to them."

"What on earth can I do? I might even have said, what can *you* do?"

"I can try. What you can do is help me spot their plane and see where they go—the operators assigned to the job."

"Yes, but how can you do anything?"

"I said I could try. If they took a night plane they are already here. If they took a morning plane they can't be here before five or so. Plenty of time to get set. You know what they look like?"

"Oh, sure. I meet killers every day. I have them in for whiskey sours and caviar on hot toast." She grinned. While she was grinning I took four long steps across the tan-figured rug and lifted her and put a kiss on her mouth. She didn't fight me but she didn't go all trembly either. I went back and sat down.

"They'll look like anybody who's in a quiet well-run business or profession. They'll have quiet clothes and they'll be polite—when they want to be. They'll have brief cases with guns in them that have changed hands so often they can't possibly be traced. When and if they do the job, they'll drop the guns. They'll probably use revolvers, but they could use automatics. They won't use silencers because silencers can jam a gun and the weight makes it hard to shoot accurately. They won't sit together on the plane, but once off of it they may pretend to know each other and simply not have noticed during the flight. They may shake hands with appropriate smiles and walk away and get in the same taxi. I think they'll go to a hotel first. But very soon they will move into something from which they can watch Ikky's movements and get used to his schedule. They won't be in any hurry unless Ikky makes a move. That would tip them off that Ikky has been tipped off. He has a couple of friends left—he says."

"Will they shoot him from this room or apartment across the street—assuming there is one?"

"No. They'll shoot him from three feet away. They'll walk up behind and say 'Hello, Ikky.' He'll either freeze or turn. They'll fill him with lead, drop the guns, and hop into the car they have waiting. Then they'll follow the crash car off the scene."

"Who'll drive the crash car?"

"Some well-fixed and blameless citizen who hasn't been rapped. He'll drive his own car. He'll clear the way, even if he has to accidentally on purpose crash somebody, even a police car. He'll be so damn sorry he'll cry all the way down his monogrammed shirt. And the killers will be long gone."

"Good heavens," Anne said. "How can you stand your life? If you did bring it off, they'll send operators after you."

"I don't think so. They don't kill a legit. The blame will go to the operators. Remember, these top mobsters are businessmen. They want lots and lots of money. They only get really tough when they figure they have to get rid of somebody, and they don't crave that. There's always a chance of a slipup. Not much of a chance. No gang killing has ever been solved here or anywhere else except two or three times. The top mobster is awful big and awful tough. When he gets too big, too tough—pencil."

She shuddered a little. "I think I need a drink myself."

I grinned at her. "You're right in the atmosphere, darling. I'll weaken."

She brought a couple of Scotch highballs. When we were drinking them I said, "If you spot them or think you spot them, follow to where they go—if you can do it safely. Not otherwise. If it's a hotel—and ten to one it will be—check in and keep calling me until you get me."

She knew my office number and I was still on Yucca Avenue. She knew that too.

"You're the damndest guy," she said. "Women do anything you want them to. How come I'm still a virgin at twenty-eight?"

"We need a few like you. Why don't you get married?"

"To what? Some cynical chaser who has nothing left? I don't know any really nice men—except you. I'm no pushover for white teeth and a gaudy smile."

I went over and pulled her to her feet. I kissed her long and hard. "I'm honest," I almost whispered. "That's something. But I'm too shop-soiled for a girl like you. I've thought of you, I've wanted you, but that sweet clear look in your eyes tells me to lay off."

"Take me," she said softly. "I have dreams too."

"I couldn't. I've had too many women to deserve one like you. We have to save a man's life. I'm going."

She stood up and watched me leave with a grave face.

The women you get and the women you don't get—they live in different worlds. I don't sneer at either world. I live in both myself.

At Los Angeles International Airport you can't get close to the planes unless you're leaving on one. You see them land, if you happen to be in the right place, but you have to wait at a barrier to get a look at the passengers. The airport buildings don't make it any easier. They are strung out from here to breakfast time, and you can get calluses walking from TWA to American.

I copied an arrival schedule off the boards and prowled around like a dog that has forgotten where he put his bone. Planes came in, planes took off, porters carried luggage, passengers sweated and scurried, children whined, the loudspeaker overrode all the other noises.

I passed Anne a number of times. She took no notice of me.

At 5:45 they must have come. Anne disappeared. I gave it half an hour, just in case she had some other reason for fading. No. She was gone for good. I went out to my car and drove some long crowded miles to Hollywood and my office. I had a drink and sat. At 6:45 the phone rang.

"I think so," she said. "Beverly-Western Hotel. Room 410. I couldn't get any names. You know the clerks don't leave registration cards lying around these days. I didn't like to ask any questions. But I rode up in the elevator with them and spotted their room. I walked right on past them when the bellman put a key in their door, and went down to the mezzanine and then downstairs with a bunch of women from the tea room. I didn't bother to take a room."

"What were they like?"

"They came up the ramp together but I didn't hear them speak. Both had brief cases, both wore quiet suits, nothing flashy. White shirts, starched, one blue tie, one black striped with gray. Black shoes. A couple of businessmen from the East Coast. They could be publishers, lawyers, doctors, account executives—no, cut the last; they weren't gaudy enough. You wouldn't look at them twice."

"Faces?"

"Both medium-brown hair, one a bit darker than the other. Smooth faces, rather expressionless. One had gray eyes, the one with the lighter hair had blue eyes. Their eyes were interesting. Very quick to move, very observant, watching everything near them. That might have been wrong. They should have been a bit preoccupied with what they came out for or interested in California. They seemed more occupied with faces. It's a good thing I spotted them and not you. You don't look like a cop, but you don't look like a man who is not a cop. You have marks on you."

"Phooey. I'm a damn good-looking heart wrecker."

"Their features were strictly assembly line. Each picked up a flight suitcase. One suitcase was gray with two red and white stripes up and down, about six or seven inches from the ends, the other a blue and white tartan. I didn't know there was such a tartan."

"There is, but I forget the name of it."

"I thought you knew everything."

"Just almost everything. Run along home now."

"Do I get a dinner and maybe a kiss?"

"Later, and if you're not careful you'll get more than you want."

"You'll take over and follow them?"

"If they're the right men, they'll follow me. I already took an apartment across the street from Ikky—that block on Poynter with six lowlife apartment houses on the block. I'll bet the incidence of chippies is very high."

"It's high everywhere these days."

"So long, Anne. See you."

"When you need help."

She hung up. I hung up. She puzzles me. Too wise to be so nice. I guess all nice women are wise too.

I called Ikky. He was out. I had a drink from the office bottle, smoked for half an hour, and called again. This time I got him.

I told him the score up to then, and said I hoped Anne had picked the right men. I told him about the apartment I had taken.

"Do I get expenses?" I asked.

"Five grand ought to cover the lot."

"If I earn it and get it. I heard you had a quarter of a million," I said at a wild venture.

"Could be, pal, but how do I get at it? The high boys know where it is. It'll have to cool a long time."

I said that was all right. I had cooled a long time myself. Of course, I didn't expect to get the other four thousand, even if I brought the job off. Men like Ikky Rossen would steal their mother's gold teeth. There seemed to be a little good in him some-where—but little was the operative word.

I spent the next half hour trying to think of a plan. I couldn't think of one that looked promising. It was almost eight o'clock and I needed food. I didn't think the boys would move that night. Next morning they would drive past Ikky's place and scout the neigh-borhood.

I was ready to leave the office when the buzzer sounded from the door of my waiting room. I opened the communicating door. A small tight-looking man was standing in the middle of the floor rocking on his heels with his hands behind his back. He smiled at me, but he wasn't good at it. He walked toward me.

"You Philip Marlowe?"

"Who else? What can I do for you?"

He was close now. He brought his right hand around fast with a gun in it. He stuck the gun in my stomach.

"You can lay off Ikky Rossen," he said in a voice that matched his face, "or you can get your belly full of lead."

He was an amateur. If he had stayed four feet away, he might have had something. I reached up and took the cigarette out of my mouth and held it carelessly.

"What makes you think I know any Ikky Rossen?"

He laughed and pushed his gun into my stomach.

"Wouldn't you like to know!" The cheap sneer, the empty triumph of that feeling of power when you hold a fat gun in a small hand.

"It would be fair to tell me."

As his mouth opened for another crack, I dropped the cigarette and swept a hand. I can be fast when I have to. There are boys that are faster, but they don't stick guns in your stomach.

I got my thumb behind the trigger and my hand over his. I kneed him in the groin. He bent over with a whimper. I twisted his arm to the right and I had his gun. I hooked a heel behind his heel and he was on the floor.

He lay there blinking with surprise and pain, his knees drawn up against his stomach. He rolled from side to side groaning. I reached down and grabbed his left hand and yanked him to his feet. I had six inches and forty pounds on him. They ought to have sent a bigger, better trained messenger.

"Let's go into my thinking parlor," I said. "We could have a chat and you could have a drink to pick you up. Next time don't get near enough to a prospect for him to get your gun hand. I'll just see if you have any more iron on you."

He hadn't. I pushed him through the door and into a chair. His breath wasn't quite so rasping. He grabbed out a handkerchief and mopped at his face.

"Next time," he said between his teeth. "Next time."

"Don't be an optimist. You don't look the part."

I poured him a drink of Scotch in a paper cup, set it down in front of him. I broke his .38 and dumped the cartridges into the desk drawer. I clicked the chamber back and laid the gun down.

"You can have it when you leave—if you leave."

"That's a dirty way to fight," he said, still gasping.

"Sure. Shooting a man is so much cleaner. Now, how did you get here?"

"Nuts."

"Don't be a fool. I have friends. Not many, but some. I can get you for armed assault, and you know what would happen then. You'd be out on a writ or on bail and that's the last anyone would hear of you. The biggies don't go for failures. Now who sent you and how did you know where to come?"

"Ikky was covered," he said sullenly. "He's dumb. I trailed him here without no trouble at all. Why would he go see a private eye? People want to know."

"More."

"Go to hell."

"Come to think of it, I don't have to get you for armed assault. I can smash it out of you right here and now."

I got up from the chair and he put out a flat hand.

"If I get knocked about, a couple of real tough monkeys will drop around. If I don't report back, same thing. You ain't holding no real high cards. They just look high," he said.

"You haven't anything to tell. If this Ikky came to see me, you don't know why, nor whether I took him on. If he's a mobster, he's not my type of client."

"He came to get you to try and save his hide."

"Who from?"

"That'd be talking."

"Go right ahead. Your mouth seems to work fine. And tell the boys any time I front for a hood, that will be the day."

You have to lie a little once in a while in my business. I was lying a little. "What's Ikky done to get himself disliked? Or would that be talking?"

"You think you're a lot of man," he sneered, rubbing the place where I had kneed him. "In my league you wouldn't make pinch runner."

I laughed in his face. Then I grabbed his right wrist and twisted it behind his back. He began to squawk. I reached into his breast pocket with my left hand and hauled out a wallet. I let him go. He reached for his gun on the desk and I bisected his upper arm with a hard cut. He fell into the customer's chair and grunted.

"You can have your gun," I told him. "When I give it to you. Now be good or I'll have to bounce you just to amuse myself."

In the wallet I found a driver's license made out to Charles Hickon. It did me no good at all. Punks of his type always have slangy aliases. They probably called him Tiny, or Slim, or Marbles, or even just "you." I tossed the wallet back to him. It fell to the floor. He couldn't even catch it.

"Hell," I said, "there must be an economy campaign on, if they send you to do more than pick up cigarette butts."

"Nuts."

"All right, mug. Beat it back to the laundry. Here's your gun."

He took it, made a business, of shoving it into his waistband, stood up, gave me as dirty a look as he had in stock, and strolled to the door, nonchalant as a hustler with a new mink stole.

He turned at the door and gave me the beady eye. "Stay clean, tinhorn. Tin bends easy."

With this blinding piece of repartee he opened the door and drifted out.

After a little while I locked my other door, cut the buzzer, made the office dark, and left. I saw no one who looked like a lifetaker. I drove to my house, packed a suitcase, drove to a service station where they were almost fond of me, stored my car, and picked up a rental Chevrolet.

I drove this to Poynter Street, dumped my suitcase in the sleazy apartment I had rented early in the afternoon, and went to dinner at Victor's. It was nine o'clock, too late to drive to Bay City and take Anne to dinner.

I ordered a double Gibson with fresh limes and drank it, and I was as hungry as a schoolboy.

On the way back to Poynter Street I did a good deal of weaving in and out and circling blocks and stopping, with a gun on the seat beside me. As far as I could tell, no one was trying to tail me.

I stopped on Sunset at a service station and made two calls from the box. I caught Bernie Ohls just as he was leaving to go home.

"This is Marlowe, Bernie. We haven't had a fight in years. I'm getting lonely."

"Well, get married. I'm chief investigator for the Sheriff's Office now. I rank acting captain until I pass the exam. I don't hardly speak to private eyes."

"Speak to this one. I need help. I'm on a ticklish job where I could get killed."

"And you expect me to interfere with the course of nature?"

"Come off it, Bernie. I haven't been a bad guy. I'm trying to save an ex-mobster from a couple of executioners."

"The more they mow each other down, the better I like it."

"Yeah. If I call you, come running or send a couple of good boys. You'll have had time to teach them."

We exchanged a couple of mild insults and hung up. I dialed Ikky Rossen's number. His rather unpleasant voice said, "Okay, talk."

"Marlowe. Be ready to move out about midnight. We've spotted your boy friends and they are holed up at the Beverly-Western. They won't move to your street tonight. Remember, they don't know you've been tipped."

"Sounds chancy."

"Good God, it wasn't meant to be a Sunday School picnic. You've been careless, Ikky. You were followed to my office. That cuts the time we have."

He was silent for a moment. I heard him breathing. "Who by?" he asked.

"Some little tweezer who stuck a gun in my belly and gave me the trouble of taking it away from him. I can only figure they sent a punk on the theory they don't want me to know too much, in case I don't know it already."

"You're in for trouble, friend."

"When not? I'll come over to your place about midnight. Be ready. Where's your car?"

"Out front."

"Get it on a side street and make a business of locking it up. Where's the back door of your flop?"

"In back. Where would it be? On the alley."

"Leave your suitcase there. We walk out together and go to your car. We drive by the alley and pick up the suitcase or cases."

"Suppose some guy steals them?"

"Yeah. Suppose you get dead. Which do you like better?"

"Okay," he grunted. "I'm waiting. But we're taking big chances."

"So do race drivers. Does that stop them? There's no way to get out but fast. Douse your lights about ten and rumple the bed well. It would be good if you could leave some baggage behind. Wouldn't look so planned."

He grunted okay and I hung up. The telephone box was well lighted outside. They usually are in service stations. I took a good long gander around while I pawed over the collection of giveaway maps inside the station. I saw nothing to worry me. I took a map of San Diego just for the hell of it and got into my rented car.

On Poynter I parked around the corner and went up to my second-floor sleazy apartment and sat in the dark watching from my window. I saw nothing to worry about. A couple of medium-class chippies came out of Ikky's apartment house and were picked up in a late-model car. A man about Ikky's height and build went into the apartment house. Various other people came and went. The street was fairly quiet. Since they put in the Hollywood Freeway nobody much uses the off-the-boulevard streets unless they live in the neighborhood.

It was a nice fall night—or as nice as they get in Los Angeles' climate—clearish but not even crisp. I don't know what's happened to the weather in our overcrowded city, but it's not the weather I knew when I came to it.

It seemed like a long time to midnight. I couldn't spot anybody watching anything, and no couple of quiet-suited men paged any of the six apartment houses available. I was pretty sure they'd try mine first when they came, but I wasn't sure if Anne had picked the right men, and if the tweezer's message back to his bosses had done me any good or otherwise.

In spite of the hundred ways Anne could be wrong, I had a hunch she was right. The killers had no reason to be cagey if they didn't know Ikky had been warned. No reason but one. He had come to my office and been tailed there. But the Outfit, with all its arrogance of power, might laugh at the idea he had been tipped off or come to me for help. I was so small they would hardly be able to see me.

At midnight I left the apartment, walked two blocks watching for a tail, crossed the street, and went into Ikky's dive. There was no locked door, and no elevator. I climbed steps to the third floor and looked for his apartment. I knocked lightly. He opened the door with a gun in his hand. He probably looked scared.

There were two suitcases by the door and another against the far wall. I went over and lifted it. It was heavy enough. I opened it—it was unlocked.

"You don't have to worry," he said. "It's got everything a guy could need for three-four nights, and nothing except some clothes that I couldn't glom off in any ready-to-wear place."

I picked up one of the other suitcases. "Let's stash this by the back door."

"We can leave by the alley too."

"We leave by the front door. Just in case we're covered—though I don't think so—we're just two guys going out together. Just one thing. Keep both hands in your coat pockets and the gun in your right. If anybody calls out your name behind you, turn fast and shoot. Nobody but a lifetaker will do it. I'll do the same."

"I'm scared," he said in his rusty voice.

"Me too, if it helps any. But we have to do it. If you're braced, they'll have guns in their hands. Don't bother asking them questions. They wouldn't answer in words. If it's just my small friend, we'll cool him and dump him inside the door. Got it?"

He nodded, licking his lips. We carried the suitcases down and put them outside the back door. I looked along the alley. Nobody, and only a short distance to the side street. We went back in and along the hall to the front. We walked out on Poynter Street with all the casualness of a wife buying her husband a birthday tie.

Nobody made a move. The street was empty.

We walked around the corner to Ikky's rented car. He unlocked it. I went back with him for the suitcases. Not a stir. We put the suitcases in the car and started up and drove to the next street.

A traffic light not working, a boulevard stop or two, the entrance to the Freeway. There was plenty of traffic on it even at midnight. California is loaded with people going places and making speed to get there. If you don't drive eighty miles an hour, everybody passes you. If you do, you have to watch the rear-view mirror for highway patrol cars. It's the rat race of rat races.

Ikky did a quiet seventy. We reached the junction to Route 66 and he took it. So far nothing. I stayed with him to Pomona.

"This is far enough for me," I said. "I'll grab a bus back if there is one, or park myself in a motel. Drive to a service station and we'll ask for the bus stop. It should be close to the Freeway."

He did that and stopped midway on a block. He reached for his pocketbook and held out four thousand-dollar bills.

"I don't really feel I've earned all that. It was too easy."

He laughed with a kind of wry amusement on his pudgy face. "Don't be a sap. I have it made. You didn't know what you was walking into. What's more, your troubles are just beginning. The

Outfit has eyes and ears everywhere. Perhaps I'm safe if I'm damn careful. Perhaps I ain't as safe as I think I am. Either way, you did what I asked. Take the dough. I got plenty."

I took it and put it away. He drove to an all-night service station and we were told where to find the bus stop. "There's a cross-country Greyhound at 2:25 a.m.," the attendant said, looking at a schedule. "They'll take you, if they got room."

Ikky drove to the bus stop. We shook hands and he went gunning down the road toward the Freeway. I looked at my watch and found a liquor store still open and bought a pint of Scotch. Then I found a bar and ordered a double with water.

My troubles were just beginning, Ikky had said. He was so right.

I got off at the Hollywood bus station, grabbed a taxi, and drove to my office. I asked the driver to wait a few moments. At that time of night he was glad to. The night man let me into the building.

"You work late, Mr. Marlowe. But you always did, didn't you?"

"It's that sort of business," I said. "Thanks, Jimmy."

Up in my office I pawed the floor for mail and found nothing but a longish narrowish box, Special Delivery, with a Glendale postmark.

It contained nothing at all but a freshly sharpened pencil—the mobster's mark of death.

I didn't take it too hard. When they mean it, they don't send it to you. I took it as a sharp warning to lay off. There might be a beating arranged. From their point of view, that would be good discipline. "When we pencil a guy, any guy that tries to help him is in for a smashing." That could be the message.

I thought of going to my house on Yucca Avenue. Too lonely. I thought of going to Anne's place in Bay City. Worse. If they got wise to her, real hoods would think nothing of beating her up too.

It was the Poynter Street flop for me—easily the safest place now. I went down to the waiting taxi and had him drive me to within three blocks of the so-called apartment house. I went upstairs, undressed, and slept raw. Nothing bothered me but a broken spring—that bothered my back.

I lay until 3:30 pondering the situation with my massive brain. I went to sleep with a gun under the pillow, which is a bad place to keep a gun when you have one pillow as thick and soft as a type-writer pad. It bothered me, so I transferred it to my right hand. Practice had taught me to keep it there even in sleep.

I woke up with the sun shining. I felt like a piece of spoiled meat. I struggled into the bathroom and doused myself with cold water and wiped off with a towel you couldn't have seen if you held it sideways. This was a really gorgeous apartment. All it needed was a set of Chippendale furniture to be graduated into the slum class.

There was nothing to eat and if I went out, Miss-Nothing Marlowe might miss something. I had a pint of whiskey. I looked at it and smelled it, but I couldn't take it for breakfast on an empty stomach, even if I could reach my stomach, which was floating around near the ceiling.

I looked into the closets in case a previous tenant might have left a crust of bread in a hasty departure. Nope. I wouldn't have liked it anyhow, not even with whiskey on it. So I sat at the window. An hour of that and I was ready to bite a piece off a bellhop's arm.

I dressed and went around the corner to the rented car and drove to an eatery. The waitress was sore too. She swept a cloth over the counter in front of me and let me have the last customer's crumbs in my lap.

"Look, sweetness," I said, "don't be so generous. Save the crumbs for a rainy day. All I want is two eggs three minutes—no more—a slice of your famous concrete toast, a tall glass of tomato juice with a dash of Lee and Perrins, a big happy smile, and don't give anybody else any coffee. I might need it all."

"I got a cold," she said. "Don't push me around. I might crack you one on the kisser."

"Let's be pals. I had a rough night too."

She gave me a half smile and went through the swing door sideways. It showed more of her curves, which were ample, even excessive. But I got the eggs the way I liked them. The toast had been painted with melted butter past its bloom.

"No Lee and Perrins," she said, putting down the tomato juice. "How about a little Tabasco? We're fresh out of arsenic too."

I used two drops of Tabasco, swallowed the eggs, drank two cups of coffee, and was about to leave the toast for a tip, but I went soft and left a quarter instead. That really brightened her. It was a joint where you left a dime or nothing. Mostly nothing.

Back on Poynter Street nothing had changed. I got to my window again and sat. At about 8:30 the man I had seen go into the apartment house across the way—the one about the same height and build as Ikky—came out with a small brief case and turned east. Two men got out of a dark-blue sedan. They were of the same height and very quietly dressed and had soft hats pulled low over their foreheads. Each jerked out a revolver.

"Hey, Ikky!" one of them called out.

The man turned. "So long, Ikky," the other man said.

Gunfire racketed between the houses. The man crumpled and lay motionless. The two men rushed for their car and were off, going west. Halfway down the block I saw a limousine pull out and start ahead of them.

In no time at all they were completely gone.

It was a nice swift clean job. The only thing wrong with it was that they hadn't given it enough time for preparation.

They had shot the wrong man.

I got out of there fast, almost as fast as the two killers. There was a smallish crowd grouped around the dead man. I didn't have to look at him to know he was dead—the boys were pros. Where he lay on the sidewalk on the other side of the street I couldn't see him—people were in the way. But I knew just how he would look and I already heard sirens in the distance. It could have been just the routine shrieking from Sunset, but it wasn't. So somebody had telephoned. It was too early for the cops to be going to lunch.

I strolled around the corner with my suitcase and jammed into the rented car and beat it away from there. The neighborhood was not my piece of shortcake any more. I could imagine the questions.

"Just what took you over there, Marlowe? You got a flop of your own, ain't you?"

"I was hired by an ex-mobster in trouble with the Outfit. They'd sent killers after him!"

"Don't tell us he was trying to go straight."

"I don't know. But I liked his money."

"Didn't do much to earn it, did you?"

"I got him away last night. I don't know where he is now, and I don't want to know."

"You got him away?"

"That's what I said."

"Yeah—only he's in the morgue with multiple bullet wounds. Try something better. Or somebody's in the morgue."

And on and on. Policeman's dialogue. It comes out of an old shoebox. What they say doesn't mean anything, what they ask doesn't mean anything. They just keep boring in until you are so exhausted you flip on some detail. Then they smile happily and rub their hands, and say, "Kind of careless there, weren't you? Let's start all over again."

The less I had of that, the better. I parked in my usual parking slot and went up to the office. It was full of nothing but stale air. Every time I went into the dump I felt more and more tired. Why the hell hadn't I got myself a government job ten years ago? Make it fifteen years. I had brains enough to get a mail-order law degree. The country's full of lawyers who couldn't write a complaint without the book.

So I sat in my office chair and disadmired myself. After a while I remembered the pencil. I made certain arrangements with a .45 gun, more gun than I ever carry—too much weight. I dialed the Sheriff's Office and asked for Bernie Ohls. I got him. His voice was sour.

"Marlowe. I'm in trouble—real trouble," I said.

"Why tell me?" he growled. "You must be used to it by now."

"This kind of trouble you don't get used to. I'd like to come over and tell you."

"You in the same office?"

"The same."

"Have to go over that way. I'll drop in."

He hung up. I opened two windows. The gentle breeze wafted a smell of coffee and stale fat to me from Joe's Eats next door. I hated it, I hated myself, I hated everything.

Ohls didn't bother with my elegant waiting room. He rapped on my own door and I let him in. He scowled his way to the customer's chair.

"Okay. Give."

"Ever hear of a character named Ikky Rossen?"

"Why would I? Record?"

"An ex-mobster who got disliked by the mob. They put a pencil through his name and sent the usual two tough boys on a plane. He got tipped and hired me to help him get away."

"Nice clean work."

"Cut it out, Bernie." I lit a cigarette and blew smoke in his face. In retaliation he began to chew a cigarette. He never lit one, but he certainly mangled them.

"Look," I went on. "Suppose the man wants to go straight and suppose he doesn't. He's entitled to his life as long as he hasn't killed anyone. He told me he hadn't."

"And you believed the hood, huh? When do you start teaching Sunday School?"

"I neither believed him nor disbelieved him. I took him on. There was no reason not to. A girl I know and I watched the planes yesterday. She spotted the boys and tailed them to a hotel. She was sure of what they were. They looked it right down to their black shoes. This girl—"

"Would she have a name?"

"Only for you."

"I'll buy, if she hasn't cracked any laws."

"Her name is Anne Riordan. She lives in Bay City. Her father was once Chief of Police there. And don't say that makes him a crook, because he wasn't."

"Uh-huh. Let's have the rest. Make a little time too."

"I took an apartment opposite Ikky. The killers were still at the hotel. At midnight I got Ikky out and drove with him as far as Pomona. He went on in his rented car and I came back by Greyhound. I moved into the apartment on Poynter Street, right across from his dump."

"Why—if he was already gone?"

I opened the middle desk drawer and took out the nice sharp pencil. I wrote my name on a piece of paper and ran the pencil through it.

"Because someone sent me this. I didn't think they'd kill me, but I thought they planned to give me enough of a beating to warn me off any more pranks."

"They knew you were in on it?"

"Ikky was tailed here by a little squirt who later came around and stuck a gun in my stomach. I knocked him around a bit, but I had to let him go. I thought Poynter Street was safer after that. I live lonely."

"I get around," Bernie Ohls said. "I hear reports. So they gunned the wrong guy."

"Same height, same build, same general appearance. I saw them gun him. I couldn't tell if it was the two guys from the Beverly-Western. I'd never seen them. It was just two guys in dark suits with hats pulled down. They jumped into a blue Pontiac sedan, about two years old, and lammed off, with a big Caddy running crash for them."

Bernie stood up and stared at me for a long moment. "I don't think they'll bother with you now," he said. "They've hit the wrong guy. The mob will be very quiet for a while. You know something? This town is getting to be almost as lousy as New York, Brooklyn, and Chicago. We could end up real corrupt."

"We've made a hell of a good start."

"You haven't told me anything that makes me take action, Phil. I'll talk to the city homicide boys. I don't guess you're in any trouble. But you saw the shooting. They'll want that."

"I couldn't identify anybody, Bernie. I didn't know the man who was shot. How did *you* know it was the wrong man?"

"You told me, stupid."

"I thought perhaps the city boys had a make on him."

"They wouldn't tell me, if they had. Besides, they ain't hardly had time to go out for breakfast. He's just a stiff in the morgue to them until the ID comes up with something. But they'll want to talk to you, Phil. They just love their tape recorders."

He went out and the door whooshed shut behind him. I sat there wondering if I had been a dope to talk to him. Or to take on Ikky's troubles. Five thousand green men said no. But they can be wrong too.

Somebody banged on my door. It was a uniform holding a telegram. I receipted for it and tore it loose.

It said: ON MY WAY TO FLAGSTAFF. MIRADOR MOTOR COURT. THINK I'VE BEEN SPOTTED. COME FAST.

I tore the wire into small pieces and burned them in my big ashtray.

I called Anne Riordan.

"Funny thing happened," I told her, and told her about the funny thing.

"I don't like the pencil," she said. "And I don't like the wrong man being killed—probably some poor bookkeeper in a cheap business or he wouldn't be living in that neighborhood. You should never have touched it, Phil."

"Ikky had a life. Where he's going he might make himself decent. He can change his name. He must be loaded or he wouldn't have paid me so much."

"I said I didn't like the pencil. You'd better come down here for a while. You can have your mail readdressed—if you get any mail. You don't have to work right away anyhow. And L.A. is oozing with private eyes."

"You don't get the point. I'm not through with the job. The city dicks have to know where I am, and if they do, all the crime reporters will know too. The cops might even decide to make me a suspect. Nobody who saw the shooting is going to put out a description that means anything. The American people know better than to be witnesses to gang killings."

"All right, but my offer stands."

The buzzer sounded in the outside room. I told Anne I had to hang up. I opened the communicating door and a well-dressed—I might say elegantly dressed—middle-aged man stood six feet inside the outer door. He had a pleasantly dishonest smile on his face. He wore a white Stetson and one of those narrow ties that go through an ornamental buckle. His cream-colored flannel suit was beautifully tailored.

He lit a cigarette with a gold lighter and looked at me over the first puff of smoke.

"Mr. Philip Marlowe?"

I nodded.

"I'm Foster Grimes from Las Vegas. I run the Rancho Esperanza on South Fifth. I hear you got a little involved with a man named Ikky Rossen."

"Won't you come in?"

He strolled past me into my office. His appearance told me nothing—a prosperous man who liked or felt it good business to look a bit western. You see them by the dozen in the Palm Springs winter season. His accent told me he was an easterner, but not New England. New York or Baltimore, likely. Long Island, the Berkshires—no, too far from the city.

I showed him the customer's chair with a flick of the wrist and sat down in my antique swivel-squeaker. I waited.

"Where is Ikky now, if you know?"

"I don't know, Mr. Grimes."

"How come you messed with him?"

"Money."

"A damned good reason," he smiled. "How far did it go?"

"I helped him leave town. I'm telling you this, although I don't know who the hell you are, because I've already told an old friend-enemy of mine, a top man in the Sheriff's Office."

"What's a friend-enemy?"

"Law men don't go around kissing me, but I've known him for years, and we are as much friends as a private star can be with a law man."

"I told you who I was. We have a unique set-up in Vegas. We own the place except for one lousy newspaper editor who keeps climbing our backs and the backs of our friends. We let him live because letting him live makes us look better than knocking him off. Killings are not good business any more."

"Like Ikky Rossen."

"That's not a killing. It's an execution. Ikky got out of line."

"So your gun boys had to rub the wrong guy. They could have hung around a little to make sure."

"They would have, if you'd kept your nose where it belonged. They hurried. We don't appreciate that. We want cool efficiency."

"Who's this great big fat 'we' you keep talking about?"

"Don't go juvenile on me, Marlowe."

"Okay. Let's say I know."

"Here's what we want. He reached into his pocket and drew out a loose bill. He put it on the desk on his side. "Find Ikky and tell him to get back in line and everything is oke. With an innocent bystander gunned, we don't want any trouble or any extra publicity. It's that simple. You get this now," he nodded at the bill. It was a grand. Probably the smallest bill they had. "And another when you find Ikky and give him the message. If he holds out—curtains."

"Suppose I say take your grand and blow your nose with it?"

"That would be unwise." He flipped out a Colt Woodsman with a short silencer on it. A Colt Woodsman will take one without jamming. He was fast too, fast and smooth. The genial expression on his face didn't change.

"I never left Vegas," he said calmly. "I can prove it. You're dead in your office chair and nobody knows anything. Just another private eye that tried the wrong pitch. Put your hands on the desk and think a little. Incidentally, I'm a crack shot even with this damned silencer."

"Just to sink a little lower in the social scale, Mr. Grimes, I ain't putting no hands on no desk. But tell me about this."

I flipped the nicely sharpened pencil across to him. He grabbed for it after a swift change of the gun to his left hand—very swift. He held the pencil up so that he could look at it without taking his eyes off me.

I said, "It came to me by Special Delivery mail. No message, no return address. Just the pencil. Think I've never heard about the pencil, Mr. Grimes?"

He frowned and tossed the pencil down. Before he could shift his long lithe gun back to his right hand I dropped mine under the desk and grabbed the butt of the .45 and put my finger hard on the trigger.

"Look under the desk, Mr. Grimes. You'll see a .45 in an open-end holster. It's fixed there and it's pointing at your belly. Even if you could shoot me through the heart, the .45 would still go off from a convulsive movement of my hand. And your belly would be hanging by a shred and you would be knocked out of that chair. A .45 slug can throw you back six feet. Even the movies learned that at last."

"Looks like a Mexican stand-off," he said quietly. He holstered his gun. He grinned. "Nice work, Marlowe. We could use a man like you. I suggest that you find Ikky and don't be a drip. He'll listen to reason. He doesn't really want to be on the run for the rest of his life."

"Tell me something, Mr. Grimes. Why pick on me? Apart from Ikky, what did I ever do to make you dislike me?"

Not moving, he thought a moment, or pretended to. "The Larsen case. You helped send one of our boys to the gas chamber. That we don't forget. We had you in mind as a fall guy for Ikky. You'll always be a fall guy, unless you play it our way. Something will hit you when you least expect it."

"A man in my business is always a fall guy, Mr. Grimes. Pick up your grand and drift out quietly. I might decide to do it your way, but I have to think about it. As for the Larsen case, the cops did all the work. I just happened to know where he was. I don't guess you miss him terribly."

"We don't like interference." He stood up. He put the grand note casually back in his pocket. While he was doing it I let go of the .45 and jerked out my Smith and Wesson five-inch .38.

He looked at it contemptuously. "I'll be in Vegas, Marlowe—in fact, I never left Vegas. You can catch me at the Esperanza. No, we don't give a damn about Larsen personally. Just another gun handler. They come in gross lots. We *do* give a damn that some punk private eye fingered him."

He nodded and went out by my office door.

I did some pondering. I knew Ikky wouldn't go back to the Outfit. He wouldn't trust them enough even if he got the chance. But there was another reason now. I called Anne Riordan again.

"I'm going to look for Ikky. I have to. If I don't call you in three days, get hold of Bernie Ohls. I'm going to Flagstaff, Arizona. Ikky says he will be there."

"You're a fool," she wailed. "It's some sort of trap."

"A Mr. Grimes of Vegas visited me with a silenced gun. I beat him to the punch, but I won't always be that lucky. If I find Ikky and report to Grimes, the mob will let me alone."

"You'd condemn a man to death?" Her voice was sharp and incredulous.

"No. He won't be there when I report. He'll have to hop a plane to Montreal, buy forged papers, and plane to Europe. He may be fairly safe there. But the Outfit has long arms and Ikky won't have a dull life staying alive. He hasn't any choice. For him it's either hide or get the pencil."

"So clever of you, darling. What about your own pencil?"

"If they meant it, they wouldn't have sent it. Just a bit of scare technique."

"And you don't scare, you wonderful handsome brute."

"I scare. But it doesn't paralyze me. So long. Don't take any lovers until I get back."

"Damn you, Marlowe!"

She hung up on me. I hung up on myself.

Saying the wrong thing is one of my specialties.

I beat it out of town before the homicide boys could hear about me. It would take them quite a while to get a lead. And Bernie Ohls wouldn't give a city dick a used paper bag. The Sheriff's men and the City Police cooperate about as much as two tomcats on a fence.

I made Phoenix by evening and parked myself in a motor court on the outskirts. Phoenix was damned hot. The motor court had a dining room, so I had dinner. I collected some quarters and dimes from the cashier and shut myself in a phone booth and started to call the Mirador in Flagstaff.

How silly could I get? Ikky might be registered under any name from Cohen to Cordileone, from Watson to Woichehovski. I called anyway and got nothing but as much of a smile as you can get on the phone.

So I asked for a room the following night. Not a chance unless someone checked out, but they would put me down for a cancellation or something. Flagstaff is too near the Grand Canyon. Ikky must have arranged in advance. That was something to ponder too.

I bought a paperback and read it. I set my alarm watch for 6:30. The paperback scared me so badly that I put two guns under my pillow. It was about a guy who bucked the hoodlum boss of Milwaukee and got beaten up every fifteen minutes. I figured that his head and face would be nothing but a piece of bone with a strip of skin hanging from it. But in the next chapter he was as gay as a meadow lark.

Then I asked myself why I was reading this drivel when I could have been memorizing *The Brothers Karamazov*. Not knowing any good answers, I turned the light out and went to sleep.

At 6:30 I shaved, showered, had breakfast, and took off for Flagstaff. I got there by lunchtime, and there was Ikky in the restaurant eating mountain trout. I sat down across from him. He looked surprised to see me.

I ordered mountain trout and ate it from the outside in, which is the proper way. Boning spoils it a little.

"What gives?" he asked me with his mouth full. A delicate eater.

"You read the papers?"

"Just the sports section."

"Let's go to your room and talk about it."

We paid for our lunches and went along to a nice double. The motor courts are getting so good that they make a lot of hotels look cheap. We sat down and lit cigarettes.

"The two hoods got up too early and went over to Poynter Street. They parked outside your apartment house. They hadn't been briefed carefully enough. They shot a guy who looked a little like you."

"That's a hot one," he grinned. "But the cops will find out, and the Outfit will find out. So the tag for me stays on."

"You must think I'm dumb," I said. "I am."

"I thought you did a first-class job, Marlowe. What's dumb about that?"

"What job did I do?"

"You got me out of there pretty slick."

"Anything about it you couldn't have done yourself?"

"With luck—no. But it's nice to have a helper."

"You mean sucker."

His face tightened. And his rusty voice growled. "I don't catch. And give me back some of that five grand, will you? I'm shorter than I thought."

"I'll give it back to you when you find a hummingbird in a salt shaker."

"Don't be like that." He almost sighed, and flicked a gun into his hand. I didn't have to flick. I was holding one in my side pocket.

"I oughtn't to have boobed off," I said. "Put the heater away. It doesn't pay any more than a Vegas slot machine."

"Wrong. Them machines pay the jackpot every so often. Other-wise—no customers."

"Every so seldom, you mean. Listen, and listen good."

He grinned. His dentist was tired waiting for him.

"The set-up intrigued me," I went on, debonair as Philo Vance in an S. S. Van Dine story and a lot brighter in the head. "First off, could it be done? Second, if it could be done, where would I be?

But gradually I saw the little touches that flawed the picture. Why would you come to me at all? The Outfit isn't that naive. Why would they send a little punk like this Charles Hickon or whatever name he uses on Thursdays? Why would an old hand like you let anybody trail you to a dangerous connection?"

"You slay me, Marlowe. You're so bright I could find you in the dark. You're so dumb you couldn't see a red, white, and blue giraffe. I bet you were back there in your unbrain emporium playing with that five grand like a cat with a bag of catnip. I bet you were kissing the notes."

"Not after you handled them. Then why the pencil that was sent to me? Big dangerous threat. It reinforced the rest. But like I told your choir boy from Vegas, they don't send them when they mean them. By the way, he had a gun too. A Woodsman .22 with a silencer. I had to make him put it away. He was nice about that. He started waving grands at me to find out where you were and tell him. A well-dressed, nice-looking front man for a pack of dirty rats. The Women's Christian Temperance Association and some bootlicking politicians gave them the money to be big, and they learned how to use it and make it grow. Now they're pretty well unstoppable. But they're still a pack of dirty rats. And they're always where they can't make a mistake. That's inhuman. Any man has a right to a few mistakes. Not the rats. They have to be perfect all the time. Or else they get stuck with *you*."

"I don't know what the hell you're talking about. I just know it's too long."

"Well, allow me to put it in English. Some poor jerk from the East Side gets involved with the lower echelons of a mob. You know what an echelon is, Ikky?"

"I been in the Army," he sneered.

"He grows up in the mob, but he's not all rotten. He's not rotten enough. So he tries to break loose. He comes out here and gets himself a cheap job of some sort and changes his name or names and lives quietly in a cheap apartment house. But the mob by now has agents in many places. Somebody spots him and recognizes him. It might be a pusher, a front man for a bookie joint, a night girl. So the mob, or call them the Outfit, say through their cigar smoke: 'Ikky can't do this to us. It's a small operation because he's small. But it annoys us. Bad for discipline. Call a couple of boys and have them pencil him.' But what boys do they call? A couple they're tired of. Been around too long. Might make a mistake or get chilly toes. Perhaps they like killing. That's bad too. That makes for recklessness. The best boys are the ones that don't care either way. So although they don't know it, the boys they call are on their way out. But it would be kind of cute to frame a guy they already don't like, for fingering a hood named Larsen. One of these puny little jokes the Outfit takes big. 'Look, guys, we even got time to play footsie with a private eye.' So they send a ringer."

"The Torrence brothers ain't ringers. They're real hard boys. They proved it—even if they did make a mistake."

"Mistake nothing. They got Ikky Rossen. You're just a singing commercial in this deal. And as of now you're under arrest for murder. You're worse off than that. The Outfit will habeas corpus you out of the clink and blow you down. You've served your purpose and you failed to finger me into a patsy."

His finger tightened on the trigger. I shot the gun out of his hand. The gun in my coat pocket was small, but at that distance accurate. And it was one of my days to be accurate.

He made a faint moaning sound and sucked at his hand. I went over and kicked him hard in the chest. Being nice to killers is not part of my repertoire. He went over backward and stumbled four or five steps. I picked up his gun and held it on him while I tapped all the places—not just pockets or holsters—where a man could stash a second gun. He was clean—that way anyhow.

"What are you trying to do to me?" he whined. "I paid you. You're clear. I paid you damn well."

"We both have problems there. Your's is to stay alive." I took a pair of cuffs out of my pocket and wrestled his hands behind him and snapped them on. His hand was bleeding. I tied his show handkerchief around it and then went to the telephone and called the police.

I had to stick around for a few days, but I didn't mind that as long as I could have trout caught eight or nine thousand feet up. I called Annie and Bernie Ohls. I called my answering service. The Arizona D.A. was a young keen-eyed man and the Chief of Police was one of the biggest men I ever saw.

I got back to L.A. in time and took Anne to Romanoff's for dinner and champagne.

"What I can't see," she said over a third glass of bubbly, "is why they dragged you into it, why they set up the fake Ikky Rossen. Why didn't they just let the two lifetakers do their job?"

"I couldn't really say. Unless the big boys feel so safe they're developing a sense of humor. And unless this Larsen guy who went to the gas chamber was bigger than he seemed to be. Only three or four important mobsters have made the electric chair or the rope or the gas chamber. None that I know of in the life-imprisonment states like Michigan. If Larsen was bigger than anyone thought, they might have had my name on a waiting list."

"But why wait?" she asked me. "They'd go after you quickly."

"They can afford to wait. Who's going to bother them? Except when they make a mistake.

"Income tax rap?"

"Yeah, like Capone. Capone may have had several hundred men killed, and killed a few of them himself, personally. But it took the Internal Revenue boys to get him. But the Outfit won't make that mistake often."

"What I like about you, apart from your enormous personal charm, is that when you don't know an answer you make one up."

"The money worries me," I said. "Five grand of their dirty money. What do I do with it?"

"Don't be a jerk all your life. You earned the money and you risked your life for it. You can buy Series E Bonds—they'll make the money clean. And to me that would be part of the joke."

"*You* tell *me* one good sound reason why they pulled the switch."

"You have more of a reputation than you realize. And suppose it was the false Ikky who pulled the switch? He sounds like one of these over-clever types that can't do anything simple."

"The Outfit will get him for making his own plans—if you're right."

"If the D.A. doesn't. And I couldn't care less about what happens to him. More champagne, please."

They extradited "Ikky" and he broke under pressure and named the two gunmen—after I had already named them, the Torrence brothers. But nobody could find them. They never went home. And you can't prove conspiracy on one man. The law couldn't even get him for accessory after the fact. They couldn't prove he knew the real Ikky had been gunned.

They could have got him for some trifle, but they had a better idea. They left him to his friends. They just turned him loose.

Where is he now? My hunch says nowhere.

Anne Riordan was glad it was all over and I was safe. Safe—that isn't a word you use in my trade.